To Conquer a Highlander

MARY WINE

sourcebooks
casablanca

Published by Sourcebooks Casablanca, an imprint of Source-books, Inc.
P.O. Box 4410, Naperville, Illinois 60567-4410
(630) 961-3900
FAX: (630) 961-2168
www.sourcebooks.com

Printed and bound in Canada
WC 10 9 8 7 6 5 4 3 2 1

*To the man who still sweeps me off my feet and puts up
with me through all my endeavors. My hero,
my partner... my husband. I love you.*

One

Scotland 1437, McLeren land

FIRE COULD BE A WELCOME SIGHT TO A MAN WHEN HE'D been riding a long time and the sun had set, leaving him surrounded by darkness. But the sight of flames on the horizon could also be the most horrifying thing any laird ever set his eyes on.

Torin McLeren wanted to close his eyes in the hopes that the orange flames illuminating the night might not be there when he opened them again. He could smell the smoke on the night air now but didn't have the luxury of allowing the horror to turn his stomach. He was laird, and protecting his holdings was his duty.

Digging his spurs into his horse, he headed toward the inferno. Wails began to drown out the hissing flames. Laments carried on the night wind as wives and mothers mourned bitterly. The scent of blood rose above the smoke, the flickering orange light illuminating the fallen bodies of his clansmen. He stared at the carnage, stunned by the number of dead and wounded. He might be a Highlander and no stranger to battle, but this was a village, not a piece of land disputed and fought over by nobles. This was McLeren land and had been for more than a century.

A horror straight out of hell surrounded him. Mercy hadn't been present here—he'd seen less carnage after fighting the English. The slaughter was almost too much to believe or accept. His horse balked at his command to ride forward, the stallion rearing up as the heat from the blaze became hot against its hide. Torin cursed and slid from the saddle. Every muscle in his body tightened, rage slowly coming to a boil inside him. Hands reached out to him, grasping fingers seeking him as the only hope of righting the wrong that had been inflicted on them.

His temper burned hotter than the fire consuming the keep in front of him. They suffered raids from time to time, but this was something else entirely. It was war. The number of bodies lying where they had fallen was a wrong that could not be ignored. Nor should it be. These were his people, McLerens who trusted in his leadership and his sword arm for protection.

"Justice…"

One single word but it echoed across the fallen bodies of men wearing the same plaid he did. Every retainer left to keep the peace was lying dead, but they had died as Highlanders. The ground was littered with the unmoving forms of their attackers. His gaze settled on one body, the still form leaking dark blood onto his land, the kilt drawing his interest. Lowering his frame onto one knee, Torin fingered the colors of his enemy. The fire lit the scarlet and blue colors of the McBoyd clan. His neighbor and apparently now his enemy.

McBoyds? It didn't make sense. These were common people. Good folk who labored hard to feed their families. Every McLeren retainer stationed there knew and accepted that they might have to fight for their clan, but that did not explain the number of slain villagers. There was no reason for such a slaughter. No excuse he would ever swallow or accept. McLerens did not fear the night, be they common born or not. While he was laird, they would not live in fear.

"There will be justice. I swear it." His voice carried authority, but to those weeping over their lost family, it also gave comfort. Torin stood still only for a moment, his retainers backing him up before he turned and remounted his horse. He felt more at home in the saddle, more confident. His father had raised him to lead the McLerens in good times and bad. He would not disappoint him or a single McLeren watching him now.

"Well now, let us see what the McBoyds have to say for themselves, lads."

Torin turned his stallion into the night without a care for the clouds that kept the moonlight from illuminating the rocky terrain. He was a Highlander, after all. Let the other things in the dark fear him.

❧

"Shannon! Wake up, girl, and quickly."

Shannon McBoyd opened her eyes to nothing but a single candle flame offering light against the dead of night. Outside the glow of that single flickering flame there was nothing but blackness. The yellow glow cast the features of her clanswoman in enough light to make out the pinched look on her face. Tension prickled along Shannon's neck and down her back.

"Here now, Gerty. What's the fuss about at this time of night?"

Shannon rubbed her eyes and shivered. The night was frigid, almost unnaturally so, and the small window across her chamber had its wooden shutters closed tight, but wind still blew through the center of it where the shutters met. The candle flame danced as Gerty moved in front of the window, and she gasped, turning her back to shield their only source of light.

"Come now, out of bed."

Shannon pushed her bedding back. Her shift was thin and worn, providing her little protection against the darkest hours unless she remained in her bed. Old Gerty didn't seem to notice the chill—that, or she was ignoring it. The old servant pushed the bed curtain aside, barely keeping the flame of the candle she held away from it.

"Yer father is calling for ye. Hurry up, girl. He's got the whisky out."

Shannon felt her stomach clench because it was not a natural time for her sire to be demanding her presence. The last remains of slumber evaporated as she tried to think of what her father wanted from her at this time of night. She crawled out of the bedding quickly because her father was never kind when kept waiting. Randal McBoyd expected obedience and promptness. Never mind that it was the dead of night, best left to ghosts and other unholy things.

"Hurry, lass."

Gerty didn't wait for Shannon to comply. The old servant was moving faster than Shannon could recall. Gerty dropped a loose gown over her head before Shannon had fully raised her arms. At least the dress was bulky enough for her to wiggle her arms into the sleeves. The fabric held the chill of the night, making her shiver again. Gerty handed a girdle belt to her and reached for the hairbrush. The servant pulled the bristles through her hair only a few times before dropping the brush back on the table. She grabbed the strands and forced them into a braid, making Shannon wince as the woman pulled too hard, but she could not appear below with her hair loose. That would start rumors that she didn't need attached to her name. She reached for her linen cap, which was sitting beside her bed, and tied it beneath her chin, grateful for the warmth it would help keep inside her. When it was blistering hot in the heart of summer, she detested the cap demanded by her father to preserve her modesty.

"Good enough. Get on with ye."

Shannon struggled to push her foot into a shoe while Gerty opened the chamber door and gestured to her frantically. There was a haunted look on Gerty's face that sent another ripple of apprehension across her skin. At least she did not sleep very far from the hall where her father would be waiting on her. Laird McBoyd always received those he wanted to see while sitting on the raised dais at the end of the great hall. A single chair with ornately carved armrests in the shape of a raptor's talon sat there on top of a costly Persian carpet.

Shannon smelled the candles burning before she saw the glow at the bottom of the stairs. Voices drifted up the stone stairs that led to her meager chamber. Many voices, and there was laughter as well. A sense of foreboding flooded her. It was an eerie mixture, the good cheer and the darkness. It felt as if she were still dreaming, because the abundance of activity did not fit with the time of day.

Something else touched her senses. She drew in a deep breath to identify the scent filling the stairway. Metallic and thick, it turned her stomach. A chill crept across her skin that left gooseflesh along her arms.

"Get on with ye."

Gerty pushed her the last few paces into the hall. As the laird's only daughter, a lowly female, she was given a loft storeroom, set off to one side of the hall, as a bedchamber. Only her brothers resided on the second floor of McBoyd Castle. She was less than her brothers in her father's eyes, a woman who should know her place and be reminded of it. The church told her that too, that she was less than a man, but her heart did not believe it. Gerty called her stubborn, often warning her that she would come to no good end if she did not learn to be content with a woman's lot.

In some ways she was content. Her chamber stairway allowed her to view the hall before those celebrating in it noticed her. She might peek in without being sighted at the large double doors at the end of the great hall. Her ears hadn't deceived her; there was much merriment indeed. But her eyes rounded with horror when she looked more closely at the men making so much noise in the middle of the night. She fought back a gasp, swallowing it before she was noticed. The scent of spilled blood was strong here. It mixed with the aroma of food, nauseating her completely. If Gerty hadn't been behind her, she would have run to the garderobe to retch.

Her clansmen were celebrating in bloodstained kilts. They laughed and jested while raising tankards of ale to one another. Shannon found her gaze glued to the dark stains marring their fingers. It was gruesome and too horrible to accept from her own kin. But a closer look showed her far more of her father's retainers sat still around the hall, in the quiet, than those celebrating. Those men sat sipping from their cups, many merely holding them with looks on their faces that said they'd had no appetite for what had happened this night.

"There ye be. What madness is this, making me wait so long for ye, Daughter?" His eyes narrowed. "Ye seem to learn nothing in church about respecting yer father."

Shannon lowered her head to give her sire the deference he always demanded from her. At least the action served to hide her frown from Randal McBoyd's direct stare. He was an arrogant laird, and the last bruise he'd left with his fist was just now fading. She was in no hurry to receive a fresh one. Such would be hers soon enough. Her sire was quick to reprimand her anytime he felt the urge. Her father was diligent when it came to reminding her she was less than a man and a disappointment to him for being born a daughter, but he could read in her eyes that she did not agree with his views completely. So it was better to just keep her gaze lowered; that preserved peace in the house at least for part of the time.

"I brought her straightaway, Laird." Gerty aimed another jab at the center of her back, but Shannon didn't need it. While she was in no hurry to get within striking range of her sire, she was not a coward either. She could suffer his strength and would not simper in the doorway like her stepmother so often did. The sight of the woman's downcast face and quivering hands always made her cringe. If that was accepting her place as a woman, she never would.

"Father."

Laird McBoyd snorted. His left hand curled around the arm of his chair while he peered at her over the rim of his tankard. He drew a deep mouthful before grunting and handing his cup off to a servant. The boy assigned the duty of holding his laird's cup was quick to take it before it fell.

"Aye, I am yer father. A fact I've detested many a time, but tonight it seems there might yet be some good out of yer mother's weakness in breeding me a daughter." He slapped the chair arm beneath his hand. "The king is dead. Scotland will be having a new family on the throne, and one that will no' be dogs begging for scraps from England's hand!"

A cheer rose from behind her, but Shannon noticed the men who watched in silence. In their eyes she could see a reflection of her own dread. It was the look of decent men who did not find war so grand a thing. But they remained silent because the laird would be followed. That was Scottish tradition, and honor was more important than misgivings.

"Ye'll be wedding the Earl of Atholl's nephew. Atholl will be wearing the crown afore the month is finished, as he should have done instead of bring James back from England. Atholl is the true and rightful heir; any clan who opposes the new order will fall under the sword like the McLeren did tonight."

"You raided the McLeren? They are at least triple our number and Highlanders—"

Her sire roared with rage. He gained his feet in a flash, and his fist connected with her cheek in the next. Shannon's head whipped about with the blow, but she never faltered from her stance. Instead she turned her face back to her father without a single whimper. She even bit her lip to ensure that it did not tremble.

"Ye'll mind that sharp tongue, girl! Mind it well, I tell ye! No woman will be speaking her mind to me. Not beneath me own roof, I tell ye."

Shannon stared straight at her sire, pain spreading across her face, but she refused to show him any sign of her discomfort. Blood trickled from her lip, but she did not raise her hand to wipe it aside. Her father snickered.

"Well, ye're a strong one, anyway. Atholl will nae be finding fault with yer spine. Ye'll give him sons worthy of being called Scottish."

He grunted before dropping back into his chair. "Aye, and wedding that boy will make sure Atholl holds true to his word to help us wipe the McLerens clean off the face of Scotland. It will be the McBoyds that become the strength here, Daughter. Atholl has promised me his retainers to see the task finished. We began tonight. As soon as Atholl's retainers arrive, we'll be finishing."

Her father reached down and pulled a dagger from the top of his boot. Its blade was still stained dark, and her father looked at the dried blood with a grin that sickened her. "I put this through the heart of McLeren's captain."

⤬

"How can I be kin to such a monster?" Shannon shook her head, trying to dislodge the memory of her father's glee over murder. She refused to believe that killing their neighbors for nothing more than power was something that brought honor to the name McBoyd. If that was because she was a woman, she was grateful to be one.

"Hush, isn't that black eye enough suffering for ye? The laird is to be obeyed, not questioned."

Shannon refused to temper her expression, not here in her chamber. Gerty clucked her tongue at her in reprimand.

"Things will nae go well for you, miss. No' with all that stubbornness inside ye. Best ye think on that while on the road to Edinburgh. Think long and hard. 'Tis for sure that yer husband will no' have any more tolerance for it than yer father does."

Think? There would be nothing else for her mind to do *but* consider the facts again and again. It was not too far into spring for travel. Yet her father was sending her onto the half-frozen road. Well, perhaps that was indeed a kindness. She had no desire to share a roof with such a monster. What manner of laird sought war when peace had been enjoyed for so long?

A greedy man, that was who.

A man who didn't know when life was good. She was not so foolhardy. Even suffering her father's dislike of her gender failed to blind her to the goodness surrounding her. There was food aplenty on the tables at all times of the year. Warm clothing for the winter and men of good conscience wearing her family colors. She had always worn her arisaid with pride and a level chin, but looking down to where the length of McBoyd tartan hung down her gown, Shannon felt shame rise up inside her. The blue and scarlet seemed tarnished now, stained just like her father's dirk. Her father had always envied his neighbor, the McLeren, even raiding them from time to time. But there was no bloodletting done. A few head of sheep or sacks of grain were the normal prize. It was more of a jest between men to see who could best the other.

Shock still held her in its grip while a trunk was packed for her journey. Her own kin had looked like savages wearing the blood of their fellow Scotsmen. That was not the McBoyd honor she had always respected. It was something borne out of greed and evil that made her cringe. As sad as it might be, she would be happy to depart. Even onto a half-frozen road.

"Here now. Let's see what can be done with yer face."

Gerty lifted her chin and studied the swelling. Her lips settled into a frown.

"Ye be a right pretty enough lass. When yer nae wearing a mark from yer father's hand, that is." She clucked her tongue once again. "With a little prayer, it might be healed by the time ye meet yer groom. Best to hope for that. No man wants a wife who needles her sire."

"I spoke a truth. The McLerens do outnumber us, and Highlanders are nae to be trifled with. There will be retribution for this night's work, make no mistake about it."

"Hush now." Gerty made the sign of the cross over herself. "Do ye want to bring a curse upon us all? Yer father burned White Hill to the ground. Every McBoyd life hangs on the alliance being made between Atholl and yer father."

Gerty snapped her fingers at the two girls packing behind them. Both had frozen in their tracks, their eyes rounding with distress as they listened in on the conversation. Somehow, Shannon didn't think that Gerty's prayer or snapping fingers would make any difference when it came to the retaliation the McLerens would be raining down on them. The maids were right to worry. She couldn't shake the tension off her back either. It sat there between her shoulder blades, twisting tighter and tighter until she ached.

"Get back to work. The sooner a McBoyd is wed into the Atholl family, the better for all of us. The alliance will be much stronger after ye've been bedded and things cannae be undone. If fate is kind, ye will ripen with a babe quickly, making the alliance even stronger for the McBoyd."

Gerty picked up an overgown of sturdy wool. "This should keep ye warm on the road."

It would be better than nothing. She had little in

the way of possessions or traveling clothes. Her single trunk was only half-full when the two maids finished their duty. Shannon made most of her own clothing during the winter, but there were not enough daylight hours during the shorter days to do more than keep up with what was wearing thin. Gerty carefully rolled up the new spring dress that was sitting on the table and placed it in the trunk along with her sewing tools.

The maids curtsied and left with only a quick glance at her. Pity lurked in their eyes, but it was much overshadowed by their desire to see the alliance sealed. That was the only thing that would see them sleeping peacefully and not watching the ridge for McLeren riders bent on vengeance.

Not that she had ever expected to wed for any other reason than her father's will. That was a daughter's duty, to wed at her father's command. Since she was old enough to recall, she had been taught such. Her mother had done the same, and the two stepmothers she had known since were no different. They arrived after negotiations and took their place in her father's bed without any manner of courtship.

Yet she had begun to hope that she would never wed. At twenty-two, she was getting rather past the age for a first wedding. Shannon didn't lament her years. In truth, she enjoyed being past the age of uncertainty. After her last birthday had passed and no groom sought her hand, a peace had settled over her. A sense of freedom that seemed to fill her with poise and confidence. She liked who she was and did not need a husband to feel complete.

Of course children of her own would be nice, but

there were many motherless babes needing care for her to fill that need. Being the laird's daughter placed her in a unique position. Taking a lover was not something she might do, because of her station. Though late at night, when the curtain that shielded her bed was drawn to keep the warmth in, she wondered what a man's hands would feel like. Was a kiss as hot as she'd heard it described? And what was passion? Her body had burned with need, making her restless, and there was no solace in prayer, no matter what she heard in church. Her dreams filled with heated visions of a lover she only knew about from gossip and books.

Maybe she would know the answer to that question on her wedding night. Or perhaps she'd find her thighs spread without a single stroke across her breasts to allow her to feel the pleasure of passion. Negotiated marriages were so often cold ones. Her newest young stepmother had wept through her first morning as a wife, while Shannon's father smirked and rubbed her bottom when she passed him. But the maids in the kitchens enjoyed their liaisons. She'd heard them whispering about how good one lad was over others. Passion seemed to be an elusive thing, only found with a few partners for women. Men seemed blessed with the ability to be satisfied with any woman they took, which seemed rather unfair, and that fact didn't leave much hope for her in a negotiated marriage.

Still, she would hope. Pitying herself had never been something she favored.

Gerty began to braid her hair. The strands were long and the color of honey. Not a true blonde but lacking the deep, dark color of brunette. Some said she was fair of face, but most ignored her because she was the laird's daughter. No springtime tumbles in the new hay for her. Each May Day she had washed her face in the morning dew alone, while the other McBoyd girls giggled and ran off into the distance for springtime fun.

Well, liaisons, really.

It wasn't making love. How could it be such when most of the couples only tasted one another before the day was over and the church's power resumed? May Day never fell to the clergy and their preaching of damnation for the lustful. All frolicked in observance of the fertility custom before kneeling in repentance the following day.

"There." Gerty finished and tied the end of her braid with a green ribbon. "Yer sweet as a spring plum. The way a bride should be. A McBoyd bride, that is."

❧

"Runner!"

Torin raised his attention from the blade of his sword. Without even looking, he drew a sharpening stone along its length in a practiced motion. The blade was already sharp, but he didn't put the stone down. Instead he watched the young boy running down the ridge toward him.

"There's a group leaving the castle, Laird." The boy drew in a few deep breaths to still his rapid heartbeat. He grinned with triumph for having something to report. "Looks like McBoyd is sending his daughter off someplace to the south."

"Dinna know the man had a daughter." Malcolm

McLeren fingered the edge of his own claymore, one corner of his mouth twitching up with satisfaction. "Now that's something I like learning about that bastard. A nice, soft place to strike back at him."

"There'll be no raping."

Torin's words weren't popular with the men waiting near him, but he held his chin firm in the face of the scowls being aimed at him. "We'll no' be mimicking the bastards, and that's my word on the matter. We're McLerens, nae savages. We're here to punish their bloody ways. Any McLeren who wants a tumble is going to have to charm it out of the lass he's chasing."

Malcolm shrugged. "When ye put it that way, I suppose I see the direction of yer thinking."

Malcolm's words earned more than just a few nods of agreement from the men surrounding them. The McLeren retainer had earned the respect of his fellow clansmen, and his agreement was something no laird might buy. That agreement was an honor, and one Torin appreciated. Being called "Laird" didn't mean a thing to him if it was nothing more than an empty title. Scotland had enough of those sorts of lairds. His father had been more to the McLerens, and he felt the need to follow in those footsteps.

Torin considered the runner. "Ye said she set out on the road?"

"Aye. With a trunk, no less. The men riding with her were no' carrying any banners, but it was her. Shannon McBoyd. I saw her plainly."

"And ye know her for McBoyd's child?"

Young Gilian grinned. "Aye. I saw her at festival

last spring. Got warned off her quick as could be too, on account she was the laird's daughter. Legitimate, they said. Her clanswomen claimed her father was dangling her chastity in front of a couple of lords and she was to stay virgin or there would be hell to pay."

Now that was interesting. Torin felt his rage subside and his brain began filtering the facts. He looked out over the men awaiting his command. Hundreds of them and more were making their way through the rocky hills above them, the McLeren colors proudly worn by all. Even in the early dawn light he could see the heather and green of those kilts. They outnumbered the McBoyd already, and these were only the fastest of the men. News was spreading faster than the fire at White Hill was cooling. The McBoyds might never have been friends, but they had never been stupid before. Firing one of his holdings had been foolish. Running his men through was pure insanity. There would be retaliation, no mistake about it. To ignore such an attack would be inviting a second one.

"This attack does nae make sense."

"Aye, lad." Malcolm tilted his head to the side and peered at him intently. "What are ye thinking, Laird?"

Torin considered the facts. Being laird was more than a title. It was a duty. His people looked to him to make good decisions. Even in the mist of anger.

"I suspect there is something brewing in Edinburgh. Something that has the McBoyd thinking he can destroy the McLerens. Something like that would take a wedding to seal."

Hands froze in midstroke across claymores. Torin

felt the weight of his clan's eyes on him while his words settled. Malcolm whistled.

"Well now. I did nae think o' that. But I do believe ye have a point. The McBoyd have nae been so bold before."

"But it's well-known that Laird McBoyd is a greedy swine." Torin looked down the ridge. "And he's being mighty smug too. No' a single man set to watch his border. He's counting on someone's men to protect him or someone else to be attacking us and keeping us busy."

Curses surrounded him, but Torin acted swiftly.

"Braden. You'll take half these men and set to making sure there are no more raids. Send a couple of runners to Connor Lindsey and let him know what goes on here."

Braden reached up and tugged on the corner of his knit cap. Torin swallowed his need to take blood for blood. Swarming over the McBoyd stronghold might quell the anger eating at him, but it wouldn't necessarily end the threat to his clan. If there was another name involved, he needed to discover who was in allegiance with the McBoyd. James I had worn the crown of Scotland precariously. His queen had delivered twin boys, but one had already died. The lords of the isles, such as Lindy and Atholl, were powerful men who were not content giving deference to a higher-ranking man. But they could not take Scotland without several of its lairds clustering behind their banners. A man like McBoyd would lend his name to a cause only if he felt there was no way for him to be cheated.

And a wedding to his daughter would buy the man,

all right. It was something worth investigating. Civil war would see more blood spilled and pit clan against clan. It was something he'd prefer to avoid. Too much of Scottish history was written in that same blood.

"I'm going to take a few men and follow the daughter. I've a mind to discover just what plot is brewing, lads. We cannae protect our families if our own countrymen are fighting each other," Torin decided.

And he could not rest if McBoyd had reinforcements riding toward his land. Standing up, Torin slid his claymore into the scabbard strapped to his back. He'd follow the daughter and keep her from sealing her father's dealings. No matter what it took to see that done.

He was laird, and his clan would have his strength above all other things.

Even above chivalry. If McBoyd was going to use his daughter in such a foul plot, then Torin would have to take her before she married the lord her father intended to bribe.

The journey was completely miserable. Unless she counted the fact that she was free of her father's house. Shannon chose to dwell on that fact. Each mile took great effort for the horses. The winter snow was beginning to thaw, turning everything into mud. She walked most of the way to save the horses from having to struggle with her weight in the wagon. It still took three days to cover a distance that would take only one during the spring. The men riding with her turned surly with their frustration.

A handful of tents were already raised when they

topped the ridge looking down on the Lowlands. Gair, her father's man, cursed when he looked down at the small number of men awaiting them. He stomped down the last of the distance and entered one of the tents without waiting to be announced. The rest of her father's men swept her along in his wake. She might have been a trunk for all the courtesy they allowed her.

"Where are the retainers promised my laird?" Gair didn't temper his voice either. A man sitting at a small table paused with his quill in midstroke. Whoever he was, the items around him spoke of money. A great deal of it. The quill had a silver tip, and sitting on a polished writing desk was a glass jar holding ink. On his hand was a signet ring, telling her he was someone others obeyed.

"Yer laird is a bloody fool." He stood, showing off the kilt of the Earl of Atholl. "I am Fergus, third secretary to my lord Atholl, the true king."

Shannon watched her father's captain bristle under the comment. Gair McBoyd turned red before spitting at the feet of the man who had insulted his laird.

"McBoyds are nae dogs to be kept on a leash."

The man raised an eyebrow. "The Earl of Atholl will be the master of your laird, make no mistake about that, or every McBoyd will end up like the McLeren."

Gair raised a fist. "We've struck a bargain with the man. We were promised retainers in exchange for his daughter."

"Aye, and you were warned to keep quiet until the king was dead and his son along with him, so that there would be no question as to where the crown went next."

A heavy silence filled the tent. Gair looked uncertain for the first time. Fergus turned his attention to her. He lifted one hand and gestured her forward. Shannon wasn't really given the opportunity to comply. The two men guarding the entrance of the tent appeared beside her and took her forward almost in the same moment as their master ordered her to move.

"Remove the arisaid from your head so I may see you. The cap as well."

One of the guards reached for her. Shannon slapped his fingers aside.

"I heard him well enough. Keep yer hands away from me."

A soft chuckle filled the tent. Fergus smiled at her while she drew her arisaid off her head, where she'd wrapped it to keep warm. His eyes were oddly intense. He studied her for a long moment, watching her untie her cap and pull it off. It was a strange feeling to have her hair completely on display after keeping it covered since she was ten years old. But she refused to quiver, it was only hair, and men had theirs on display quite regularly.

"The girl appears acceptable."

Gair snorted. "When will the retainers be here, man? That's what I want to be knowing."

Fergus frowned. He moved closer to Gair, his face darkening. "You Highlanders never understand the value of patience. The king is dead, but the queen escaped with her whelp. There are those who give her shelter and want to crown her son."

Shannon gasped. She couldn't contain the sound. There was a chill in Fergus's voice that sent a shiver down her spine. He turned to look at her once more, but his attention did not linger. He faced Gair again, and his expression was as hard and cold as ice.

"Attacking a neighbor who outnumbers you was ill-advised when the wedding had not yet taken place. There will be no retainers until the bedding."

"Ye sound like a bloody Englishman."

Fergus responded with a small curving of his lips. The secretary turned and returned to his chair. He didn't appear to mind that everyone waited while he settled himself in comfort.

"I was in the company of the king while he was being held in England. How else do you suppose I earned his trust?"

"A trust you betrayed, now didna ye, laddie?" Gair snickered in spite of Fergus's narrowing eyes.

"I make the best alliances for the times. If a man wants to succeed, he must be willing to see where the future is and not cling to the past. James the First was the past. My lord will be a bright future for Scotland."

"He'll nae be wearing any crown without the McBoyds following his banner."

Fergus remained silent, but Shannon could see in his eyes that his mind was anything but idle. There was a calculating look to the man, one that sent horror through her. He spoke so calmly of murder, the man's soul must be rotten.

"Still, the agreement was a wedding before any action was to be taken against your neighboring clan. You shall have the agreed-upon retainers only when the first condition has been met."

"But we fired one of their keeps and killed the retainers. We need the men now." A hint of desperation entered Gair's voice. "I want them now, man."

Fergus remained unconcerned. "As I stated. Yer laird is a fool. There is more than one clan attached to this. The queen has supporters who want her son crowned king. My lord Atholl needs all of his retainers. The fight your laird picked with your neighbor is your own affair."

"They'll wipe us out, down to the last man."

Fergus lifted one eyebrow again. "Then I suppose you had best make haste for Edinburgh so that the wedding may take place. My lord will not move against your enemy until he has a solid pledge of loyalty from your laird. Something that cannot be undone if your laird panics when the time for action arrives."

Gair sputtered, his lip curling with a snarl. Rage shook his body, but Fergus remained unmoved. The secretary raised his hand.

"That will be all."

❧

"You there. How long does it take to rub a horse down? And why are the pair of ye working on the same animal, for Christ's sake?"

"Just doing me duty."

Torin kept his face down. He felt naked without his claymore, but it was worth it. His hands moved in practiced circles over the horse. Secretary Fergus O'Bien liked his things along with him when he traveled. His horse was housed directly behind his tent, making it an easy task to listen in on his conversations.

Malcolm looked at Torin over the back of the horse, a gleam in his eyes.

Bending down, Torin picked up the handle of a wheelbarrow that was piled up with the animal's leavings. Malcolm shouldered a yoke with buckets on either side and fell into step behind him. It was an effort to keep his pace slow, but he needed to play the part of a servant doing only what he had to. He itched to rip the House of Atholl plaid off his back too.

It was the colors of traitors, men who conspired against a unified Scotland. They were worse than the English. James I had been a Scot, and there was no king Torin would rather swear his loyalty to. Anyone who had helped murder him deserved to die.

"Damn nasty bit o' business we've discovered here." Malcolm dropped the yoke the moment they were out of sight. The sun was gone, making it easier to escape into the night. For a Highlander, the night was nothing to fear. Let Fergus and his men huddle by their fires and think they provided protection. Nothing would shield them from the wrath of a McLeren laird.

Torin's men waited for him, still as stones and hidden among the rocks that dotted the landscape. He sensed them before he ever saw them.

"Well then, what's yer thinking, Laird?"

Torin cast a look down at the flickering fires. When Scotland's isle lords bickered over the crown, Scotland became too weak to keep England on her side of the border. His father had sworn on bent knee to James I, and Torin had done the same. Now he would raise his claymore in defense of James II, rightful heir to the Scottish throne.

"I want the daughter and the secretary. The rest die like the traitors they are. We need the secretary to expose this plot and the daughter to prove McBoyd's guilt."

There was a ripple of agreement from his men. They stood up, shadows among shadows, and he listened to their swords being pulled free. Blood for blood. But it would be the right blood spilled. That of their true enemy. McBoyd was a puppet who was too stupid to know he was being controlled. He would die another day.

But first he'd be exposed for the traitor lover he was and he'd see his daughter on her way to McLeren land.

Two

MOST OF HER BODY ACHED FROM FIGHTING THE MUDDY
road, but sleep remained elusive. How could it not?
When had the world gone insane? Shannon stared off
into the night and heard the wind whistling through
the hills as it had always done. But tonight the sound
didn't bring a smile to her lips. Instead it sounded
cold and forbidding. Lying on her back in the bed of
the wagon, she didn't even find comfort in the stars
above her. Thick clouds covered their twinkling light,
wrapping the night in dampness. She could smell the
water in the air. By tomorrow there would be rain to
further clog the road.

She would not lament that. There was no hurry in
her heart, even if it meant a fire to warm her toes by
in Edinburgh. She would rather suffer the chill than
join the swirling plots at court.

The wind whistled more strongly, but something
else teased her ears as well. A soft gurgle and a crunch
of gravel. Both were barely audible. Like whispers.
Wrapped in the moonless night, she questioned if
it was real or the product of her imagination. The

Highlands could do that sometimes. The older generation claimed it was the ghosts of the past.

Another crunch and Shannon rolled onto her side. Her heart accelerated, and she clamped her lips together to remain silent. Pushing her head up, she peered over the side of the wagon where she'd left the cover turned back. Meager light drifted up from Fergus's tent, where lanterns burned. Just a fleeting bit of light that washed over the forms lying on the ground. She stared at them, her mind refusing to absorb what their positions meant. With arms flung out and knees buckled, they lay in unnatural positions, their long pikes several feet from their open hands.

Another crunch of gravel and this one was directly beneath her nose. The sound sent fear through her, her breath freezing in her throat, her hands pressed against the hard surface of the wagon bed. Her view of the bodies was cut off as a shadow rose in front of her. Huge and black like the night, she smelled more than saw him. Every muscle tightened and bunched, and energy pulsed through her in a flood. It was instantaneous. Without giving herself time to think, she pushed her body away from the looming shape and back across the wagon bed. Her fingers clawed at the bundles, seeking anything heavy enough to throw. Instead she was trapped with the cover tied tightly on the opposite side of the wagon.

"Alarm!"

That single word confirmed what she already knew. Horses screamed from behind Fergus's tent, and the night was suddenly filled with the sound of running. A soft word came from the man watching her. So soft, but that didn't disguise the frustration with which it was uttered.

"Do nae make a fuss—"

Her hands closed around a chest, and she heaved it toward him before he finished his warning. She would not go quietly to her death. The chest smacked against his body with a very satisfying sound. Noise was all around her now. The harsh sound of metal meeting metal. The grunts of men fighting and the unmistakable sounds of defeat. Soft, gurgling sounds of bodies being run through or the heavy thump of blows landing on human flesh.

It was sickening. Her body surged away from the cursing form watching her. He snarled and knocked the chest aside. One huge hand curled around the top edge of the wagon, and the entire bed rocked as he vaulted over the side. Shannon frantically shoved against the cover, and it gave way with a tearing sound. Her body was pressed against it when it split, dropping her onto the ground in a heap. Pain raced through her legs and hip from the hard landing, but the need to escape overrode it. She kicked at the fabric of her gown and scrambled away from the wagon. The main battle was clustered around Fergus's tent now, the few McBoyd retainers left to keep her inside the wagon lying on the ground where they had fallen.

The horses were still standing near the front of it. Shannon tore a feed bag off the muzzle of one and gained its back before any of the men around her noticed. She tried not to look behind her but couldn't resist a quick peek. She fumbled with the leather strap securing the horse to its teammate when she caught a look at the man trying to get to her.

He was a demon from hell.

He had to be. Men didn't grow that large, not without help from the devil. He swept the remains of the wagon cover aside with one motion of a thick, muscled arm. The light from Fergus's tent cast him in a shimmer of light, his silhouette sending horror through her mind. He jumped to the ground and landed on two perfectly placed feet, his legs bending to absorb the impact before he straightened to a height taller than any of the men she knew. With a toss of his head, his hair settled over his shoulders, and he stared straight at her. His hands came up, the fingers open and grasping, but the strap connecting the two horses came free, and Shannon dug her feet into the sides of the surprised steed.

The horse jumped forward but stopped, nervous from the attack surrounding it. The animal was bred for its strength, not for speed, so it had never been trained for warfare. Its back was wide, making it hard to grasp with her thighs from her astride position. Hooking her fingers in its mane, Shannon dug her heels in once again.

"Come on now. Let's be gone from here." She leaned down across the animal's thick neck, hoping her voice would penetrate the fear holding the horse in a nervous side-to-side prancing.

"Go on now. Make for the forest…"

Another dig with her heels and the horse didn't need any further coaxing. It shot forward, using all its strength to speed up the rocky incline toward the trees. Shannon remained down across its back for fear of being tossed. For the moment there was no hope of directing where the animal went, since it took all her strength to remain on its bouncing back. Each time its hooves came down, she clung tighter as her stability was threatened, but then it would dig into the rocky ground and surge forward with a power that left Shannon in awe, leaving a tingle of excitement invading her belly, even given the dire circumstances.

They made the tree line and the horse slowed, forced to temper its pace as the number of trees increased. Her heart was racing too fast, her breathing a harsh panting that made it difficult to hear. Forcing her mouth closed, she turned her head, searching the dark shapes of the trees for shadows that moved. The need to flee pounded along every muscle, but she forced herself not to panic. The horse was nervous enough. Smoothing a hand along its neck, she kept her heels pressed into its sides to urge it farther away from the attack behind her.

"There she is!"

Shannon gasped, whipping her head around to see who had followed her. She heard more than saw them, the hard pounding of their horses' hooves telling her that they rode stallions trained far differently than hers. But she refused to give up. Life was suddenly too sweet, too precious to surrender.

"Come on now. Ye can do it."

In the darkness it was impossible to tell where the next threat was coming from. The night was pitch-black, and the sound of riders bounced off every tree and rock.

The thunder of hooves was nearly deafening and almost enough to snap her control over her emotions.

Unanswered questions flittered through her head. Who was attacking the camp below? Did they mean her any harm?

But she didn't have time for such ponderings. She couldn't take the chance that all they wanted was Fergus and his group of traitors. They might consider her guilty simply by her apparent association with those who had murdered a king.

A strangled cry escaped her as she was dragged from her horse. Hard hands pulled her over a saddle, and her cheek smacked against the warm flanks of the animal, its scent filling her senses. She pushed against it, rising up, refusing to lie docile.

"Here now. Have a care, lass. It's a long way to the ground."

Her captor tried to push her head back down, but he didn't credit her with much strength, using only a single hand in an attempt to control her. Shannon twisted, attempting to sit all the way up. Bare tree limbs raked across her face. Icy and frozen, they sent pain through the exposed skin of her face and neck, but she pushed on, struggling against the hand that latched onto her arm. She slid right down the flank of the horse, her legs crumpling when she hit the ground. Tucking her chin against her chest, she rolled, trying to escape the sharp hooves of the animal.

"Damned McBoyd."

She landed in a heap, her thin gown soaking up the melted snow. It was icy cold, making her shiver, but there was no time to worry about that as she fought to free her feet from the tangle her gown had become. Shannon pushed to her feet, frantically searching for any place to hide.

"What's the matter, Devyn? Cannae ye keep hold of a wee lass?"

"She's stronger than she looks. And she has a wild temperament."

Her pride stung, her temper heating up enough to make the wet spots on her gown unnoticeable.

"We'll be seeing about that. Spirit or no, I'm no returning to me laird without the prize he's wanting." Smug and arrogant, one of her would-be captors wasn't interested in what his comrade thought of her.

She dived away, but too late. The words brushed her ear right before two solid arms clamped around her, the strength in them bruising. He squeezed the breath right out of her, but she kicked and bucked in spite of the spots that began to dance in front of her eyes.

"At least she's no' a screamer."

Shannon angled her head down and sank her teeth into the arm trapping her own against her chest. Her captor growled, but his grip lost its iron hold, and she dived away from him. She hit another hard body. This one wrenched her arms behind her back and shoved her face-first into the muddy ground.

"We'll be seeing, will we? What I saw was her getting loose from you." The man on top of her chuckled. "She's a feisty one, all right."

"Aye, well, let's keep hold of her. The laird is nae going to be too happy about how far she made it."

A hard knee jabbed into her back, right between her shoulder blades. Another man pressed her down on her bottom. Her face turned scarlet, but she was helpless beneath their heavier bodies. Something rough was looped around her wrists and pulled tight.

"Now, I was nae going to tie ye up, lass, but ye gave me no choice."

"No choice? Ye're mad!" she snarled. "Whatever yer quarrel is with Fergus, I am no' part of it. Get yer hands off me!"

They pulled her off the ground with an ease that stung her pride even more. Dead leaves and chunks of muddy snow fell off her, making soft plopping noises when they hit the ground. A shiver shook her frame, the chill of the night too much for her temper to fend off.

"Me laird thinks otherwise, lass. So ye are going, even if I have to sit on ye again."

In the night he was nothing but a specter, but the hard grip on her upper arm was solid and unrelenting. Her wrists ached where they were bound behind her, the rope irritating her skin. The horses surrounded them, and the men on either side of her lifted her right off her feet and up to another one of their clansmen. He didn't take any chances on her struggling away from him. He locked her against the horse with one hard knee across her back. With her hands bound behind her, her head bounced with every step the animal took. Nausea twisted through her belly, and more spots decorated her vision. The black void of unconsciousness beckoned with a promise of relief from the pain and cold, but she resisted, unwilling to be handed over so simply.

There was light twinkling through the trees now. As they drew closer, she lifted her head to stare at it. Her neck ached, but she couldn't remain ignorant of what she was being returned to. Nothing but a few lanterns, but they spread their glow over the spot that only an hour past had been a camp of McBoyds. Now it was occupied with McLerens. Shannon gasped, unable to keep her horror contained inside her, her gaze glued to the colors of the kilts worn by these men. She understood now. There was no way to hold out hope that there was any misunderstanding. Her father had started a clan feud, and the McLerens had risen to the challenge.

Her father's retainers lay where they had fallen. There was no mercy in the eyes of the men who stood near the fallen bodies. They wiped their claymores on their victims before sliding them back into the scabbards strapped to their wide backs. A soft chuckle met her return and then another, until the clearing was full of male amusement. Her face burned again as she felt herself being handed down.

"Whose daughter are ye?"

A lantern was held up to bathe her in light. She blinked as her night vision dissipated in a painful pinch. Whoever he was, his gaze fell on her arisaid and the McBoyd colors woven into the wool.

"Answer me."

The man was accustomed to being obeyed, his voice edged as sharply as the claymore strapped to his back. Shannon lifted her chin, refusing to give him the satisfaction of an answer. Let him wonder.

"She is Shannon McBoyd, the daughter of yer enemy, Laird McLeren," Fergus babbled from where he was poised on his knees. The secretary looked at her with hungry eyes and hope on his face. Shannon only stared at him. He was pathetic. All his fine things and powerful signet ring didn't mean anything now. The tent was leaning and torn, his horse being stroked by a Highlander while the man himself whined in the mud. "Take yer vengeance on her. I have nothing to do with yer quarrel."

"What I see is that me men had to tie her up to get her here, and you fell on yer knees without a single protest. Not that I expect any more from a traitor."

Disgust edged his voice. His gaze settled on her, raked her from head to toe with a sharp look that didn't miss any detail. His men waited on his will, their attention on her and what their laird made of her. Shannon held her chin steady, the sight of Fergus nauseating her completely. She might be a woman, but she was no coward.

Laird Torin McLeren was someone she'd heard much about, but it still hadn't quite prepared her for meeting him. The fact that his men stood alert, in anticipation of his next words, spoke volumes about how much respect they had for their laird. His word would be law.

"Yer father is dealing with traitors and making war on my clan."

"Then I wish ye luck in dealing with him. Ye'll find him back on McBoyd land. I'll bid ye good-bye and best of luck in securing peace."

There was a snort of amusement from one of the men behind him that died quickly when Laird McLeren didn't join him. Quiet surrounded them, the wind the only sound Shannon heard. Hearing it magnified just how silent his men were.

"Ye'll be coming with me, Shannon McBoyd."

Hard authority edged his tone again. Disregarding the fact that the man was a full head taller than herself, she gave her temper free rein. What good were polished manners when lawlessness surrounded her?

"I have no intention of doing any such thing."

"Ye see why we had to tie her up."

Laird McLeren took a step closer to her, but his attention was directed over her shoulder to the men behind her. "Aye. What I do nae understand is why she looks like ye rolled her in the mud first. I did send four of ye after her, aye?"

"But ye told us no to hurt her. That was the part that took the doing."

Laird McLeren made a soft sound beneath his breath that she only heard because the rest of his men were so silent.

"Enough prattle. We've ground to cover before dawn, lads." He pulled a dirk from the top of his boot, and the lantern light glistened off the polished blade. Shannon snarled at the weapon. He heard her and his eyes narrowed.

"Do nae give me grief, McBoyd. Yer clan has been spilling the blood of my kin without cause, and I'm set to see yer father pay for it."

"By spilling my blood?" It wouldn't be the first time. She should have counted herself lucky that she wasn't already on her back being soiled before her throat was cut. Her skin crawled with revulsion at the idea, but pride kept her chin steady. Very few in this life were granted an easy death by fate. She should nae expect different.

His fingers curled around her arm, but he controlled his grip, keeping it from biting into her. That surprised her.

"I will nae be lowering myself to the same deeds that yer father has. I said ye are coming with us. That way I can stop this wedding that will destroy the unity Scotland has known."

He pulled her forward, and she stumbled right past him. The hair on the back of her neck stood up with him behind her. But he held her steady, and she felt the blade kiss the skin on the inside of her wrist.

"Give me trouble, and ye'll be thinking me men were gentle with ye."

He sliced the rope that held her wrists together, but the freedom was short. With a twist of her body, he pulled her hands in front of her in spite of her resistance. Within moments her hands were tied, the rope circling each wrist with a small amount of play between her hands. He held her close, much too close for her comfort. She could smell him again, and this time she noticed that it was an agreeable scent. Surprise made her pull against his grip. A soft weakness behind her knees alarmed her. He was a hardened warrior, one that she'd best be well away from, for he had every reason to treat her harshly. Liking anything about him was insanity.

"Mount up, lads."

His men moved in the same moment he spoke. Their horses must have been kept off in the distance, because now there were rows of them, each one strong and unfearing of the blackness surrounding it. A younger lad brought a huge stallion closer to his laird. The animal pawed at the ground, snorting with impatience. Torin gained the saddle with one powerful motion of his large body. Shannon found herself staring at the graceful way he moved. Almost beautiful. There was nothing clumsy about him.

He held his hand out to her. A gasp passed her lips, and her face turned scarlet as he caught her watching him. With a shake of her head, she backed up, away from that hand.

He grunted, and a moment later her feet left the ground as his men lifted her up, tossing her rather precariously onto the back of his horse. She had to duck her chin to avoid being hit by the thick scabbard of his claymore. The horse moved and she felt herself slipping over the other side of the huge beast, the fabric of her gown making it simple to slide across the sleek hide of the animal because she wasn't close enough to the man to share the saddle.

Torin caught her bound wrists and stopped her. He lowered his head and eased her arms down his body until her bound wrists were settled in front of his belly. Her face was pulled tight against his back while he pushed her arms down over his chest. She sputtered with outrage, but the man simply settled her arms around his waist without any concern for her modesty. The length of rope he'd left between her hands made it possible for her to sit up once her arms were lower, but if she raised them, her face had to be pressed against his back because of how large his chest was.

"I told ye, Shannon. Ye are bound for McLeren land with me."

He sent the horse up the hill in the next moment. She bounced in a jumble of fabric and legs, landing on the saddle with a harsh jolt that traveled all the way up her back to slam her teeth together.

"Tighten yer arms around me, and grasp the horse with yer thighs, woman, or ye'll nae be able to walk for a week."

Cursed Highlander.

Yet he was right. Her only other choice, an ill-advised one, was to suffer being bounced like a sack, leaving her with an aching body, and her most tender parts would receive the most abuse. But grasping him sent a shiver through her. He was hard, his body covered in muscle that was warm beneath her hands. A strange enjoyment flooded her when she opened her fingers and laid her palms flat against his belly. The touch, disturbingly intimate, startled her, and she closed her hands quickly in response.

But the next bounce forced the breath right out of her because she was not concentrating on keeping her jaw set. Her teeth hit each other, sending pain through her head. The motion continued down her spine, snapping her like a length of leather. Sweat popped out on her forehead, while the pain lingered. Torin never hesitated. He kept his stallion moving, keeping his word.

Forcing her fingers open, Shannon laid them against his belly again. This time she scooted up behind him and tightened her legs around the horse beneath her. She thought she heard a sound of approval come from him but didn't dwell too closely on it. Her pride was already suffering. She had to move in unison with him, her hips flexing forward and back in harmony with the motion of the stallion. Her arms needed to remain firmly around him to keep her seat from returning to the jarring bouncing.

Her face turned scarlet and remained that way in spite of the chilly night. She'd spent many an hour thinking about what she'd missed on May Day, and tonight that lack of knowledge was proving difficult to bear. She'd never suspected that a man would feel so good in her arms, that holding him would send little fingers of sensation into her flesh. The hard muscles covering his back didn't feel unyielding; instead they seemed to impart a sense of strength and protection that began a tightening in her belly. Even the way he smelled didn't repulse her—fresh and earthy, making her achingly aware of his masculinity, drawing her attention to his body and the strength lying under her fingertips. This close, she noticed just how much stronger he was than any other man she'd met.

She snorted at her own thoughts. Aye, stronger, and the man was her captor. Her father's lands were considered middle ground in Scotland. Torin McLeren was a Highlander. He surpassed every tale she'd ever heard about how adept they were in the art of war and getting what they desired. Being tied about him was certainly proof enough of that. Yet so was the way he guided the stallion through the darkest hours of the night. There was no missing his skill. She'd have to be blind not to see him for what he was—a fine warrior.

Which only opened the door to despair. While more ground fell behind them and the sun began to turn the horizon pink, she couldn't help but feel the bite of foreboding. Even being sent off to marry hadn't stolen so much of her spirit, because at least there was honor in becoming a wife, even one desired for nothing more than her bloodline.

Now she was a hostage instead of a bride. She would be a McBoyd among McLerens, who had recently lost kin to her own clansmen. That promised her a chilly reception once Torin reached his Highland fortress. The rope around her wrists was a hard reminder of just what position she held now that her father's retainers had failed to protect her. If the king truly was dead and her father sworn to following those who had helped to murder him, a dungeon on McLeren ground might be a kinder fate than she would have faced in Edinburgh. She just wished she didn't feel so helpless. Dread dug into her belly, and she hated it. Never once had she felt so much fear. The taste of it was bitter indeed. She pushed it down, forcing herself to ignore it, but it proved a constant battle that made every minute feel longer.

Curse men and their greed, for tonight it was costing her dearly.

Three

Torin raised his hand just after daybreak. His men pulled up and dismounted quickly. The horses were allowed to walk toward a small stream, where the animals lowered their heads to drink.

Her captor lifted her hands over his head easily and lowered her to the ground with one arm. Her feet were numb and her knees wobbly, but Shannon stiffened her legs while pushing her loose gown down from where it had dried against her skin, the mud acting like glue to keep her dress raised.

"You may relieve yerself behind that outcropping there. Go any farther, and I promise ye I'll be right on yer tail, and for the rest of our journey ye'll be relieving yerself with me standing beside ye."

Beast.

The man was the furthest thing from chivalrous there could be, but she turned and headed where he pointed before he took offense. It was humiliating having to be grateful for the privacy, but she was.

"And be quick, or I'll be up there looking for ye."

She didn't answer. The man wasn't her father or

even a relative, so she didn't owe him any respect. Besides, she'd been playacting for years with her sire, making it look as though she gave him the deference the church claimed she owed him. Maybe that was why fate had turned so ugly against her.

Shannon stood for a moment to ponder that idea but simply couldn't force her mind to absorb it. She refused to believe she was less in the eyes of heaven because of her gender. Many would brand her a heretic for thinking such, but all around her there was male and female, and neither could exist without the other.

The forest around her was full of sounds, the new day being greeted by birds beginning to return from their winter grounds. Patches of snow still lay beneath the branches of the trees, but it had melted where the sun shone directly on it. Spring would be arriving soon, and all the bare limbs would be sporting buds. But for the moment, the land was still held in winter's grasp. She might run but would face freezing once the sun set tonight. Her pair of robes was not constructed from fabric heavy enough to protect her from the elements, and her arisaid was not thick enough to keep her warm. Building a fire would only serve to draw Torin to where she was hidden, and not building one would see her dying a slow death from the winter chill.

Returning was her only real option, even if her pride balked at thinking it. Attempting escape was only setting herself on a path to death or being run down. Torin wouldn't be an easy man to elude, of that she was sure.

She was clumsy with her wrists still tied, making raising her gown more cumbersome than normal, but she wasn't going to ask the beast for help relieving herself. She'd manage.

It chafed to return, but with no better option, Shannon dragged her feet back toward the McLerens. She rounded the outcropping and jumped back a pace when she ran into Torin. Her feet landed on the back of her gown, pulling the fabric tight enough to rob her of her balance. She raised her face to his as she felt her body tumbling backward. He looked more surprised than she, his large body reacting with a jerk and a reach toward his claymore. Shannon landed on her backside at his feet, and with her wrists bound, she couldn't keep her body from rolling all the way into the damp snow. It soaked through her robe, sending a gasp past her lips.

Torin muttered something beneath his breath and reached for her.

"I'll manage myself." She batted at his attempt to help her, slightly shocked at how easily she'd struck the man. It had been an impulse, and one that rose up so fast, she didn't have any chance to temper it with reason.

He frowned at her. "Oh aye, I can see how well ye are doing."

Her cheeks colored. "Ye're a beast to make fun of me, considering that ye are the one who bound my wrists. I'll wager that you would find it a bit of a strain to manage yer kilt with rope knotted about yer hands."

She did not worry if his pride took injury from her words. She refused to care at all about his ego. Her robes were a tangled mess around her knees now, baring her legs to his gaze. His expression darkened, a muscle on the side of his jaw twitching. He reached down and hooked her upper arms while she struggled to sit up, trying to get her feet under her in some sort of ladylike fashion, without spreading her thighs wide.

"Are ye daft, woman? Wearing shoes out in this weather? Where are yer boots?"

He stood her on her feet and continued to aim a hard stare at her. She had to tip her chin up to maintain eye contact with him. The urge to scoot back rose up inside her, and she clamped down on it.

"And who struck ye?"

Now his voice was deadly. The tone confused her, for it struck her as protective. She looked away, too unsure to continue looking at him. The man was her captor, not a friend she might look to for comfort.

He cupped her jaw and raised her face to his once again. The contact of his fingers against her jaw was jarring. She was stepping away from him out of pure instinct, but he reached out and caught her wrists where the rope bound them to keep her near.

"Ye'll be telling me what I want to know, Shannon."

"I will not." She jerked her chin out of his hold, gaining another frown from him. His eyes were as dark as midnight, along with his hair, two things the night had prevented her from noticing before.

"I owe ye no obedience."

That muscle twitched on the side of his jaw again. Dark hair covered his chin now, but the shortness of the beard told her he normally shaved. The dark growth gave him an even harder look. But his lips suddenly twitched up into the briefest of grins.

"Well now, I suppose I can see where ye might think that's a fact."

Amusement danced in his eyes for a moment before it died and his face returned to a hard expression. "But it does nae change the fact that I will have what I want from ye. One way or another, lass. 'Tis yer choice how harshly you wish me to deal with ye."

He gave a tug on her bound wrists, and she tumbled toward him. Before she hit him, he bent one knee and lowered his shoulder. A startled cry that was more anger than fear escaped her lips, as the beast surged upward with her body slung over his shoulder.

"Put me down!"

He slapped a hand on top of the backs of her thighs instead.

"Enough orders from you. While ye ride with me men, ye'll be following my commands."

"I would be happy to be gone from the company of ye and yer men."

"I would not." Firm and resolute, his tone granted her no hope that he might be softening in his intention to take her onto McLeren land.

Her long braid swung like a tail down to the ground, pulling her hair, while he turned and covered the few paces back to where his men waited. He dropped her onto her feet without so much as a grunt to hint that lifting her was any great effort for him. In fact, she caught a glimmer of smug satisfaction in his eyes before he turned to face his men.

"Devyn, Donald, Kevin, and Brockton."

His men answered instantly, moving forward to face their laird while taking quick, narrow glances at her.

"I'll be knowing which of ye laid yer hand across

this woman's face. My orders were clear; there was to be nothing in the way of retribution."

Torin's men all moved closer; even the horses seemed to still. Shannon felt her face turn hot as every set of eyes settled on the blackened and bruised side of her face. She bristled beneath their attention, her pride rejecting such notice of something she considered insignificant.

The men in question all frowned. Devyn spoke up first. "Not a one of us did, Laird. I'm a McLeren retainer; I do nae strike women."

Torin never altered his stance. His shoulders were set stiffly, his hands locked around the wide leather belt that held his kilt in place around his waist. He turned his attention to her, but it wasn't his expressionless face that captured her attention; it was the look being sent her by the four men who had run her down last night. She saw herself in their eyes, an enemy of their entire clan, who was inflicting yet another wrong on them by angering their laird.

"It does nae matter a bit. Think you that I am hurt? I am not. It is of no concern at all."

Torin raised one dark eyebrow at her tone. Surprise appeared on several of the men's faces, but she didn't lower her chin. Let them be aghast that she was arguing with their laird; he was not *her* laird.

"'Tis a matter of my orders being followed, and I will nae have any man riding with me who does nae respect what I say. Give me the man's name, or I'll strip all four of them of their rank and standing as my retainers."

Shannon felt the blood drain from her face. Her hand flew up to cover her mouth as horror flooded her. His words were harsh. What he threatened was a high dishonor for the men standing there awaiting his word. All activity froze; even the horses sensed the tension in the air. Confusion wrapped around her in a thick curtain while she stared at the hard determination on his face. There was no hint of yielding, not a single glimmer of mercy. Worse than that, behind him, she watched his men cast her angry looks. Guilt slammed down on her shoulders, threatening to buckle her knees because she knew they were innocent; she understood all too well what it was like to suffer punishment for something that you could do nothing to change. She had stood so often in front of her own laird and father while injustice was handed down to her.

"Does something about my intentions bother ye, Shannon McBoyd? If so, speak up. I won't give ye another opportunity to set the matter straight. Who struck ye?"

Torin watched her intently, his gaze feeling as though it were burning right into her soul and seeing every thought that raced through her head. She wanted to refuse him, almost needed to deny him what he wanted, because of the rope binding her wrists, but the guilt was too heavy for her heart to bear.

"Yer men have told ye the truth; none of them raised their hand against me. My father struck me, before I left his land. I would think a Highlander would know the difference between a fresh bruise and one that has been healing for a few days."

He stepped closer and reached for the side of her face. Shannon shook her head, refusing to stand steady for his touch. He seemed so much larger with no space between them; her feet stepped away without any thought on the matter.

"Ye have yer answer. Do nae touch me."

A soft chuckle was his response. Amusement sparkled in his eyes, and his lips rose back into that grin. He raised a hand to dismiss his men, but he stepped closer, blocking her view of them. She kept her chin raised and their gazes locked to make sure the brute didn't think he frightened her.

It wasn't a lie, not if he assumed it. She thrust her fear down, refusing to spend her last day of life whimpering.

"Ye have a stubborn nature, Shannon." His tone still carried his amusement, but the glimmer in his eyes hardened when his attention settled on the side of her face still bearing the mark of her father's displeasure. "But that is no reason for a man to strike a lass."

Surprise drew a scoff from her lips. "The church would disagree with ye, and there is nothing stubborn about not being loose. Yer hands do nae belong on me, and that's a fact."

"Is it now?"

He was toying with her. Wasn't that just like a Highlander? They were fearsome warriors and held a notorious reputation for tossing skirts whenever they might. She shivered as the idea of having his hands on her thighs cut through her thoughts.

Shannon shook her head, but Torin captured the rope binding her wrists together once more, keeping her in place and leaving her no defense except her words.

"It is, and ye should know it, unless ye are as savage as I hear Highlanders are. I had thought that gossip was not to be believed." She made sure the beast understood that she was rethinking her position on the matter.

His grin melted back into a firm line, while his keen stare settled on her face. He stroked the bruise, lightly fingering it with a touch that was so delicate, no pain resulted from it. She shivered anyway. Her skin had become sensitive, so much so that she was aware of each fingertip resting on her face. Gooseflesh covered her throat and traveled down her body beneath her gown. Never once had she been so aware of a touch.

"Take yer hand away. I am nae a slut to be seen by others with a man's hands on me. Grant me that respect, if not my freedom."

He didn't remove his hand. Hard determination glittered in his eyes, and she met it with just as much resolve.

"Does that mean that ye would be more receptive to my touch in private?"

Excitement rippled across her skin, her imagination offering up an idea of him pulling her against him for a reason other than taking her north as his captive. A flicker of heat appeared in his dark eyes, shocking her with how wild her ideas were.

"It doesnae."

Her palm itched to connect with his smug face, but guilt gnawed at her as well because she was more angry with herself than him. She jerked against his hold on her bound wrists but only succeeded in pulling herself off balance when he didn't give even a single inch. Her body tumbled forward a step, drawing a snarl of frustration from her, but at least her face was no longer in his hand.

He stiffened and stepped back, releasing her completely. "All right, lass. I believe I understand ye."

"I doubt it." She hissed at him in a low tone, because now that he'd moved, she could see that most of his men were still watching them. Amusement decorated their faces.

"I suppose ye think I deserve to be humiliated because I am a McBoyd. Is this what I am to expect from a Highlander?"

"It is not." His tone hardened now, every hint of playing vanished. His expression tightened too, the grin completely gone.

"Then what is yer game?"

He raised one hand, and another lad brought him his horse. He grasped the reins in a large hand that drew her eyes. A tingle went across her cheek with the memory of having those fingers against her skin. She shook off the strange feeling, ordering herself to stop looking like a demented fool.

"I sought to understand what sort of a person ye are, Shannon McBoyd. Wanted to know if you would watch others suffer when ye held the power to keep it from happening. I do know the difference between a fresh bruise and one that has been healing for a few days."

He swung up onto the back of his stallion with an ease that still amazed her. He wore a pair of trews beneath his kilt to protect him from the cold weather, but the soft fabric still showed her the corded muscles that covered his limbs. He clamped those powerful legs around his mount and kept the animal still while he leaned down and offered her his hand. A challenge lit his eyes, and there was no mistaking why. The man wanted to see if she knew when she was beaten.

She took his hand of her own doing, because if she didn't, his men would place her behind him. The only choice she had was to decide if she wanted only *his* hands touching her, or others' as well. In a way, the beast was giving her what she'd demanded, but that didn't make it easy to lift her hands toward his. She gritted her teeth while she did it, cringing when his fingers curled around her wrist. At least she was able to jump and help gain the back of the horse faster.

He lifted her bound wrists up and over his head once again. Her body scooted up close to his without hesitation.

"I can't see as how it might matter what sort of person I am."

Her head was pressed against his back now, and her words soft. His men were mounting, the sound of leather and metal filling the air.

"It matters because it is very possible that I am going to have to keep ye, Shannon McBoyd, and I do nae fancy the idea of having someone under me roof who will slip a dirk in me back while I sleep."

"I'm happy to leave the killing to you men." And she would certainly not be going anywhere near the man's bed. Even if his touch was inviting and strangely enjoyable.

"Yer father started the blood spilling, but I aim to end it, even if that means taking you back to Donan Tower with me."

"Trust a man to think that is not a harm."

"I never said it was not a harm, only that I will do it because I see no alternative. Ye cannae be allowed to wed the man yer father has struck a bargain with."

There was an odd note of compassion in his voice, one that her frayed nerves wanted to cling to. For just a moment, she allowed herself that luxury. But once she dispensed with her fear, her body began to notice his far more intently. The scent of his skin was clean and strangely enjoyable. Shannon bit her lip, firmly ordering herself to think of other things.

"I'll see ye treated decently on my land, for ye seem to be a honest lass."

"And if I hadna passed yer test?"

She was mad to ask the question, but the words passed her lips before she was able to remind herself that agitating him was not wise. Not when her wrists were tied and she was helpless.

He turned his head, looking back at her. "I'd be forced to treat ye as such actions deserved."

"I force nothing upon ye." She couldn't help but pull against her bound wrists. His hand suddenly landed on top of hers, stilling the motion.

"Which is why ye have my word that ye will be treated decently."

With a sure hand, he pulled the stallion's head about to face north. He was taking her to the Highlands without hesitation. She flinched when the horse began moving.

The chill increased in spite of the sunlight throughout the day. More snow became visible, and Torin had to steer his horse around patches of slick ice. Shannon found herself grateful for his warmth as the sun began to set. Her legs shivered with the cold, and she found herself looking with envy at the knee-high leather boots worn by the other men. Her little shoes let the winter cold in to torment her toes, and her ankles ached.

The clouds pressed down on them, finally beginning to rain near sunset. Becoming soaked completed her misery. Shannon gave up the fight to think of positive things; she felt the icy droplets soaking into her clothing and running down the front of her body.

Torin suddenly pulled his horse to a stop, the animal dancing sideways in protest. The horse wanted to be in its warm stable, not standing on the road in such weather. Torin turned and reached behind her to raise her arisaid up. Her jaw would have dropped open if her face hadn't been pressed against his back. The fabric became wet, but at least it helped cut some of the chill.

"Yer father is a harsh man to send ye out in shoes."

Torin didn't give her a chance to answer; he raised his own plaid up to shield his head and gave the stallion its freedom to continue up the path. The last of the light shimmered off a long loch, and her belly began to rumble. No one seemed to have provisions.

Of course they didn't. The harsh truth cut into her thoughts with the glaring fact that these men had ridden out from their homes to defend their land against a raid. They hadn't returned home for comforts but had pressed on until they discovered those guilty of killing their kin.

Highlanders. They were feared for good reason. If you expected them to act like other men, you would be shown the error of your thinking quickly. Maybe it was the harsher climate into which they were born; or perhaps it was bred into them. Whatever the reason, Highlanders possessed a determination that was unmatched. As the light faded, the only complaints came from Fergus. The rest of Torin's men pressed forward, focused on gaining their home before they rested.

"There."

Shannon heard the word as much as she felt it. Torin's chest rumbled beneath her arms. She shifted her head under his arm to look.

"That's Donan Tower, lass."

He was proud of it too. And relieved to have made it back home. Dread punched clean through her heart, the combination of his elation at seeing his home and the sight of it rising up from the rocky landscape too much for her.

For her, it was to be a prison.

Donan Tower sat on a rocky pile of land surrounded by Loch Alsh on three sides. A long bridge led to its gate. It was more than a single tower—one larger keep sat in the center of several other buildings. On the shore surrounding it was a village full of thatch-roofed homes with smoke rising from them. Even in the rain, the sound of work drifted on the night air. Sounds from the blacksmith and sword makers as they hammered. There was also the sound of sawing and the scent of stew cooking over fires. People began appearing as they were sighted. The villagers didn't let the rain intimidate them. With McLeren plaids covering their heads, they emerged from their shelters, waving to the returning retainers. Torin's men sent up a roar that sounded as ferocious as it did joyful.

Shannon found herself nursing self-pity. That tower was naught but a prison for her. There would be no friends there for the daughter of their enemy. Her father's disdain would feel quite warm in comparison.

They reached the village and were forced to slow down. Not a simple task, because the stallion wanted to gain its warm stable and knew where to head. Torin pulled up on the reins to keep from trampling anyone. Shannon felt the stares of his people on her and her McBoyd tartan. They gave her harsh glares and a few even spit when they sighted her. A sudden feeling of gratefulness for being on the back of Torin's horse swept through her. She had to be grateful that the man wasn't leading her by a length of rope behind his horse. It would not have been the first time a captive received such treatment, considering the circumstances.

Torin was being quite decent to her, just as he'd promised he would.

She banished the good feelings toward her captor instantly. The man was her captor, not her friend. Even if he were the gentlest man in Scotland toward her, his people would only hold that fact against her and hate her more. Aye, she saw the hate in their eyes. Some weren't so harsh, but many glared at her with the anger at her father's raiding written on their faces. The first touch of hoof to the stone bridge made her cringe. The chill crept inside her until it encased her heart, loneliness wrapping tightly around her.

If her captor noticed her quivering, he never let it impede his progress toward the raised gate on the other side of the bridge. The steady clop of the stallion's hooves cut into her like a knife.

Once inside the curtain wall, she could see that the tower and its surrounding buildings rose several stories into the air. The stone was gray and darkened with age, except for one building that was lighter than the rest. New construction spoke of a wealthy clan, because there were enough resources to add on to the castle. Her father was more fool than he knew. A clan that could afford new additions to their towers was also bound to be valued as a friend to other clans too. Making war on the McLeren could very well bring down the wrath of any other clan that wanted to be aligned with one doing so well.

So foolish and such an unkind fate for her...

Torin pulled up in front of the wide stone steps that led up to one of the outer buildings. He pulled the dirk from the top of his boot, and she felt the rope holding her arms around him give way. A soft sound of relief passed her lips as she was able to sit up completely. The muscles along her back complained bitterly of the hours they had been held in a single position. Torin swung one leg right over the lowered head of his mount and jumped down while she was gently stretching out her spine. A second later he reached up and grasped her, his large hands easily closing around her hips.

"What are ye doing?"

She sounded breathless and clamped her mouth shut to try to compose herself. Her feet landed on the ground, and Torin grasped one wrist. He pulled the rope off and studied her skin.

"Welcoming ye to Donan Tower."

"Welcome..." The man was clearly insane. Her

jaw dropped with shock. "Now there is a misused word if ever I heard one."

He shrugged, but his face remained stony and impossible to read. "It can be what ye make of it. I do nae plan to lock ye in the dungeon unless ye give me reason to place you behind iron bars. I made ye a promise, and I will keep my word."

"Why would you consider anything you said to me a promise?" She pushed her soaked arisaid back so that she might look up at his face. The man loomed over her, the top of her head only rising to his shoulders.

His eyes narrowed at her question. "Because I spoke the words, Shannon McBoyd, and I keep my word."

"Most men wouldn't consider anything said to the daughter of their enemy a promise."

He stiffened. "I am a Highlander."

His fingers remained curled around her wrist, and his tone was solid steel. He used the grip to tug her along behind him as he climbed the stairs and entered a large receiving hall. The air inside felt hot against her chilled face. Two large hearths were set into the side of it, and both had fires blazing in them. Her belly began rumbling as the scent of food hit her. Her stomach was so empty, it ached. Torin's men were filing past them on their way toward the hearths and the women tending the large iron pots hanging over the fires. But everyone in the hall was busy staring at her. Conversation died down, leaving only the crackle of the fires and the footsteps of the returning men.

"This is Shannon McBoyd, daughter of Laird McBoyd."

Eyes narrowed in response to her name. The happy expressions that had greeted the return of their laird and retainers were replaced with hard looks. All of them aimed directly at her.

"She will be treated decently, or ye will answer directly to me." Torin pulled her farther into the hall. "And she is no' to leave the tower."

He released her and turned to mount a set of stairs built into the wall opposite the hearths. He climbed them without any hint of distress and disappeared through a doorway at the top. Conversation resumed, and she heard her name being repeated. The women at the hearths began dishing up bowls of steaming food for the retainers, and benches scraped against the stone floor as they sat down to enjoy their meal.

She was suddenly grateful for the scorn her father held for her. Standing in front of a hall full of people staring at her was nothing new. Her cheeks did not turn hot, and her chin remained firmly in place.

She would endure, because Shannon McBoyd was no coward. Such was the only thing she had control over, but she didn't miss the fact that no one watching her cared.

❧

"What are ye planning to do with the lass?"

Malcolm followed him often. Most of the time Torin was happy for the counsel; today he wasn't. He untied his scabbard and set his claymore aside before looking back at the other man.

Malcolm grinned back at him. "Did ye think no one would ask, on account of ye are laird now?"

"I was hoping."

Malcolm sat down in front of the fire that was warming the outer solar and stretched out his feet toward the flames. "She's a bonny thing."

"She is a bundle of trouble that I do nae need on my land, old man. Douglas will nae be pleased to hear she's imprisoned beneath my roof."

Malcolm responded by laughing. He gave in to a full-bellied chuckle that filled the chamber.

"Och now, only a young man would look at a sweet lass like that and call her trouble."

"She's a McBoyd. The earl will nae consider it a light matter, even in these times. He might order her hung for her blood. There's a duty we can do well without."

Torin shook his head to dispel the distaste filling him. Shannon McBoyd had a spark of life in her that he would hate to see strangled. Even if the king's counsel ordered her death, Torin doubted he'd find the discipline to carry out the sentence. He withdrew his claymore and began to dry the long blade so that it would not rust.

"Oh aye, my mind still works well. The earl is known for his ways of killing off the relatives of those who strike at him. That's the only way to gain a crown if ye weren't born wearing one." Malcolm stroked his white beard. "But there's a beauty in having that girl here, don't you know. A more perfect way to pay back McBoyd, I cannae think of. Knowing his daughter is here will surely drive him insane. The man cannae cry to the earl without admitting what he was doing sending his daughter south. I'll sleep better tonight, knowing that he's boxed in and unlikely to do any more raiding."

"What it will do is send him south to Atholl looking for men to come up here to slaughter us all." Torin held up his sword and inspected the blade. "With his daughter here, he has an excuse to feed his hunger for killing McLerens."

"All ye need do is threaten the lass. Her father will nae need to know that we McLeren are not so ambitious as he is, and would not follow through with harming her."

Torin slid the claymore into a dry scabbard and placed it against the wall.

"Except that I believe McBoyd would prefer we kill his daughter, because that would give him the excuse to validate his attack on White Hill by saying that we were plotting to steal her. It would be my word against his."

Torin turned away from Malcolm to hide the rage that took command of his features. For the first time in his life, he was in favor of stealing a woman. He wasn't sorry, not one bit, about bringing Shannon back with him as his captive. She had too much honor in her to stand anywhere near her bastard father.

Malcolm resumed stroking his beard. A pensive look entered the old man's eyes.

"Well then, I suppose it is a good thing ye took the girl before she cemented this bit of business. The Douglas will nae be letting Atholl march on the Highlands."

There was that. Both earls might want to quarrel, but the Highland Douglas was stronger, and Atholl knew it. Torin pulled his wet clothing off without a care for the other man in the room. Being alone with his thoughts wasn't the best of ideas, not when he was spending too much time dwelling on Shannon and not enough on the plot that she'd been the seal on.

Not any longer. She'd stay right where he'd put her until he was satisfied that the true king was sitting on the throne. But that would take quick work on his part. Highlanders enjoyed staying far away from Edinburgh and its plots, but today, that was not a luxury he might afford. His fellow clans could not remain in their Highlands while the queen was fighting for the rights of her son.

Action was needed.

At least that turned his thoughts away from his captive. He'd send riders to the Douglas and the Lindsey. The Earl of Douglas was a powerful man, who would help bring an end to the threat. There was no other choice but to keep Shannon, even if he didn't enjoy the idea of it. Donan Tower was his home, and he didn't much care for anyone viewing it as a prison. But he'd do what had to be done for the sake of his people. That was his duty.

Torin drew in a stiff breath. There was more to his actions than just the plot against the king. A deep satisfaction was moving through him now that he had succeeded in bringing Shannon to his home.

She was a bonny thing, as Malcolm had said. But what he found snaring his attention was the way she'd held her chin steady while surrounded by Highlanders who'd reduced grown men to whimpering heaps. Shannon McBoyd possessed a spirit that he couldn't help but admire. There were few men he held the same respect for, and that knowledge was tugging on his attention, refusing to be discarded in favor of focusing his thoughts on what was happening in Edinburgh.

Torin discovered his thoughts centered on something far closer to home, the bonny lass whom he'd stolen.

Four

"STOP STANDING ABOUT. THERE'S WORK TO BE DONE, or didna yer McBoyd mother teach ye anything about how a house is run?"

A McLeren woman sneered at her before shoving a large wooden tray at her. The retainers had finished eating, and the long tables were covered with dirty dishes now. The tray was scarred and had an uneven rim, but it was still useful for gathering up things that needed washing. Shannon gripped the edge and pushed the opposite side against her hip in a practiced motion. She was already swiping abandoned bowls off the table before the woman turned away from her, but Shannon still witnessed the smug look that appeared on the woman's face.

Well, that was to be expected.

She continued clearing one of the long tables, the cold remains left in the bowls drawing a long rumble from her empty belly. There was still stew simmering over the fire, but the McLeren women standing near it didn't offer her any welcome to join them.

Quite the opposite. They sent her harsh glares, and a few nodded with approval to see her acting as their maid. Shannon gave them her back when she reached the end of the table and began to work her way along the other side of it. She felt them watching her but didn't concern herself. She knew how to lend a hand, and that was for certain. Her father had never allowed her to be the pampered, highborn woman of the house. For the moment, she was grateful for that fact. She would not be sniveling because no one made her welcome. It was better than the worst that might have happened, considering the circumstances. She doubted her father would have treated Torin's sister so well if he had her in his possession.

That was a sad fact. Her father's face came to mind, but she only saw him with a scowl, which was a lament, to recall her sire only in a sour mood. A soft sigh passed her lips for the happiness that she had never known from him. She doubted she would ever see him again.

She stacked the bowls with a practiced hand, keeping the tray balanced and her feet from stepping on her hem. She kept two of the fuller bowls toward the center of her tray and made sure not to pile anything on top of what would serve as her supper. There were crusts of bread left on the table too. Most of it crumbled, but again, it would be more to her taste than begging at the hearth.

She followed her instincts toward the back of the cooking area and found a long washroom. The sound of moving water filled her ears while she took careful steps down a long stone staircase that took her to the ground level. She stood at the back of the main tower, where the water moved in a current toward the river that ran beneath the bridge they'd ridden across and on past the village.

Castles needed a water supply in case of siege. Donan Tower had plenty, with the loch surrounding it on three sides. It made for simple cleaning. The room she'd stepped down into was long and had sinks built along one wall with small rounded stones and mortar. She could hear the waterwheel turning on the other side of the wall, and see the glitter of the moonlight off the water of the loch through large windows that were set into the wall. Water was flowing through the sinks and on to places cut away in the wall that allowed it back outside. She could hear it splashing on the surface of the loch when it returned. The sinks sat at an angle to allow that and to make sure that muck did not collect. The room didn't smell of mold, telling her that Donan Tower had a good head of house.

There was more than one set of sinks as well. She walked the length of the room, impressed by how long it was. At least the length of two of the large trestle tables sitting in the hall. There were four sets of sinks, which meant four waterwheels. The room was full of the sound of water moving, and there was a chill that tickled her nose, but the cleanliness of it impressed her further. It was clear that food was kept only at one set of sinks, which left the others for laundry.

Very modern indeed.

For the moment the room was deserted, and it offered her the first true privacy she'd known since being awoken by Gerty. She suddenly realized how badly she ached. It felt as though every muscle was bruised or strained. One ankle hurt more than the other and felt like it was swollen inside her shoe. Her belly was in a knot so tight, she wasn't sure if she wanted to eat or retch.

She turned in a circle and returned to the sinks where the dishes were cleaned. Picking up one of the bowls, she didn't linger over the meal but ate it quickly before any of the McLeren women appeared to order her to another task. Even cold, it was pleasant. Yet her belly gave a slight heave when it hit, making her slow down.

The sound of the water was soothing, but it made her feel every bit of grime that clung to her skin. There would be a bathing house somewhere too, but she doubted that it would be empty, with so many retainers newly returned. She likely had that fact to thank for her current privacy. If the bath house was full, most of the maids would be there lending a hand.

But there was water and soap here. Opening her oversleeves, she unhooked the cuffs of her chemise and pushed them high above her elbows. The soap was kept in a pottery dish near the sink. It was soft and easy to dig up with her fingers. Which was better for cleaning dishes than boiling that same soap until it might set into bars.

She shivered at the first touch of the water. Her skin rippled with the chill, but gaining relief from feeling soiled was far more pressing. She plunged her arms into the water and cupped her hands to bring it toward her face. The bruise from her father's hand stung, but once the first touch of cold water passed, all that remained was a sense of freshness.

She scrubbed every inch of skin that she might, casting quick looks behind her at the stairs, but no one appeared. That allowed her to open her gown and use a small cloth to clean her neck and chest. She longed for a true bath but knew that she wouldn't be gaining such a luxury anytime soon.

At least she wasn't hungry. Returning to the tray, she ate more before beginning to scrape the leftover food into a large bowl that stood near the sink. Waste brought need. Even the scraps might be used to fatten the fish on the loch and keep them returning to a place that would be easy to catch them from.

She worked quickly because her back ached. Her face felt clean, though, and she kept her mind on that. Her privacy ended as the other women appeared with trays full of more dishes to do. They promptly left them piled near the sink with little smirks while they went back up into the hall without tending to any of the chores.

They most likely thought it fitting to use her like a slave. In truth, that word fit all too well. Her spirits sank lower, until even the knowledge that she knew what she was about failed to cheer her. She felt the bite of the cold water more, and the burning along her back and hips became nearly intolerable.

She finished with a soft hiss and turned her back gladly on the sinks. The wash house was still empty, but she didn't wonder why. Even with the water filling the room, she knew full well what was happening up in the hall. She could see the light shimmering around the doorway.

There would be a celebration happening now. Whisky, strong cider, and ale, most likely, being passed about in honor of the return of their men. The girls would take to dancing, while merriment filled the hall.

She had no taste for it. Loneliness wrapped around her so tightly, she ached even more. But she tossed her head and began searching the washroom for other doorways that would take her up to the main floor of the tower. She didn't want to appear in the back of the hall so that her captors might raise a toast to their captive as well.

She was quite sure they would not need her to do that.

She found another set of stairs and climbed them. The sound of the water died, and she did indeed hear the music floating down the hallway from the hall, but the corridor was dim due to its thick stone wall. It was also cold. The wind whipped the bottom of her gown because all the window shutters remained open to draw the smoke away from the hall hearths. Lanterns hung every twenty paces, telling her that the shutters normally remained open and that the corridor was often used after supper. Otherwise the candles in the lanterns would not be wasted. They were costly lanterns too, made of tin folded into cylinders that had cuts to allow the light out. Open candles might have blown out or posed a fire danger with the breeze. It was quite clever planning, placing the tower so that the night wind blew through it, to keep the smoke from collecting in the rooms. She kept going, because there was one thing she had learned from her father, and that was that there were often storage rooms on the same floor as the great hall.

She rounded a corner and stopped at the open windows. The moonlight was magnificent on the surface of the loch. It rippled with the night breeze, all cast in silver moonshine. The soft music filtered to her ears, making it impossible to ignore the beauty laid out before her.

A splash drew her attention, and she leaned into the window. Her jaw dropped slightly as a man rose from the silvery water. He climbed up onto one of the rounded rocks that rose above the surface of the loch. There was no hint of strain from him as he climbed confidently up the side of the smooth boulder like a hero from a legend who was able to grip what appeared to be a smooth-faced stone. He gained the top of it with a few long motions of his limbs. He stood there, completely bare, with nothing but water streaming down his bare flesh.

She should have looked away.

But she didn't.

Her teeth went into her lower lip as she moved closer to the wall. Her hands rested on the smooth stones lining the window opening, but the chill beneath her palms was quite welcome. Somehow her blood was moving quickly through her veins, her heart beating at a faster tempo. Her gaze moved over him, fascinated by his body, huge and set with wide shoulders. His hair lay across those shoulders in curling tendrils that still drained water. It slithered down over the hard ridges of muscle that coated his back, like liquid silver in the moonlight. He lifted his head, tilting his chin toward the moon, and drew a gasp from her lips.

He was pure magnificence. The embodiment of legend and lore such as no ballad could ever convey.

All her life she had heard tales of Highlanders and how strong they were. This man was the living proof of those stories. A shiver rippled along her skin, and she refused to blink, else he dissipate like a spirit. His shoulders tapered down to a trim waist and a pair of buttocks that were tight. His legs were thick and cut with more ridges of muscle that moved down past his knees and over his calves to his feet.

She wanted to see all of him.

It was a shocking idea, but one that she could not lie about. It burned through every lesson on propriety and correctness that had ever been preached to her. Suddenly it felt as though she had to see him from the front. She would have sworn that she needed to know what the rest of him looked like, if only to have it confirmed that he was more attractive than any mortal man might be.

As if he sensed her thoughts, he turned his head and looked back toward the tower. His jaw was set in a firm position that seemed to portray pride. He stood entirely still, only a few last trickles of water sliding across his firm body. The loch continued to ripple and gently slap against the rock he stood on. His hands opened, displaying large palms, and he slowly rotated to face her.

The breath froze in her chest, but not because it was cold. Her body was warm and hot inside, completely the opposite of the cold stone her hands rested on. The chill in the night air cooled the flush on her face. Blood surged through her body, warming every inch of her, right down to her smallest toes. She heard her heart working and noticed the time between each beat.

It was Torin McLeren, her captor, but knowing that didn't make her turn away. There was a part of her that enjoyed having the man at a disadvantage. But more of her simply enjoyed the sight of him.

He had truly looked a legend, rising from the loch in the dark of the night as the church warned.

Yet she felt no fear, not even hesitation. Part of her even contemplated climbing through the window to join him on his stone throne. The reason was simple; she longed to touch him. Was he as cold as the loch or warm like a mortal? She yearned to know.

There were other men in the water, but her attention was captivated by the one standing on the boulder. He drew her gaze to him, and there was none left for the others who bathed near him.

"Laird, Lindsey's on the road. Coming up the bridge now."

The shout came from the curtain wall. Shannon felt her eyes widen, and she pushed away from the window with a strength that sent her tumbling back across the corridor to avoid being caught. The magic of the moment shattered, leaving her gasping because she'd somehow forgotten to draw in enough breath. She had been absolutely fixated on him, like they had been enclosed in a moment of intimacy.

Shame bit into her, threatening to choke her. But the worst torment was the way her memory recalled in vivid detail what Torin looked like. She leaned against the wall, too shocked by her need to stare at him to stand up straight. Never once had she behaved so wantonly, even if she had to admit to thinking about it from time to time. Thinking and looking—staring really—were two different things entirely.

She far preferred the looking…

Her cheeks heated, but how could they not? He was magnificent.

She closed her eyes and moaned softly. Now things were even worse, and she hadn't thought such might be possible. She shivered again, the memory tormenting her with how much she had enjoyed looking at his bare form.

How much she had wanted to touch him… and yet she did know what the man felt like pressed against her.

With a gasp, she forced her sagging body to straighten. Her circumstances were bad enough. If the only thing she might control were her own thoughts, she was not going to allow them to run wild. Not when they might lead her toward an even worse fate that involved her virtue being forfeited to her captor. It was one thing to suffer being taken against her will, but her heated thoughts were going to make her a willing participant before much longer.

She would not do such. Yet her body was growing too tired to resist its impulses. It was always easier to give in when you had gone too many hours without rest. The tension of the day was gnawing away at her reserves. She cast a look about, seeking refuge from the McLeren. All she needed was some time to rest and regain her strength. For the moment, no one seemed to care where she was, and that was a kindness of fate that she intended to make the most of.

Moving along the corridor, she sought out any deserted workroom that might serve as good shelter for the night. Several workrooms lay down the next corridor. These rooms faced the east and would catch the morning sunlight well. In spite of the bulk of winter being behind them, one of the rooms was still half full of raw wool. She sniffed at the air and found it fresh enough. The wool had been washed before being stored. Taking one of the small lanterns from where it hung in the corridor, she carried it farther into the room. Lifting it high, she allowed the light to illuminate what was there. Thick cloaks hung from pegs on the walls, yet another sign of the McLeren's wealth. Garments such as these were costly, and yet they remained in the workroom for any maid who discovered herself chilly while working the spinning wheels that sat near the windows. The wooden shutters were closed now, but she could still hear the wind whistling on the other side of them. But they did not rattle, telling her that they were in good repair.

Reaching for one of the cloaks, she swung it around her shoulders. A shiver shook her as her body anticipated being warm. Returning to the doorway, she moved into the hallway to replace the lantern. Keeping it would have told anyone looking for her where she had gone, and Shannon discovered it satisfying to know that she had slipped away. Maybe that was only an illusion, because she was still within the tower walls, but it was a comfort, and one that she would hug tightly to her chest.

The cloak began to cut the chill of the night quickly. But with the relief of being warm, her body began to fail her. The sleepless nights and long days of fighting her way through icy mud took their toll. With her belly full, there was nothing to keep her eyelids from drooping. Reaching for the second cloak, she laid it across some of the wool waiting to be carded. It made a fine-enough pallet, maybe even softer than the barley chaff one she had used back in her father's fortress. Lying down on the cloak, she shook out the first one on top of her. Curling the edges of the bottom one up and on top of her, it made for a very pleasant bed.

It would not have mattered if it were uncomfortable or not. She doubted anything short of true pain would have kept her eyes open. While the mind was willing, her body demanded rest. She would not return to the hall and appeal to her captors for a bed to rest in. She wasn't helpless. She'd see to her own needs by using her wits. There was always a way to endure.

Always.

❦

Connor Lindsey was pure Scots. Torin enjoyed the way the man didn't let the night stop him from going where he was needed. The neighboring laird paused as the gate was hoisted to allow him entrance, but his stallion danced in a circle while the heavy gate was moving upward. The moment it was high enough, he lay down across the neck of the beast and charged forward, with his retainers on his heels, not waiting for it to be high enough for him to remain sitting upright in the saddle.

Aye, that was a man of action right enough.

"Torin, ye sorry excuse for a friend! What's this I hear about ye having fun and no' waiting for me to share it with ye?"

Connor was off his horse and up the stairs in the same amount of time that it took for him to speak.

"The king is dead. Murdered."

His friend sobered instantly, all traces of teasing leaving his face. His features may have been fair, with light hair and eyes the same color as the loch when the sun shone on it, but there was nothing light about the look that took control of the man. Torin took the last step and stood on even footing with him.

"I'd hoped that rumor would play out to be false."

"White Hill is still smoldering."

Connor cursed. "Then it's true, and the McBoyd are plotting with that traitor Atholl."

There was distaste in the man's tone, the same bitterness that Torin had tasted throughout the journey home. Behind Connor, his retainers' expressions tightened. They wore different colors than his own men did, but at the moment they were all Scotsmen. Something that would cease to be, if they allowed Atholl to tear the country apart for his own gain.

"Come, my friend, we've matters to discuss."

Connor Lindsey grunted and followed him into the tower. The hearth fire was burning low, but a flick of his fingers sent the women to building it back up. The hall was still full, a sense of joy in the air, but the conversation dwindled away until the pop and crackle from the fire became dominant. Connor sat down at the high table along with his captains while Torin did the same.

It was time to talk strategy.

Five

THE CHURCH BELLS RANG AT DAWN.

Shannon sat up quickly and gasped when her back protested. Her muscles were tight and sore. Pain snaked through her when she raised a hand to rub at her eyes. She was not used to riding so many hours, but there was nothing to be done about the agony. Sitting still would only see her hurting longer. Better to get moving and work the torment out of her flesh.

Light filtered into the room now, illuminating the edges of the wooden shutters. Reaching up, she unlatched them and opened them wide. The water of the loch sparkled with the newly risen sun, the rays of light dancing off the ripples. Shannon stared at the distant shore, trying to judge the distance. It would be too far to swim.

Of course it would be. The towers would not be safe if the loch might be crossed. The surface wasn't smooth, hinting at powerful currents that were most likely stronger than she thought.

Yet Torin had braved them...

Her cheeks heated, and it had naught to do with the morning sun. Her memory was crystal clear, offering up an image of Torin standing so confidently last evening. Her attention moved to the boulder that he'd stood on. In the morning light, it was just another smooth stone, one of hundreds that she could see on the surrounding mountains.

The church bells began ringing again, this time in a steady rhythm meant to call the inhabitants to morning service. Her blush burned hotter as the sound mingled with the memory of what she'd spied last night. Suddenly she understood why the church preached against good Christians wandering during the dark hours. The night truly was filled with temptations to sin. Something about the darkness had indeed made her bolder, more passionate than she had suspected she was.

Her attention strayed to the boulder once more, and this time she noticed that it was only thirty feet from the shore. Beyond it lay a large expanse of choppy water that would claim her life if she attempted to swim it. The boulder Torin had stood on was the farthest one out, telling her that the loch deepened past it as well.

She heard footsteps in the corridor now. They didn't stop but continued on toward the front of the tower. The bells continued to beckon, and she followed the sound without really thinking about her actions. Every morning she went to service, just as every member of the clan did. Such obedience was instilled in every child from the moment that their mothers recovered from birth. Old and young alike gave deference to the church.

The eating hall was empty when she reached it. Crossing the large area was much simpler today. The double doors that led to the yard were open, and she reached them without protest from anyone. Below her, she could see the last of the McLeren making their way toward the church that sat off to the right side of the gate. It had a steeple that the bell hung in. The few people in sight were hurrying toward the open doors, their hands reaching out quickly to dip into the holy water waiting near the door. She could hear the monks beginning to sing the first verses of the morning Mass.

But she froze on the top step, a tingle shooting down her nape. Raising her head, she looked up onto the curtain wall and found several men watching her. These were burly retainers, their chests covered in mail tunics. On their heads they wore helmets that were secured into place by sturdy leather straps beneath their chins. They stared at her, and she recalled all too clearly the way their laird had ordered that she remain within the tower.

Did the beast mean to deny her the Mass?

She looked back at the church and the distance between the tower and its doors. No one stood between her and the sanctuary. Why had she not thought of it before? The church would shelter her. Even a Highlander laird would not challenge the authority of the priest.

Of course, that meant she would have to become a nun. Nothing was free in this earthly life. Not even from the church. If she sought shelter in the church, she would be expected to pledge herself as a bride of

Christ, making her dowry the possession of the church. It didn't matter that her father had not given her his blessing to become a nun; the church would hound him until he consented and gave her dowry to them.

She nibbled on her lower lip, indecision tearing at her thoughts. Part of her enjoyed the idea of knowing her father would be pressed into submission just as he had so often done to her and everyone around him. Laird McBoyd would have to kneel in obedience to the church or face being excommunicated.

It was unkind of her to wish her father ill, or anyone for that matter. She needed heaven's goodwill now more than ever; turning spiteful was sure to see the angels and saints turning deaf ears to her prayers.

That should have been reason enough to turn her against the idea of becoming a nun, but it was the vision of Torin standing on that boulder that clouded her thinking. Just a few hundred feet across the yard and her honor might remain unsullied forever, but she'd never know what it felt like to run her fingers over the firm flesh of a man. Never get close enough to smell the clean scent of his skin again.

It was a truth that she'd make a poor nun, one who was less than dedicated. That in itself would not be uncommon. A third-born daughter was always promised to the church. Her father had avoided the demands of giving a portion of his wealth over so far, but with two sons, the priests were watching her new stepmother to see if the woman produced any more daughters.

Pain snaked through her lip as she bit it too hard. She was not debating the loss of the possibility of touching Torin McLeren, only the loss of the possibility of ever having a husband. He was not a man to whom she would be yielding anything such as her touches. The man was her captor, and he'd earned every bit of scorn that went along with that term. She would find a way to banish what she had seen from her thoughts.

"You'll be needing to step back into the tower now, lass, as I warned ye to stay inside these walls."

Shannon turned in a flurry of her robes, one shoulder pressing tightly against the door frame she stood in out of a need to know that no one might sneak up behind her. She knew his voice instantly, and it raised the tiny hairs on the back of her neck. But the sensation was not confined to just her nape; it rippled down her body, touching off an awareness of the man that was too intimate for her comfort.

Torin McLeren eyed her from beneath lowered eyebrows. He gripped his belt, the fingers of his hands looking larger than normal to her. Maybe it was the purple background color of his plaid that drew her attention so strangely, or the way his kilt seemed to suit him. He wore only a shirt, with one edge of that plaid pulled over his right shoulder and crossing his chest. It was folded neatly, showing the signs of having been pressed. His household staff took excellent care of their laird if they ironed his kilt.

Better to think of the efficiency of his staff than accept that his hands drew her interest.

"You mean to deny me the Mass?"

He stepped forward until he was sharing the doorway with her. Another shiver raced down her spine in response. The certain knowledge of what he looked like beneath his clothing sent a blush burning across her cheeks. It seemed impossible to ignore how much he pleased her, at least in the matters of the flesh.

Which was sinful and bound to lead her astray.

"I told ye that ye may not leave the tower." He moved closer, positioning his body between her and the steps that led down to the ground. "My word will be honored, or I'll set a guard on ye."

"Ye're doing a grand duty of that right now."

His lips twitched, the corners rising ever so slightly before he pressed them back into a hard line. His dark eyes flickered with something that confused her, his gaze settling on her burning cheek for a moment.

With a startled gasp, Shannon turned away from him, stepping back into the hall because it was the only path open to her. But a soft chuckle sent her spinning back to lock eyes with him. She drew in a deep breath, because the man was wearing a grin now, and it transformed his face into a charming vision that must be kin to Lucifer. A temptation that drew innocents to fall from grace with fascination.

"Ye'd make a poor nun, Shannon."

Just because she'd thought the same thing, didn't mean that she was going to allow him to tell her something so personal. She tossed her head and felt her chin rising to meet the arrogance staring at her.

"Ye do nae know a bit about me. It is a fact that I'm a faithful woman. I may take very well to the life of a nun."

His attention dropped to her blush again. His lips thinned once more from the grin they had risen into, a hard line that lacked the cold determination she'd come to expect to find on his face. This was something different; it looked almost like hunger.

"You won't." His tone was deep and rich with arrogance. "I do nae question yer devotion, but I cannae ignore the fact that yer eyes enjoy the sight of me. Ye'd be a discontented bride of Christ because yer bed would be a cold one."

Shannon sucked in a harsh breath. The man was brash indeed. "I do nae enjoy the sight of ye." It was a lie, boldly spoken, and it sailed right out of her mouth on the wings of her pride. "And ye are overly bold to say something such as that out loud."

His lips twitched again, rising into a smug curve that mocked her. Male pride lit his eyes, and she felt something inside her rising to meet it. His teeth appeared as his lips split.

"Even if it is the truth?"

Each word was spoken like a challenge. Her chin lowered, but she looked at the floor for a moment because she didn't want him to see the agreement shimmering in her eyes. She did like to look upon him, with nothing man-made to inhibit the view. A hot flicker of need snaked through her, twisting her belly; denying it would be another lie, and one she knew he'd read right on her face.

A warm touch startled her away from her thoughts. Torin reached out and stroked her cheek while she was foolish enough to have her attention on the ground. She jumped, stumbling over her own feet, which seemed too clumsy to recall just where she needed them placed to keep her balanced.

Torin caught her.

One of those large hands darted across the space between them to clasp her upper arm and steady her.

"Yer hands—"

"Do nae belong on ye?" His grip tightened. Just a fraction, but the look that flickered in his midnight eyes told her he did it to make sure that she understood that he would not be bent by her will.

"Yer memory is sound, McLeren, even if yer understanding of Christian values is not."

"We're nae in church, lass."

"But I am the last woman ye should be touching."

He blew out a breath that she heard because the hall was so quiet. No one was near, and that heightened her awareness of him. Her heart beat faster because she knew they were alone. Every sense became sharper, making her keenly aware of details that she normally didn't notice. The way his lips curved or the manner in which his eyes darkened when he looked into hers.

And she could not deny that she was enjoying having his attention upon her.

"Maybe I need to show ye that my touch does nae have to be that of a barbarian. You were correct when ye told me to seek out yer father. My quarrel is not with ye, Shannon."

His voice deepened, and his grip on her arm loosened, becoming almost as gentle as the touch he'd lain against her cheek. She was keenly aware of it. The skin on her face still felt warm where he'd touched her. And on her arm, the layers of her robes did little to protect her from noticing how warm he was.

"Does that mean I am free to leave?"

"No, it means that I am left wondering what exactly is between us, since it is no' a quarrel."

Excitement leaped up inside her, shaming her with how quickly it heated her belly.

"I prefer the quarrel, for you are nae to my liking. I have never fancied a Highlander."

He grunted softly, her barbed words finding their mark. Fury danced across his eyes, and a moment later he tugged her forward. She stumbled past him and ended up in the corner with the stone wall at her back. Her captor took one long step and caged her there with his huge body, both of his hands flattening on the wall behind her.

"Be careful what ye demand of me, lass. I am a Highlander, and part of me will be happy to prove ye truthful in what ye say I am."

Her heart froze and then jerked hard beneath her breast. Her lungs began working faster to keep pace, and that drew his scent into her once more. This time her body responded with another twist of excitement running through her belly. The heat stained her cheeks, flowing lower and lower until it encased the tender globes of her breasts. The delicate skin tingled with a longing that shocked her but also added to the growing excitement pooling in her belly.

"But that is no' the way I'd like things to be between us." His gaze touched on the mark her father had left on her face. "What is it you long to return to, lass?" The emotion that crossed his eyes was one of distaste, and that was something that no amount of talking might have convinced her of. There was sincerity in his eyes that she witnessed only because she was so close.

His hand lifted and gently touched the healing bruise. She shivered, jerking her head away from his fingers, only to feel them sliding along her cheek once more. Slowly, gently, but there was nothing soft about the man. His hands were covered in smooth skin, but other than that he was as hard as she had witnessed last night.

Which made his tender touch too sweet to ignore.

"I want to return to what I know, my kin. It is where I belong." There was firm determination in her tone.

"What ye have known appears to be a hard life best left behind."

Shannon discovered that she liked his words far too much. She reached up and pushed his hand away from her cheek.

"No one chooses who their parents are. It's my duty to return to my father."

His gaze settled on her bruised face again.

"As it is mine to keep you from doing that."

She gasped but saw his determination to do exactly as he said burning in his midnight eyes.

"You are being unreasonable, acting like a barbarian, keeping me here against my will." She had to force each word out, past protesting lips that did not want him to give her leave to depart. It was insanity, but she craved more of his touch, which was why she had to escape before she lost the will to resist.

"Yer father should have found you a man worthy of yer spirit. The right sort of man would give ye a place to utilize all the passion brewing inside ye, and it would not be by insulting him with that sharp tongue of yers."

"I've no' ever met the man he sent me toward. It's unchristian to think ill of a stranger."

Torin chuckled, the sound deep and very male. "As ye noticed, lass, I'm nae feeling very Christian at the moment. But more of the barbarian ye accused me of being."

"Bringing me here as yer captive was barbaric."

"Hmm… but as ye noticed, I am a Highlander, and we steal women from time to time." His eyes darkened dangerously. "Especially when their kin is nae worthy of them."

His fingers slid down until they touched her lips, one single fingertip teasing her lower lip. Insanity shot through her. It stole her breath and every logical thought from her mind. There was suddenly nothing save the twisting of excitement in her belly and the way her lips enjoyed being touched. Never once had she noticed how sensitive they were. She was suddenly frightened by how much sensation roared through her, uncertain if she would recover from it.

"I'd prefer a strike when ye are displeased with my words."

His lips parted to show her his teeth while a large, wolfish smile beamed at her. "But ye've no' yet had a sample of the alternative." His voice deepened, dropping low and turning husky. "Ye cannae make a good choice unless ye have experienced both, sweet Shannon."

"I'll take yer word on the matter—"

His mouth sealed whatever else she might have

said inside her own. She turned her head away, but he followed her, the contact becoming a firm kiss that refused to allow her to escape. But it wasn't hard. His hand cupped the back of her head to hold her captive, and still the hold wasn't brutal.

No, what was brutal was the assault on her senses.

His lips were hot against her own, slipping along the sensitive surfaces while his tongue boldly licked along her lower lip. That unexpected action sent a shaft of hot delight through her. He enticed her to move in unison with him, and she discovered a need to do exactly that. She angled her face so that their lips met more completely, and the reward was sweet pleasure. It flooded her senses, intoxicating her. Her boldness drew him forward, almost in the moment that she moved to bring their lips closer together. His large body pressed against hers so that her softer curves yielded to his harder form. A gasp rose up and opened her mouth in spite of her initial thought to resist his kiss. He took instant advantage of her parted lips, pressing her mouth to open wider with his own. The hand cradling the back of her head tilted her face upward toward his, while his tongue invaded her mouth.

She shivered but not in revulsion. Sweet sensation surged through her as powerful and uncontrollable as a spring river. She felt as helpless as a tree branch being tumbled in the turbulent current. The only solid thing in reach was Torin. Her hands sought out his strength, and she quivered once again when her fingertips landed on the hard ridges of muscles that were solid and unyielding, just as she'd imagined him to be.

The church bell rang, its loudness raining reprimand down on them both. Torin stiffened, the hand cradling her neck tightening as though he wanted to refuse to release his captured prize. His eyes glittered with hunger that threatened to make true her hasty words. He looked pagan, felt like the legend that she'd heard whispered near the glowing remains of a fire late in the night when there was no clergy to warn them of the dangers of such stories. He muttered something in Gaelic, low and deep, before pushing himself away from her with the hand that was still flattened against the wall. His huge body was stiff with protest, and he turned his back on her for a long moment.

She was grateful for that.

So damned thankful for a moment to compose herself, she didn't seem to have the strength to stand up on her own. Instead she leaned against the wall, using its sturdy construction to remain on her feet. Her entire body yearned to be pressed against his again. She wrapped her arms around herself because her body was so pitifully needy. It was not just in her sex, where she expected lust to pool; it raced along in her blood, touching every part of her. Little shivers of regret rippled over her skin, and her nipples had drawn into hard points that were irritated by the fabric of her undergown.

The bell rang again, telling them that the service was drawing to a close. The sun had fully risen now, and even the most faithful had chores to be attended to. For certain she would welcome the McLeren women back, including their scowls.

"As I said, Shannon McBoyd, you'd best take care what ye call me, for it appears I like to help you speak the truth."

"That is no' fair to blame your lack of discipline on me."

He turned and tilted his head slightly, while considering her with an expression that told her little about his mood. She suddenly saw herself through his eyes and didn't care for the picture she must make, leaning so feebly against the wall where he'd left her. Straightening her spine, she squared her shoulders once more.

"But I suppose ye'll just be telling me no' to expect fairness from life."

That was a solid truth if ever she had known one. Better to speak it herself than listen to him tell her that.

Torin shook his head, his lips rising just a bit at the corners to offer her a grin. He closed the distance between them as they both heard the church doors open. The sounds of the monks chanting drifted on the morning air.

"I will tell ye again that ye will stay inside this tower or I will run ye down on the road."

"Because ye want to torment my clan by keeping me yer captive?"

He shook his head and moved even closer. Her body responded instantly, her heart speeding up once again, but he stopped with a single pace between them. Hunger danced in his eyes, making her mouth go dry.

"Yer father's home is no sanctuary, and I'd be committing murder in allowing ye to return there before justice has been done. You'll stay here, Shannon. Ye'll be treated more fairly here than ye might be on yer father's land when justice is handed out for his murdering my kin and plotting against the king."

His tone was hard, without any hint of yielding.

"And I still say ye'd make a poor nun, the fact that you kissed me back confirming that ye are not meant to sleep in a cold virgin's bed yer entire life."

"That does nae mean I will be lying in yer bed." She had no idea where such boldness came from, but her words were spoken before she considered the challenge they presented to him. He'd already stolen her. Telling him that he couldn't charm her into his bed was a sure way to get the Highlander to try his hand at seducing her.

She suddenly understood why women were told to remain silent. But his teeth flashed at her, confirming that her knowledge came too late. There was a flare of unmistakable determination in his dark eyes now.

"Well now, lass, we'll be seeing if ye can keep yer eyes off me. I promise that I will nae ignore ye if you cast yer attention toward me." He shrugged. "'Tis a barbarian code of honor."

❧

"Brute."

Torin McLeren heard her, but he didn't stop. Once he'd delivered his words, the laird had turned his back on her and started across his great hall. The longer pleats of his kilt swayed slightly with each powerful step. She wanted to scream. The urge was almost too great to ignore. Frustration nipped along her body, tormenting her with how much she noticed his warmth being gone now.

Indeed, she wanted to yell like a child, and the hardest part to bear was the fact that she was frustrated by being denied what she craved.

Which would never do.

She couldn't long for Torin McLeren. Not the man who had tied her wrists and imprisoned her amid people who hated the sight of her. There had to be a way to resist him. The rest of the women were chatting on their way back up the steps. They fell silent when they spied her.

"Well, come on then. Ye seem to know a thing or two about kitchen work."

Shannon felt a tiny spark of satisfaction begin to burn away some of the heat Torin had left tormenting her.

"I dinna know why that surprises ye. I'm no' wearing velvet and pearls like some princess."

One of the McLeren women took offense, her eyes narrowing. "Ye have some nerve to be taking that tone."

"I offer ye what ye give me." And Shannon discovered that she wasn't in the mood to be sneered at. Torin was correct about one thing, she would make a poor nun, but only because she wasn't meek.

"Why you—"

"Enough."

It was an older woman who spoke, and her voice carried authority. The other women looked to her with their lips pressed closed. She fingered the edge of her arisaid with wrinkled hands while her gaze swept Shannon from head to toe.

"She speaks a truth. There be no cause for unkind tones. The lass does her share as well as you do."

"But Margot, she is a McBoyd." The offended woman propped her hands onto her hips, unwilling to accept being reprimanded. There were more than a few faces that tightened in agreement.

The older woman lifted one charcoal eyebrow. "No one asked me who I'd like for me parents, Anise."

Anise lost a great deal of her confidence. "Well, I suppose that's a fact. But there is still work to do."

The women followed Anise toward the hearths, while the men waited until they were summoned for the first meal of the day. Shannon followed the McLeren women because the idea of being left to stew in her own thoughts was far worse than suffering the scathing looks she gained. But there were no more insults, at least spoken ones. The older woman's word was being heeded well and truly. The McLeren women turned to pressing her with multiple tasks, working her harder and harder, without any reprieve.

Shannon gave them measure for measure right back. She paused in the back kitchen to wipe her forehead because sweat was beaded across it. Even with her breathing slightly too fast, she still smiled when she went back through the door frame and caught a few of the women looking surprised to see her so soon.

She was stubborn, but for the moment that was in her favor. No one would be calling her lazy. At least they wouldn't be speaking the truth if they did. That knowledge gave her satisfaction. It spread through her, burning away some of the despair that had lodged so deeply in her chest.

"You have a troubled look on your brow."

Connor Lindsey spoke quietly, but that didn't keep his words from irritating Torin.

"You didna need to be poking about in me thoughts, man. Ye're nae that good of a friend."

Connor offered him a smug smile. "Yes, I am, because if I were nae, I'd offer to take that little bit of fire out of here."

Torin growled. It was a sound that most men took notice of. Connor merely widened his lips to flash his teeth at him.

"But I understand you well enough to know that you have set yer mind to finishing what ye have begun."

"Aye, that's the truth of it. Ye may thank me for that when Douglas lays down his word on this matter. Being anywhere near Shannon McBoyd won't be in any man's favor."

Connor laughed, low and deep. "Her kiss would be worth it."

"You will never know what her kiss tastes like."

Torin shot his words off too quickly, but even knowing that his temper was misplaced did not make him regret them. Things were becoming more complicated than even he'd thought they might. Shannon McBoyd was sweet. Her lips had a taste that was going to haunt him, and that was for certain. Torin watched Shannon as she tended to a chore of cutting meat. There was no hesitation in her motions, no hint of sickness because her task included raw meat. It was a fact that her father had not allowed her an idle life beneath his roof. His clanswomen were testing her, working her harder than they themselves were toiling; in short, they were trying to break her.

Torin had to resist the impulse to intercede, and that surprised him. A protective urge was worming its way up from inside him, but his help wasn't needed. He watched his kin frowning when Shannon rose to their challenge, with a satisfied look on her face.

He found that impressive, which led him back to frowning at his captive. She finished the piece in front of her and carried it toward one of the large iron kettles that the women were beginning a stew in. His fingers curled on the tabletop when he noticed the wool clinging to her long braid.

"Baeth."

His head of house looked up without any fear. The woman had run the house for his father, and she knew her duty well, even when that included dealing with his displeasure. Baeth made her way in a steady pace toward the high table.

"Laird?"

"Where did ye place my… guest last night?"

Baeth ran his entire house: there was no woman set above her in authority. She had a sharp wit and wisdom from her years. She blew out a soft breath, surprising him because it was very rare that the woman admitted she had failed at anything, but she never lowered her gaze. "'Tis a shameful truth that I neglected the lass, and my staff followed my example. I was with my son last night, Laird."

Torin felt his temper rise. He was accustomed to better control over his emotions, but the heat threatened to boil over in spite of years of learning to temper his words. Being laird meant thinking before he spoke. His words were often taken as law. That was a responsibility that his father had spent many an hour trying to instill in him, even though Torin had not been in the direct line to claim the McLeren lairdship. His uncle had been laird, but his fine, noble-blooded wife had never produced any children. Torin's father married a girl he had fallen in love with; she'd come with nothing but that affection. Without ties to noble houses, Torin had not been favored to inherit. His father had raised him to temper his words in case fate decided he should be laird.

"Where would ye like the lass to sleep?" Baeth asked the question quietly, waiting to see what he would do with a captive. Although stolen brides were not uncommon in the Highlands, a stolen woman who wasn't being claimed by a man was. Half his kin were already assuming that he'd be enjoying Shannon McBoyd in every sense.

Guilt chewed on him because his cock didn't think that was such a bad idea, which made him the barbarian Shannon McBoyd had labeled him. But if he didn't claim her, some of his men would consider trying their hand at taking the vengeance they craved to take on her kin on her. He'd have to keep her close or risk failing to protect her as his father had taught him to do. Maybe his sire was gone now, but honor was something that did not pass on the wings of death. Torin was grateful to his father for teaching him to hold himself accountable, even when it was difficult.

Having Shannon McBoyd beneath his roof was going to test him, and that was a solid fact.

"Place her in the south chamber, on the second floor."

Baeth's eyes widened slightly, but she held her tongue. His own chamber was one floor above, and everyone would begin speculating about why she was sleeping so close to him. If he gave her a chamber near the other maids, his men would begin trying to charm her before the month was out. Her McBoyd name wouldn't keep the men from noticing how bonny her face was.

It hadn't kept him from noticing how sweet her kiss was. Baeth began to turn away, breaking him out of his thoughts.

"And I will be most unhappy to see her wearing muddy robes again. This tower is nae so poor that anyone I bring here should be reduced to wearing travel-stained garments."

Baeth lowered herself in a quick curtsy. "As ye wish, Laird." She turned and began her way back toward the women who worked under her command. Their hands still moved, but they had fallen silent in an effort to hear what was being said. When the head of house displeased the laird, they could expect to feel her wrath, even if he did consider the woman fair.

"Ye left her loose?"

Connor was not teasing now. From one laird to another, the man wanted to know if he had gone soft in his thinking.

"I am no' in the practice of imprisoning women. If she were a man, I'd have clamped her in chains as I did with that traitor her father sent her to." He paused, thinking about what keeping Shannon McBoyd loose in his hall had led to this morning. Connor raised an eyebrow when he grew silent too long.

"She has nae given me any reason to treat her unkindly. It is her father whom I've business with." Frustration edged his words, while his attention remained on Shannon.

"Well, she's the one ye've got drawing yer gaze now."

"Only because I'll no' see any woman mistreated who has nae earned such."

Connor didn't respond, but there was a guarded look on his friend's face that Torin had seen before. The man knew him too well.

"Do nae look at me like that."

Connor ignored the warning, his expression becoming more pensive. "Ye sent for me because ye knew this was bigger than McLeren or Lindsey."

"She is a woman and no' part of what her male kin are doing. Don't ye have a Chattan bride waiting for ye whom ye dealt with her father for? Shannon McBoyd obeyed her father, and that is not a sin."

Connor abandoned his hard stance. "Aye, I see yer point there."

"I'll be treating the woman gently until she gives me reason to change that."

"Fair enough." Connor turned a smug look toward him. "Who knows? She might grow on ye. It certainly looked that way this morning, while everyone was in church."

Torin snarled softly, but his friend only chuckled.

"What's the matter, Torin? Did ye think because I've got a bride contracted that I've gone blind and cannae see what a sweet little guest ye have? Or that I'd no' do exactly the same as ye and keep a good eye on where she is?"

"From what I hear of yer bride, ye'd better reconsider what takes yer notice."

Connor sobered, his eyes filling with dark thoughts. "Well, that's another matter, my friend. One I'll be looking into once this matter with Atholl is finished. I have heard the rumors as well."

Torin lifted an eyebrow, but Connor shook his head. There was a set to the man's face that disturbed Torin, but the matter with the king was more pressing. Connor Lindsey had come to the position of laird unexpectedly, but he was a good one. The man did not place his own troubles before those of the clan.

"I'll be waiting to hear yer tale, my friend."

Connor shrugged. "As ye pointed out, I contracted her through her father. If my bride has set her heart on another, I'll have to seek a bride someplace else. Maybe I'll do ye a favor and take young Shannon there. Douglas will most likely hang her father and brothers, leaving the lass in need of a husband."

"If anyone marries her, it will be me."

Connor glared at his friend. "Why? Because ye stole her or because ye kissed her?"

"Both."

"That may not be enough to save her from the noose, my friend. There will be many who say her blood is tainted."

Connor was correct, but Torin didn't want to admit it out loud. He debated the situation, his mind trying to work it into something easier to deal with.

Wedding Shannon would not be an uncommon way of dealing with the matter. But Connor was very correct that there would be many opposed to leaving any alive who were kin to the traitors who murdered the king.

Baeth wasted no time getting to her ordered task, snapping her fingers at two others and pointing at the laird's captive. Shannon McBoyd was not impressed with his order that she be offered better. She shook her head and resumed cutting with a stubborn set to her lips.

Lips that he knew tasted sweet. His fingers curled into a fist, and he struck the top of the table. Connor chuckled at his frustration.

"That one burns hot enough to melt sand into glass. Keeping her will nae be a simple matter."

"Aye, that's a fact."

The only part he did not like was that he was beginning to look forward to clashing with her.

He stood up and covered the distance between him and Shannon quickly. The women stepped away from him, knowing the look on his face and the fact that it promised he was not in the mood to be challenged.

Shannon lifted her multicolored eyes to stare into his. There was a hint of heat in those orbs, but stubbornness outshone it.

"Ye may have noticed that I rise to the challenges ye cast toward me, lass."

She hissed at him, but her cheeks began to turn pink. She wanted to argue with him, but he reached out and plucked a tuft of wool off her shoulder before she made her protests. Her eyes widened when he held it up.

"I refuse to believe that ye enjoy being filthy or being left to sleep wherever ye could find a space. Such will be corrected. Baeth will see to ye, or if ye persist in refusing her offer, I will do it myself."

Each word was edged in solid promise. She should have been familiar with the man's unyielding nature, but she still wanted to argue. Shannon bit her lip instead. She felt the weight of too many stares resting on them. Torin was laird here, even if he wasn't her laird. Since she could not leave his holding, his word would be carried through.

Her gaze dropped to his hands, the same ones that had touched her so tenderly and yet imprisoned her so completely.

"I dinna need help tending to myself, so tell yer women to leave me be."

He drew in a stiff breath. "And I've told ye before, Shannon McBoyd, yer kin have been killin' mine, so ye will go where I say until the Earl of Douglas sorts out this matter."

Shock held her tongue still for a long moment. "You sent word to the Douglas that I am here?"

He nodded. Relief flooded her. It swept away the fear that she hadn't even noticed was gnawing away at her insides. Once it was gone, she blushed with shame for the rude manner in which she had been speaking. His keen stare didn't miss the emotions that crossed her eyes, and he let out a frustrated grunt. With a flick of his fingers, he sent Baeth and the other women away from them.

"I'm a Highlander, true enough, but that does nae mean I am without honor. Quite the opposite." Pride edged his words. "But I'm owing ye an apology for no' telling ye that I sent to Douglas. There will be justice done, but no' revenge. I brought ye here to keep yer wedding from happening."

Which was a kindness, and a great one. She doubted many other men would conduct themselves so honorably. But she could hear the women near the hearth whispering now, and she would have sworn that she felt their cutting looks on her back.

"Yer people want revenge." However justifiable, it stung to feel their glares on her.

"Aye." He stared straight into her eyes without pity for the fact that they were talking about her own kin. "But revenge will nae bring peace, and that is what we need in Scotland."

She couldn't help but respect him for saying that. It was such a contrast to her father. She could not resist the urge to admire him. Her feelings must have become visible on her face, because one of his dark eyebrows rose in question.

"Does that mean ye find me more to yer liking, Shannon?"

His words were edged with a temptation that she would be wise to ignore. The man began to grin at her, and she found the expression too mocking to tolerate.

"I find ye fair, which is more than I expected and a compliment to be sure, but that has nothing to do with liking. So ye can just remember that. I told ye before that I am nae a light skirt, so ye can stop being so brash as to use my name so familiarly."

He chuckled, barely loud enough for her to hear. She caught herself leaning toward him and stiffened. His eyes flickered with approval and that same hunger that had fascinated her when they were alone. Only they were far from alone now, and she heard the whispers increasing over at the hearth. Her cheeks turned hot, and the worst part was that Torin noticed, his attention moving to the growing spots of color and lingering there for a long moment. Shannon berated herself but seemed to be powerless to control the physical response. Her blush burned hotter.

"Aye, lass, ye have told me that, but it's the fact that ye find me attractive that I'm finding more interesting."

"I do not… find you any such thing." She had to stop and lower her voice. The women might have moved away, but it was clear that they were doing their best to hear every word. Merriment danced in his dark eyes, and she realized that she'd leaned toward him in her attempt to keep their voices from drifting. It brought him too close for her comfort. She was keenly aware of him, noticing little details about his face and lips that she'd never taken interest in with other men. Sensation rippled across her skin beneath her clothing, touching off little flickers of excitement.

"Enough. Ye are imagining things. You brought me here with rope around my wrists. Attraction is not what is between us."

His expression darkened, and she was almost sorry to know she'd caused it. Regret nibbled at her, reminding her how handsome a man he was when his eyes sparkled like the stars against a moonless night sky. But he suddenly shook off his ill temper, offering her a mocking grin once more.

"Well now, lassie, since ye are nae a light skirt, tying ye around me was the only way to bring ye home with me, and I do have me reputation as a Highlander to think of. Stealing brides is tradition."

She slapped the tabletop, drawing a few gasps from those watching.

"Trust a man to say something like that. You gain from my loss of reputation, and I am not yer bride." She stumbled over the last word, excitement threatening to embarrass her by making her voice unmistakably cheerful over the idea of being wed to him.

He tilted his head slightly, clearly enjoying her temper. But he suddenly rolled the wool still clenched in his hand. Lifting it up, he stared at it for a moment, his face becoming pensive.

"Ye were in the back hallways last night during supper."

A tingle went down her nape, and she straightened up, withdrawing, back across the table. But that wasn't nearly far enough. Torin shifted his keen stare away from the wool to her face, his eyes burning into hers.

"The wool is stored in the back workrooms, and no McLeren woman goes there when me and my men return. But ye would nae know that, would ye, lass?"

Shannon willingly held her tongue, but she felt her cheeks turning scarlet. His dark eyes moved to the stain, studying it. When he looked back into her eyes, there was a flicker of hunger lighting his gaze. Excitement flared back up deep in her belly.

"Well now, Shannon McBoyd, I believe I'll no' be offering any apology for this morning." His lips rose into a mocking curve. "And I'm going to enjoy the compliment ye paid me good and well."

"I offered ye no words of praise."

He shrugged, his wide shoulders moving easily beneath his shirt. Shoulders that she had seen last night and was still thinking about despite the bright light of day.

"On the contrary, lass, ye have paid me the sweetest form of praise a lass can offer a man." He flattened his palms on the tabletop without a care for what he might touch. The tender skin of her lips actually tingled as she watched him leaning closer and closer. The man was completely mesmerizing.

"Ye kissed me back because ye liked what ye saw last night, and that is the highest form of praise from a virgin."

Shannon stiffened, backing away from the table and the glaring truth of his words. His expression was smug, and it irritated her immensely. No man should be so confident of her. Especially not Torin McLeren. It was too much for her pride to bear, too much to stare at, so she turned her back on him. The women watching sucked in stiff breaths, but what sent her teeth to grinding was the warm male chuckle that drifted over the worktable to her ears.

Brute. Highlander brute!

❧

The bathrooms were indeed on the opposite side of the great hall. Another set of waterwheels pulled water up from the loch here. Yet there was another large hearth with coals glowing ruby in the morning light. The water was dumped into another stone trench, but it wasn't divided into sinks. Instead the water flowed along the wall past eight large slipper tubs. They were pushed up beneath the trough that the water flowed through, and directly above each was a section of wood that might be pulled up to allow the water to spill down into the tub waiting below.

It was ingenious.

Shannon looked at the design, impressed by its simple solution to hauling buckets. Large copper kettles hung over the hearth, telling her that the only water you needed to move was the hot water. The stories she'd heard about Highlanders bathing often suddenly took on more truth. With such a bathroom, she would gladly bathe often. Her skin suddenly itched, her undergown feeling grimy.

"Yer clothing will need to be washed, so we'll find ye something else to wear for the day. I am Baeth, the head of the house."

Baeth spoke softly but with a firmness that spoke of her confidence in her position. A large ring was secured to her belt, and from it hung an assortment of keys. Large and small, they were a symbol of her position.

Two other McLeren women had followed them, and one set a kettle over the hearth. The water dripped on the outside sizzled when the heat hit it, and then the room was filled with the sound of water hitting the bottom of one of the slipper tubs. They were copper tubs, yet another thing that proclaimed how solvent the McLeren clan was. Metal cost money. The row of tubs accounted for a hefty investment.

Well, she was going to enjoy the benefits of her captor.

The word "captor" stuck in her thoughts now. Torin might be a brute, but he was not dishonorable. He'd sent to the Earl of Douglas, and it was startling just how much that bit of knowledge was comforting to her. The man could have shut her away and ordered his kin to keep their lips sealed. It might have been years before someone spilled the secret at a spring festival. Years that she would have spent living as the lowest person on the land.

She was grateful for his honor but at the same time fearful of what would happen when the Douglas heard. With the king murdered, there would be blood demanded. Her father was deep into the plot, and it was very possible that she would share his fate.

Unless Atholl gained the crown, which was not such a difficult thing to agree with. His grandfather had married twice and dissolved the first marriage, but there were many who believed the children from that first union should have inherited the throne. James I was descended from the second marriage.

That idea surged quickly into her mind, filling her thoughts completely. If Atholl became king, anyone who opposed him would fall. The McLeren were strong, but not mightier than all the Lowland clans combined. It would be Torin who paid for interrupting her journey. The cost would undoubtedly be his life. Icy dread dug its claws into her, suspending her thinking while she fretted over what might happen to the laird who had brought her home with him. She suddenly gave a huff and reached for one of her shoes to begin unlacing it. The man didn't need her efforts to shelter him.

No, he was already blessed with the strength of legend. She'd seen that so clearly last night.

Her cheeks burned again, frustrating her. Blushing had never been her habit, and it was one that she was not happy to discover becoming part of her every waking hour. She pulled at her shoes and clothing, removing it all quickly to keep herself busy.

She was spending far too much time thinking.

The last thing she did was untie the strip of leather that kept her hair in a braid. Once free, the strands began to loosen and rise up in an unruly cloud. Once she washed it, curls would appear, and they would be even harder to control. She suddenly missed Gerty greatly, for getting her hair combed and rebraided was going to be very hard without another set of hands. But she refused to remain dirty when a bath was within reach.

She gave no notice to the McLeren women watching her. Bathing was never private on McBoyd land either. But these women eyed her. She felt their stares moving over her, so she lifted one foot and stepped into the tub before the hot water was added.

A gasp passed her lips, but she steadied herself and picked up her other foot. Remaining on display was worse than the icy-cold water. Setting her teeth, she sat down and shivered when the water rose above her waist.

One of the women snickered.

"Meanness is a sin that I've little tolerance for."

Baeth spoke quietly and without looking at either of the women, but they both straightened instantly. One turned to pull the kettle out of the hearth with a long iron hook. Steam rose from the spout now, and Shannon looked at the wispy white vapor with longing. A moment later, the hot water was poured into the tub. Moving it around with her hands, she smiled as her fingers encountered the warmth.

"I hear tell that you had a trunk with ye. I sent one of the kitchen lads off to see if any of yer things made it to the Highlands."

"Thank you."

Baeth seemed set on keeping a conversation going. Shannon suddenly realized how much she missed the little remarks that were so often part of her everyday routine. Since leaving her father's house, she had been ordered, instructed, and told what was expected of her, but no one spoke to her.

Well, except for Torin, but the man only sparred with her. Maybe the lack of conversation was the reason she rose to contest his words so quickly.

Baeth lifted a ladle and dipped it into the water still flowing along the wall.

"Mind yer eyes."

The water hit her head, clearing out any cobwebs that might have been there. Shannon blew out a stiff breath but smiled because her skin felt cleaner already.

"Spring will bring some welcome warmth."

Shannon didn't answer because she was busy scrubbing away the mud from traveling. She didn't think she had ever felt so dirty, and she didn't care if the soap stung her eyes. She scrubbed her face twice before sighing with relief. The kettle was brought back with only warm water to rinse her hair out. The woman holding the kettle stood watching in wonder as the water left behind hundreds of curls.

"Ye have lovely locks."

"Lovely until you are the one who must try and keep them out of the fire."

Baeth clicked her tongue. "As troublesome as it might be, ye'll be the bonniest sight on May Day morning."

Would she? Shannon lifted her face and looked up toward one of the open windows. They were set higher into the wall, with half shutters that kept anyone in the yard from looking into the bathroom.

"I'm not allowed out of the tower."

The two women looked at Baeth. The older woman considered her thoughts for a long moment while Shannon stood up and reached for a length of linen to dry off with.

"All the lasses go out on May morn. I think ye should be no different. That's tradition."

Yet she was different; she always had been set apart from even her own clanswomen on May Day. However, many believed in the rite of May morning. It was fabled to bring good luck to the land and those living on it. The belief was rooted in their druid past. The church might do its best to banish it, but the festival would be held.

"The lads will be watching ye for certain. That's something that clan colors dinna hold any authority over. A lad likes what he likes, and many a father has tried to interfere, only to hear that his daughter has married who she loves."

The other two women laughed, only it was a lighthearted sound now. Naughty smiles appeared on their lips, and that gained them a raised eyebrow from Baeth.

"Love is a fine thing, and that is not to be confused with lust, even if you younger lasses haven't the wisdom to know one from another."

Had it been lust that saw her kissing Torin back?

Heat curled through her belly, moving over her skin as she pondered that idea. The day was fair, and she dried quickly, but her nipples remained hard and tight. Hunger licked at her, and her lips tingled with just the memory of his kiss.

He'd labeled it attraction. Was that just a soft way of telling her that he knew she lusted for him?

A set of footfalls interrupted her thoughts. A younger woman entered the room, her arms draped with a set of gowns. The other two women wasted no time. They took up the garments and helped place the softer underrobe over Shannon's head. The second one followed, and in spite of her pride, she couldn't help but appreciate clean clothing. The last thing lying over the girl's arm was a length of plain brown wool.

"I didna think ye would be wanting a McLeren plaid for an arisaid, but yers is in need of a washing."

"It is." There was an awkward moment that felt like it lasted an hour. Shannon broke it by reaching for the brown wool and draping it over her back. It was still too chilly to go without an arisaid, and the truth was that the McLeren girl didn't think a McBoyd should be wearing McLeren colors. However, as they were both being civil enough, it would be best to allow the matter to pass without a comment. While she wouldn't call it kind, she could agree that there was a lack of meanness among those in the bathhouse.

It was the truth that she was becoming confused about just what she thought of remaining at Donan Tower, or of Torin, for that matter. He had honor, and that didn't lend itself to her thinking ill of him.

"That will do for the moment, but if yer own things are nae here, we'll have to find ye something else for May Day. This blue does nothing for yer eyes." Baeth eyed Shannon critically, and her fellow McLerens joined her.

"I've no need to look pretty."

The head of house actually smiled at her. It was an expression that spoke of her wisdom and the fact that she considered herself more experienced than anyone else in the room.

"Every lass needs to feel pretty on May morn. Celebrating the spring is a tradition that brings good luck. Don't be turning yer nose up at that, or those naysayers in the clergy will be getting their way and we shall never see another maypole dance."

Shannon had to nod with agreement. For all that she had never been allowed a May-morning tumble, there was the dancing and merriment that helped drive the last of winters bitterness away.

There is nothing preventing me from having a tumble this year.

That idea stole her breath and flooded her with excitement. It began to pound through her, touching off little ideas of just what lovers did. Little recollections of overheard conversations overlapped inside her mind, tormenting her with the possibility of having Torin for her lover.

"Well now, let's do something with yer hair, lass. It seems to have a mind of its own."

Shannon sat down, her thoughts absorbing her. She was grateful for the help and too preoccupied to stubbornly insist on fending for herself. Her mind must be going soft. Such was often the fate of a captive. Only she'd expected to last a bit longer, retain some of her pride for more than a few days.

That's what came of spying. The clergy knew what they preached, for her one moment of weakness was pulling her farther away from the path of goodness.

His kiss had been good and full of pleasure…

She shivered, a delicate motion that rippled over her skin. Her lips were keenly sensitive once more, yearning for another kiss. She might want to argue against it, but she could not lie to herself. The pleasure had taken command of her, every muscle and all her thoughts too. There had been nothing, save the desire flooding her.

A rush of water broke through her brooding. One of the women had pulled a rope off the wall that had a hook tied to the end of it. She'd hooked it through a bail on the high end of the tub and pulled on the rope until the tub tipped up onto the lower end. The water spilled out and ran down the sloped floor of the bathroom. Shannon stared at the way the floor was built up on one side of the room to allow the water to run downhill. It rushed toward an iron grate that was set into the wall at the farthest corner. The water easily escaped, and she heard it splattering on the stone foundation of the tower.

Ingenious. If it weren't for the laird, she just might discover herself pleased with where she had ended up. Life at Donan Tower would be comfortable.

If she didn't mind her thoughts, she'd find herself being drawn back toward that man for more of what she did find pleasing about him.

❧

"Ye are playing a game."

Shannon looked up to see who was talking to her. He had to be speaking to her, because there was no one else in the back kitchen. Up the stone steps she could hear the sounds of conversation filling the hall while everyone ate the last meal of the day.

Connor Lindsey filled the door frame, his shoulders just as wide as Torin's. But he had light hair instead of dark.

She preferred Torin…

Her hands curled into fists as the thought just blossomed in her mind. Connor Lindsey noticed and offered her a mocking grin.

"If ye didna want to be noticed, ye should be in the hall instead of trying to prove those McLeren women wrong in thinking they are giving ye too much to do."

"I'll suffer with yer noticing. Now go gloat to someone who is interested. There is no one here to notice ye tormenting me for sport."

Connor Lindsey moved down the steps instead. Shannon propped her hands on her hips and raised her chin. He watched her with narrowed eyes. They were as keen as Torin's, but she did not have any trouble recalling that he was someone she was best to keep at arm's length.

"I could take ye away from Donan Tower."

"Oh could ye now?" Shannon didn't care if her tone was mocking; the man was toying with her.

"Ye don't find that appealing?"

"I suppose it depends on where ye were planning to take me."

His lips split in a roguish smile that flashed his teeth at her. "To Lindsey land, of course. I've a fine tower north of here. Birch Stone has a view of the sea from her towers."

"Spoken like a true Highlander."

He frowned at her, but his eyes sparkled with merriment, betraying the fact that he was still trying to tease her.

"The Highlands are beautiful, lass. I'll be happy to show them to ye."

He moved closer, doing it slowly to keep her gentle.

"That's close enough."

"I dinna think so."

She'd misjudged how close he really was and noticed exactly why when his hands appeared from where he'd kept them tucked between the folds of his kilt. He caught her upper arm, because her hands were still propped on her hips, making her elbows point out.

She snarled at him, but he pulled her easily into his embrace.

"Release me!"

He flattened his hand against her back instead, smoothing along her spine. The touch relieved some of the tension that leaning over the washing sinks had left in her back, but Shannon preferred the ache to his touch. She balled up her fist and sent it toward the underside of his jaw. One advantage to having only brothers was that she had heard a fair bit of coaching on fighting from her father during supper.

Connor Lindsey apparently knew a great deal more about fighting, because he turned his head and caught her fist in one of his large hands. She was free from his embrace, but only for a moment before he twisted her arm behind her back with his grip on her fist.

"Now is that any way to be, lass?"

"When ye force yer touch on me… aye!"

His eyes darkened; his gaze dropped to her mouth. "I'm just thinking that ye could use a comparison to what Torin offered ye this morning."

She gasped, completely startled by the idea. No one had ever kissed her, and now she had two different men doing it on the same day? Her mind froze with shock.

Connor took advantage of her uncertainty, bending down to place his mouth on top of her own. She rebelled, pulling her head back as far as her neck allowed. Connor followed her, his hand releasing her fist to slide up her spine and clamp around her head. He held her steady for his kiss, his lips becoming demanding when she refused to open her mouth for him. She could smell his skin, but it didn't seem as pleasant as Torin's had; in fact, all she did notice was how much more she preferred Torin's kiss.

Lifting her knee, she sent it up into the folds of his kilt with all the force she could.

"*Sweet Christ.*"

Connor Lindsey jumped back, releasing her. She'd been straining away from him so much, she stumbled and ended up against the sinks. Reaching into the sink, she pulled out the heavy clay pitcher she'd been cleaning up. It dripped water all down her front, but she gripped the handle tightly.

"Get away from me, ye demon."

Connor drew in a deep breath and straightened up. Something glimmered in his eyes that made her shake the pitcher threateningly.

"I'll bust this across yer skull if ye dare touch me again. I swear it."

He grinned at her, only it was far from a friendly expression. There was a spark of challenge in his eyes that told her he wanted to try her.

"If ye have some notion about taking me away, I suggest you go argue with yer friend who brought me here and told me I cannot leave the tower. The pair of ye are well suited to one another with yer barbarian manners."

Connor Lindsey laughed. He threw his head back, and his chest shook with his amusement. Shannon felt her temper explode. She turned and scooped up a pitcher full of cold loch water.

Once more Connor Lindsey moved faster than she'd anticipated. He closed the distance between them and grasped the top of the pitcher. His larger hand spanned the opening, and he forced her to pour the water back into the sink. She could have struggled to keep the pitcher but released it in favor of moving away from him.

"I've already had a bath today, lass, and we don't need me walking through the hall dripping water for the gossips to notice."

"Ye're not worried about my reputation; ye just want to avoid having yer friend hear that ye offered to take me home with ye."

Connor Lindsey shrugged, his expression becoming guarded.

"Well now, Shannon McBoyd, I admit that I am more concerned about Torin. The man is my friend, and that is not something I say lightly." His expression hardened. "I needed to know if ye kissed him back this morning because ye are nae above using his lust against him. I'd have to take ye out of here if that were so."

"You kissed me to see if I was—"

"A slut."

He said it firmly and without a hint of a flinch. Her temper boiled, and her hand closed into a fist once more. Connor Lindsey held up his hands in surrender, taking one long step away from her. That shocked her again.

"Oh, get on with ye. I've got better things to do than suffer yer company."

He snorted with amusement. "That's the first time I'm no' offended that a lass told me washing dishes is more to her liking than I. Ye are a hard one, Shannon McBoyd."

"That seems to please ye and yer sense of protecting yer friend Torin McLeren. So grant me some peace by leaving."

"Aye, ye understand, then. That's a point in yer favor. One I'm grateful for because I will nae have to

battle with my friend over ye. Torin would have tried
to keep ye out of his sense of honor because he's the
one that took ye."

"You would have fought with a friend over me?"

Connor tilted his head slightly. "As sure as I enjoyed
stealing a taste of ye."

He paused with one foot on the bottom step. His
blue eyes studied her for a long moment.

"But I'd be a poor friend to leave him with ye if
you were going to try and twist him about yer finger.
I owe the man better than that."

"But ye have not the same sense of honor when it
comes to how I am treated?"

He shrugged. "If ye act the slut, ye dinna deserve to
be treated with respect." He pegged her with a hard
look. "Torin is an honorable man; sometimes I have
to save him from himself."

A shiver went down her spine. His eyes were icy
cold now, telling her that leaving with him would
have been a mistake. A very large one. Shannon
turned her back on him. She heard him chuckle, but
the sound grew softer and softer as he left.

Relief flooded her. The urge to wipe her mouth
across her forearm was strong, but that only made her
frown. Connor Lindsey was a fairly handsome man.
There was no reason for her to loathe his kiss or to
reject it so violently.

Yet she had. The impulse to struggle had been
fierce. But worse still was the budding feeling of
achievement that was working its way through her.
She'd passed Connor Lindsey's test, and that pleased
her. It shouldn't have. On principle alone she should

refuse to care at all about what either man thought of her character.

She sighed, her hand freezing on the edge of the sink. To do that would be to become shallow. She did care, did notice that Torin was an honorable man, which was why he fascinated her so. Connor Lindsey was more ruthless, but not without honor. The man would be loyal to those he deemed worthy of it.

Torin McLeren had earned Connor's friendship, something that would not come easily. That made her close proximity to Torin all that much harder to bear, because she was beginning to respect him herself; that sort of thing might lead to liking him, and maybe more. She'd just have to be grateful that he slept in a different part of the castle than she did. Distance would be her greatest ally.

&

"It's a fine chamber, hopefully as well as the one ye had beneath yer father's roof."

Baeth snapped her fingers at the girl working in the small fireplace that was set into the wall. The head of house was contemplating Shannon's reaction to the chamber she was being given. It was far better than the storage room she'd occupied growing up.

Except that it was one floor beneath Torin's chamber.

"'Tis too fine. The workroom is well."

"Nay. The laird bid me place ye here. It's fitting, you being the daughter of a laird."

The girl stoking the fire nodded, but it was the look of approval that made Shannon want to squirm. There was more than a hint of suggestion on both women's faces and a little too much excitement brewing in her belly. There was no point in arguing; Torin's staff wouldn't go against their master. Especially for the daughter of their enemy.

The world had certainly gone mad in the last week and taken her along with it.

"The bed is strung well and tight. We even found a few of yer things. I'm pleased to see that my kin took the time to bring yer possessions along."

That was a kindness that she hadn't dared to expect. Walking across the room, Shannon looked down at the new dress she'd been working on. It had only been a fortnight, yet she reached out to touch the half-sewn skirt as though it had been years.

"Good night."

Shannon looked up and inclined her head without thinking about it. Baeth shot her another pleased look before motioning the other girl out the door before she followed. The door shut with a soft snap, and Shannon stared at the smooth wood that composed it. There was no way to bar it. Well, there was no point in quibbling over what she did not have. Somewhere within the thick curtain wall, Fergus was no doubt longing for better than what he'd been given. She doubted Torin had been kind to the man, even if he was a secretary to the Earl of Atholl.

Yet he was being kind to her.

Sweeping her gaze across the chamber, she took in the furnishings. They were sturdy and well made. A table was set against the wall, and her dress was laid out carefully on its smooth top. Fabric was expensive, no matter whether you were servant or noble. Her new dress was placed with care for that fact of life. Candles sat in two holders there, ready to be lit should she decide to work. The fireplace was small, but it warmed the chamber well. It also had a chimney to draw the smoke out. Set near the fireplace was a bed, hung with sturdy wool curtains and covered with a canopy to make it cozy during winter. A thick ticking was lain over the ropes that were strung through the frame. It was wide enough for two people, unless the other person was Torin. The man would dwarf the bed frame.

Why did she keep thinking about the man like he was going to be her lover?

Visualizing him in the bed meant she was longing to have him sharing it with her. For certain she was going mad to allow such ideas to flourish.

Heat licked across her cheeks, and it did not come from the fire. She turned her back on the bed, only to find herself facing the window. The shutters were closed and locked against the night, but her hand itched to reach for the latch.

Her blush grew hotter as she realized that the chamber overlooked the spot from which she'd spied on Torin the night before.

Was he down there tonight? Curiosity taunted her with how simple it would be to look down on what she desired.

With a snort, she sat down on the small bench near the table and picked up her skirt. She would not open the shutters. The night would be long enough without another glimpse of how much perfection Torin

McLeren was blessed with. She was already thinking about how much more she liked his kiss compared to Connor's. She began to pull the needle through the skirt while her mind continued to tumble with her troubled thoughts.

It was a curse for her. One that brought longing and hunger from which there was no escape. Not so long as she was imprisoned within Donan Tower.

Or was there?

If she weren't a child living beneath her father's rule any longer, the rules were different. She looked up, soaking in the details of the chamber. Things were very different and very uncertain. Her teeth went into her lower lip as she contemplated the facts. Who knew how bleak her fate might be? Accepting that fact somehow made her more hungry for the things that she had been denied. A thirst for more of life's pleasures began to torment her. It was as if she craved a reward for braving the harsher side of reality.

There were so many things she had never done, so many experiences she had never sampled. Torin's kiss surfaced from her memory, and she did not banish it. Instead she let the sensations flow through her again, smiling at the way her lips tingled. It had been delightful. Every one of her senses clamored for more.

And why not?

Was she not a woman? No one would believe she was still a maiden after being held in the Highlands anyway. The needle was frozen halfway through a stitch, and her gaze returned to the closed shutters. But she remained on the bench and pulled the needle free, taking up the slack in the thread.

She'd think a bit more. Just because she'd decided she might do as other women did, didn't mean she would run to toss up her skirts. A tumble wasn't what she craved. She wanted a lover. Maybe Torin, and then again, maybe she'd send the arrogant laird away. She wanted a lover who would hold her tenderly and tease her with sweet kisses, not brand her with passion hot enough to leave an obsession behind.

If there were such a man living outside a book, that was.

But she'd finish her spring dress and listen to Baeth. She did want to look fetching on May morn. It would be interesting to see what Torin McLeren thought of that.

She'd not be the only lass staying in the tower. May Day might be a tradition as old as time, but so was weighing the choice to lie with a man. Only a fool failed to think long and hard before going out to dance around the maypole. She'd happily look into Torin's face when he noticed that she was following her will and staying behind in the tower instead of following his tempting offer of going out to dance on the green.

Six

"THE LAIRD IS GONE."

Brockton McLeren looked her straight in the eye the moment she came down the steps from the second floor, where her chamber was. The man was clearly standing there to make sure he didn't miss her.

"So I'm charged with making sure ye're here when he returns."

The man's tone left little doubt that he wasn't pleased with his duty. His expression was surly, and he'd crossed his arms over his chest like a child beginning to pout. Shannon had to resist the urge to smile at him.

"Well, I suppose I'll tell ye that I plan to go to church this morning, and don't be telling me that it is nae permitted."

Her words were overly bold, but she held her chin steady and stared straight into Brockton's face. The burly Scot frowned, and his forehead furrowed until his eyes were nothing more than slits. He finally grunted and shrugged.

"I dinna see any reason to tell ye nay. The priest would likely be hounding me by the week's end if he

didna see ye in the pews. I dinna need that hassle, and
that's a fact."

Shannon gave him a nod and let him think it was
his choice. Her pride was bristling, but arguing with
the man would only gain her an enemy. That would
be a poor choice, especially when she considered the
sunlight just beyond the open doors of the great hall.
It beckoned to her, shimmering and promising relief
from the stale air inside the hall.

Moving forward, she paused on the top step.
Excitement curled through her as she descended the
first few steps and no one sent out a cry. It was April
already, and the winter was quickly losing its grip. The
air was still brisk, but the sun was cheerful. It would
rain instead of snow now too. Already the hills were
beginning to sprout with new growth. She noticed it
more than she had before. Losing the right to venture
outside had taught her to savor every detail she might.

But the church bell rang, so she hurried to join
the other members of the congregation. Her McBoyd
colors stood out among the McLeren ones, but the
priests sent her a smile of welcome.

❧

Baeth frowned at her son Brockton. "Did ye nae think
that she might try to become a nun if ye let her go to
the church? They'd give her sanctuary, and the laird
would have the devil's time getting her out of there if
she were of a mind to stay."

Her eldest son shrugged. "At least that way I'll
no' have to worry that she won't be here when the
laird returns."

His mother snorted at him.

"Ye know so little. Why is it we don't understand anything until age has passed its hand over us."

Baeth wasn't asking her son the question. It was more of a statement. Her son frowned while he followed her toward the church.

"Becoming a nun sounds like the best thing she could do. Her father's a traitor, and I doubt the Earl of Douglas will be letting the man live much longer. No one will have her to wife after that. The best she might hope for is to become someone's leman. If she becomes a nun, it will solve a great many things. The earl will nae have to decide if she needs to die with her father. She'd be a bride of Christ; the earl would let her live."

Baeth clicked her tongue. It was a sad truth that many men would be agreeing with her son. Well, a fair number of women too. But she wasn't one of them. A daughter had no choice in what her father did. Baeth gained the entrance of the church and saw Shannon sitting in one of the pews. The McLeren women sitting in the same row made sure there was a space left between them and where their McBoyd guest sat.

Baeth smiled slowly. Wisdom came with age, and she enjoyed the authority that had come from her years of service. Making her way down the aisle, she slid in next to Shannon and sat down beside her. Whispers instantly rose but died when the priest turned to glare at the pews.

She shot a smile back at the man when his chin dropped in surprise.

❦

"Ye're poor company tonight, Torin." Connor listened to the night with a practiced ear. They had allowed the fire to burn down to coals, blanketed by thick ash. The moon provided all the light they needed. Nestled in between jagged rocks on the side of a hill, they took time to rest their horses until the sun rose.

"Marry that bride who is being groomed for you if ye want someone to worry about pleasing ye."

Connor frowned. "I'll attend to Deirdre Chattan soon."

Torin eyed his friend suspiciously. "For a bride that ye worked so hard to contract, ye dinna sound very enthusiastic."

Connor scowled at him. "And for a man who holds love so highly, ye stole another man's bride and rode home with her tied around yer body."

Torin growled. "Now I know something is wrong with yer impending match, because ye are trying to start a fight with me."

His friend offered him an arrogant smile. "If I wanted to annoy ye, Torin, I'd confess that I cornered that Lowland sweet ye have stashed in yer tower and stole a kiss from her."

Torin felt his blood run cold. He glared at Connor while battling the urge to send his fist into his face. His friend laughed at him.

"Ye're jealous."

Torin frowned. "I am not. I barely know the lass and wish I'd nae needed to take her."

"Well now, if that is so, there's no reason for ye to be upset."

Torin made a fist and sent it into his opposite hand in warning. His friend raised his eyebrows. Torin snorted at him. He and Connor had spent the very first day they'd ever met fighting. Connor had spent his youth fighting those who sneered at him for the sin of his parents. Torin had joined the young boy in many of those battles, refusing to see him beaten for something he couldn't control. They'd lost more times than they'd won, but their friendship had grown strong.

Connor drew in a stiff breath. "All she did to me was try and smash her knee into me pride."

"So is that the problem with claiming yer Chattan bride? Smashed… pride?" Torin snickered. "I can see how that might be an impediment to wedding vows. It will nae be very good for relations between yer clans if the bride wakes up the day after her wedding still a virgin."

"Shannon McBoyd did nae get that big of a jump on me. Even if she was a fiery thing. She's a virgin. I've no doubt of that." Connor lost his teasing look, his expression turning dark.

"But ye doubt Deirdre Chattan's purity?"

Connor looked dangerous. He was not a man to cross with dishonesty. "I'll see what she has to say on the matter. But I hear dark rumors that she's been riding out to meet young Melor, despite our bans having been read."

"That's a mess, my friend. Ye'll have the church fighting ye if ye try to refuse her."

"Unless she confesses."

Which would be foolish of the girl. She'd likely

be cast out by her father and forced to seek her lover. If her lover rejected her, life would be very cruel. Connor sighed.

"When did we become so responsible, Torin? I miss the days when the only ones who suffered for our fighting were ourselves."

"Fate had other plans for us."

They were both laird, in spite of neither being born into the right position to inherit the title. They'd been raised to expect nothing and instead had gained what many men hungered for. Torin laid his head on his forearm and pulled his plaid close around his face. He was laird, and he'd do the position justice. Fate had placed him in charge, and he would do his duty with honor.

He closed his eyes, and Shannon's face surfaced in his mind. She was sweet. Too sweet for the plot that threatened to pull her down into its swirling depths.

Death felt like it was blowing on the wind. Torin felt the icy touch of it on his face. He shouldn't be so personally concerned. Shannon wouldn't be the first child who lost her life because her family ended up on the wrong side of the king.

The way her mouth had moved beneath his reminded him that she was very much a woman. One who was innocent but passionate too. The temptation to teach her what she longed for was tearing at him, taunting him with how sweet it would be to introduce her to passion.

It was a bad idea at best. Dishonorable and bound to tarnish his reputation with gossip of lust. Shannon would be the one to suffer most at the hands of the gossips; women always did. That only made it more important that he resist her.

Important, indeed, but it was proving impossible.

❧

Shannon found her frustration rising over and over throughout the next few weeks. Brockton watched her diligently. The man peeked around corners and stood outside the bathroom when she was in it. Discovering that he was Baeth's son only made everything worse, for she was thankful to the head of the house. It would not do for her to complain about the woman's son. Baeth kept her from having time to fret by putting her to work. The labor truly helped her settle in, for it was the same chores that she had always done. Somehow she had never really thought about the fact that no matter what color her arisaid was, she was still a woman doing exactly what other women did every day across the country. It was only the presence of Brockton, watching her like she was suspected of something evil, that kept her neck aching.

But it was Baeth who helped solve that dilemma. She snapped her fingers, and a maid brought her a pile of freshly washed and pressed sheets.

The head of the house pointed one of her weathered fingers at Shannon. "Up the stairs with you and change the bedding. Tuck the corners tight."

The maid didn't want to give the sheets to Shannon. She gripped them tightly, wrinkling the freshly ironed fabric.

Baeth looked down her nose at the girl.

"Have ye gone simple?"

The girl pressed her lips tightly together, still refusing to relinquish the sheets. Shannon held her chin steady. It wasn't an easy task. Somewhere in the last few weeks she'd convinced herself that those working around her didn't resent her so much anymore. It appeared that she was the fool. It hurt more than she cared to admit, pain spiking through her while the sheets became more crinkled.

"These are the laird's sheets."

Baeth snorted. The maid jumped, clearly realizing that she'd overstepped her place.

"As if I don't know that. Stop acting like a simpleton. If Shannon is above stairs changing sheets, there won't be any question of her being inside the tower, now will there?"

"Oh… well, I see."

The sheets landed in Shannon's arms instantly. Baeth snorted with frustration.

"She sees nothing." With a huff, the woman shook her head and aimed an exasperated look at Shannon.

"What I thought was to give ye and my son a bit of peace. You'll have the tending of the upper floors in the afternoons when the laundry is done. That way I can toss my son into the yard and out from beneath me skirts."

Brockton snorted, but his mother lifted that finger again. "Get on with ye. I do nae know what men do with themselves during the day, but I'm sure yer father taught ye. So get to it. I know what a lass should be about while the sun is shining. The girl will stay above floors or answer to me, and don't be making the mistake of thinking I don't notice every person who uses those stairs."

That finger was pointing straight at her, and

Shannon felt the authority streaming out of it. She lowered herself into a curtsy without thinking but gained a nod of approval from the formidable woman. She peeked back over her shoulder as she took the first step, and Brockton was indeed heading toward the open doors of the great hall. His step was lighter than she'd ever seen, the longer ends of his kilt swaying with his fast pace.

"Go on, Shannon McBoyd. Enjoy a bit of peace. I expect the laird will be returning soon."

So take what solace she might?

There was no point in putting the words to voice. While each day was a blessing, it was also one more that brought her closer to the judgment that was certain to come her way.

"Keep order and act like the noblemen you are said to be. Scotland needs her lairds united, not fighting one another."

Quinton Cameron stood firmly in place as half the men around him yelled out protests. Holyrood Palace had seen its share of heated debates, but today a man could feel the tension in the air. Torin watched the men making the most noise; they were the ones he wanted justice from.

Torin stood up and pointed at Atholl. "Atholl sent raiders onto my lands, and I demand justice. The man is a traitor."

Atholl's supporters were quick to jump to their feet with their voices raised in protest.

"Laird McLeren is correct."

The room fell silent as Archibald Douglas swept into the room with two retainers guarding his back. Each laird had been restricted to no more than two men apiece, but that didn't ensure that there wouldn't be a bloodbath before sunrise.

Torin stared at Douglas, as did every man in the room. The Earl of Douglas was as powerful as the Earl of Atholl, and one of them wasn't going to survive this meeting.

"Walter Stewart, Earl of Atholl, is the true king." It was Laird Gilson who spoke up, but no man was willing to stand behind him.

Douglas fixed him with a penetrating look. "More than one man in this room claims royal blood; that does not grant any one of us the right to send armed men after the crowned king. It was murder, and justice will be dispensed, or we'll be reduced to an unruly lot so busy fighting with one another, England will be able to invade us. Scotland's alliance with France will only stand strong if there is a king of Scotland who is followed by all her lairds. Young James will wear the crown; that is the word of the Douglas."

There was grumbling around the room, but many heads nodded. Laird Gilson looked worried, glancing behind him to see if any laird would support him. None did.

"Atholl is a traitor and will die one. Those who shook hands with him will face the same."

Torin felt his mood darken. Shannon's face rose from his mind while the day wore on. Mercy was never discussed, and he brooded over the fate of his captive. The only grace fate afforded him was the fact that Douglas was focused on Atholl, but Torin knew it would not last past the moment that the Earl of Atholl was executed.

Quinton Cameron stopped him outside the chamber at the end of the council.

"Rumor has it, ye took McBoyd's daughter."

Torin glanced down the hallways, making sure they were empty before he answered. "The man sent her to wed Atholl's kin after he fired one of my holdings. It was a bloody scene."

Quinton drew in a stiff breath. "I suppose it was a deed well justified if ye kept the daughter from placing a seal on the deal. I'd wager my own lands would have been next on McBoyd's list."

"Very likely."

Quinton Cameron was a good neighbor, who didn't raid McLeren property or steal his sheep. He spent more time at court than Torin did, but he still wore a kilt like the Highlander he was.

"And what are yer plans for the lass?" Quinton kept his voice low, but there was no mistaking the tone.

"I have nae decided."

Torin turned and left, his task completed. He'd acted justly and taken his fight to court instead of launching his men onto McBoyd land as he was deeply tempted to do. Now he favored returning to Donan Tower to resume chasing Shannon through its hallways. A man at war couldn't enjoy breaking down the defenses of a lass.

Life was full of choices; he'd made his.

He was returning to McLeren land.

Another fortnight passed with nothing but normal chores. The routine was soothing to her soul, smoothing away the last of her worries. It became so much easier to relax with normalcy surrounding her. Every day there were duties to perform. When the sun began sinking in the afternoon, Baeth kept her word and sent her to the upper floors to work. With the aid of arches, the tower rose three stories above the great hall. But it appeared that no one slept in the bedrooms. A slight stain touched her cheeks when she realized why. The laird's chamber was here, and the chambers on the second floor were intended for his family. What drew a blush from her was the fact that her small chamber was on the second floor, where only Torin's family should be.

Or his mistress…

She shook her head to dispel that thought.

It had been by his order that she slept there, and she didn't need to think about why he'd done what he had. It was impossible for women to understand men anyway.

Shannon ground her teeth and scoffed at her thoughts. She had somehow turned into a wanton. Torin McLeren simply wanted her accounted for so that when his overlord came looking for her, it would not be hard to produce her.

Aye, and hand her over like a prize.

Even without sheets to change, there was plenty to clean above stairs. The open shutters allowed dirt to be carried in on the breeze from the newly turned fields. Spring was bringing longer days, and the hills were alive with new plants that soaked up the warm sunshine. Flowers began to bloom, and the loch swelled with the runoff of melted snow.

She did not mind cleaning. Gerty had shown her the way of it when she was too young to recall. It took every pair of hands to make life good. The women saw to the home while the men went to the fields. Pausing for a moment, Shannon looked out one of the large windows in Torin's chamber. The iron hinges that held the shutters in place needed cleaning and oiling to keep them from rusting. She'd done every window in the tower before forcing herself to reenter his private chambers.

She practically felt the man in the room with her. If that was sinister or of the devil, so be it. Alone with her thoughts, she could not lie to herself. The chamber was large, rather fitting for its master. Her attention strayed to the bed. It was a huge one, set with bedding that must have cost a fortune for how much cloth was needed.

Again, it suited Torin. He was an honorable laird and deserved the best. There were plump pillows and a mattress filled with goose down. To lie on it must be delightful, she thought. Just changing the sheets had been a feast for her senses. She pressed her fingers against the soft surface, just for the thrill of testing it.

Her cheeks heated more. She'd had to almost lie on the bed to reach the heavy coverlet in the center and pull it over the sides. The creamy, smooth sheets had beckoned to her with a wicked suggestion of what it might feel like to lie completely nude amid them. That thought was completed by the idea of having Torin, just as she'd seen him, in the bed with her.

If Torin were atop her, his larger body would press her down into that softness…

Wicked, but so fascinating, her mind allowed the thought to surface again and again. As the spring warmed the air, her passionate ideas heated her cheeks.

So working alone suited her full well. She took each task Baeth gave her and set off to complete it to the head of house's satisfaction. The other McLeren women checked up on her, peeking in to see if she was working or daydreaming. When she caught them spying on her, they walked toward her as bold as might be and ran their fingers across whatever she had been cleaning. But they became less amused by the game as the days passed.

"I didna bring ye here to be a maid."

Shannon jumped and fell against the window ledge she was working in. Her upper body went right through the open space in the wall, and her feet slipped on the smooth floor. For a moment all she saw was the ground, her eyes widening at how far away it was and how impossible it felt to stop herself from tumbling toward it.

A solid hand gripped her back; fingers dug into her arisaid and yanked her away from the window. She stumbled back inside the chamber and right across the floor as she heard the sound of her dress ripping.

But it was the sound of Torin's voice that took precedence in her mind. She landed against his bed; her hands flung out behind her to absorb some of the impact, but her legs still knocked against the frame, with painful consequences.

"Sweet Christ. Ye have no business leaning out of windows if ye're so taken to fright."

Torin McLeren was angry. His face was a mask of fury while he stood in front of the open window with his arms crossed over his chest. The pose made him look larger and more undefeatable than he normally appeared.

"Ye should nae have crept in here like an assassin."

He snarled, but she raised her chin, the dark sound rubbing against her pride. She should have been frightened of the huge man, but she wasn't. There wasn't a single hint of any reserve inside her; in fact, she was eager to tell him he was wrong.

"This is my private chamber." His voice was low and sharply edged. "I do nae need anyone telling me how to enter it."

"Except that yer head of house sends her maids here to see to the keeping of it, so ye should nae be so astonished to find someone working here."

He grunted at her words but pressed his lips together in a firm line instead of arguing. He wanted to. She could see that shimmering in his eyes, but his gaze lingered on her face for a long moment, and something else flickered in his eyes. For just a fleeting moment it looked like he was happy to see her. It did not last long, because his attention shifted behind her, to the bed she was still leaning against.

His bed…

Shannon straightened, drawing her hands away from the bed. Torin watched her, and it was impossible not to stare back at the man. She shouldn't be happy to see him again, but that didn't stop the rise of emotion inside her.

"Why are ye acting as a maid? I never ordered you to such a position."

He sounded perplexed, and that drew a small grin to her lips. She did enjoy knowing that he found her difficult to understand.

"Why do ye assume that being a McBoyd means I am lazy?"

"Ye're McBoyd's daughter, no' just a McBoyd."

Her eyelashes fluttered, cutting off his ability to look into her eyes. Her father's disdain for her suddenly felt shameful. As the laird's daughter, no one would think she was accustomed to serving anyone except her immediate male relatives. That was why the McLeren women had enjoyed watching her clear the table so much. They thought her shamed and belittled by their demands.

"That has nothing to do with anything. I work in trade for what I eat." She headed for the door, intent on escaping. But she had to stop when he moved into her path, blocking the door frame with his large body. Sensation rippled along her arms and beneath her clothing to tease her skin all the way across her chest and belly. Memory rose thick and hot with exactly what it felt like to be held against him.

"You owe nothing, since it was my decision to bring you here, Shannon. It is not my intention to have you humiliated."

His words were coated in fairness and his tone kind. Her pride didn't care for it, because it was too close to pity.

"Well, it was my choice not to sit about waiting for the earl to decide what to do with me."

His eyebrows lowered, his expression becoming brooding. "I'll no' see harm done to ye, Shannon."

Something in his tone disturbed her; a hint of kindness that she only heard after someone was dead. She looked at Torin and saw the mud dried on his boots. His hair lacked the clean look that she'd come to expect from him too. Clearly the man was fresh from the road.

"Well, I do nae desire yer protection. Whatever ye just came from, I'll face it and be happy to be finished with this mess."

He unfolded his arms. "Nay, ye will not face it. There is nothing out there but death for the kin of those who enacted this plot against the king."

She shivered. There was no stopping the response. It raced down her spine, shaking her with icy dread.

"Go on, then. Tell me what ye were off seeing. Do nae think ye are softening the blow by hesitating. I can stand steady for whatever news ye have."

Admiration flickered in his eyes. She had not wanted to impress him, but she liked it just the same. She lifted her chin and stared him straight in the eye.

"Atholl will be executed for murdering the king. Young James will be crowned, with the Douglas standing behind him. I expect Archibald Douglas to be named lieutenant general."

Which meant the Earl of Douglas was king in all but name. His word would be law, and it would be in the man's best interest to hunt down all the supporters of the plot. That was the only way to secure his position.

"Well then, it appears that justice has been done." But what made her words sound hollow was the certain knowledge that revenge had yet to begin. She could see it in his eyes.

"It is far from finished, Shannon."

His voice was grave and dark with the promise of retribution for what her father had done.

Footsteps came up the stairs, and she felt each one like a dagger puncturing her skin. She looked beyond Torin toward the doorway to see who was coming. Her belly tightened with fear as she contemplated seeing her executioner.

A warm hand cupped her chin instead. Torin raised her face so that their eyes met again. She'd not even noticed the man close the space between them, and now she was torn between the excitement he bred inside her and the terror those footfalls instilled. There was no possibility of hiding her fears; the best she might do was bite into her lower lip to keep herself silent.

Torin gently pulled her lip free with his thumb. The faint scent of leather and horse clung to his skin. She inhaled it deeply, seeking out the scent of him beneath those things.

"Easy, lass. I'll keep my word to protect ye."

"But how—" She clamped her mouth shut, despising how pathetic she sounded. With a shake of her head, she broke his grasp on her chin. "I'll weather it quite well. No matter what comes my way."

The footsteps had stopped, and she drew in a deep breath before leaning over to see what was waiting for her. Her belly was queasy, but she forced herself to look. Connor Lindsey peered back at her with blue eyes that were full of curiosity.

"Well now, should I leave the pair of ye in peace?" His lips rose into a mocking grin that annoyed her.

"Nay." She uttered a single word before Torin pressed his thumb over her lips in warning.

"Leave us, Connor."

"There's the thanks I get for riding with ye. Thrown over in favor of a pretty lass."

Shannon shot a glare at Torin and then wished that she had not. The man was staring at her with eyes that glittered. His hand was curled around her face, his grip light, but she knew the strength tempered by his control.

She heard Connor leaving and hissed over the thumb pressing down on her lips.

"I told ye that I didna want yer protection."

"And I told ye that I will see to ye. Nothing ye say will change the fact that I am responsible for you being here, and that means that I will be having a say in what is done. When it comes to others, my commands will be heeded."

Each word was delivered in a solid tone that didn't leave room for argument. Shannon shook her head, dislodging his thumb.

"Very well, but since ye sent yer friend away, I'll speak my mind. Get yer hands off me."

"No."

The hand holding the side of her face slid back to cup her head as he moved forward to capture her mouth with his. The kiss was demanding. He pressed her mouth open with his, seeking out her tongue with his own. It was bold, and she resisted, trying to step away.

Torin didn't grant her any reprieve. He followed

her, one strong arm encircling her body to bind her against him. She inhaled his scent now, that male scent that pleased her senses far too much. Passion did not build slowly this time. It erupted like a bolt of lightning splitting the sky open. Need rose up from her belly, hot and demanding. Her tongue met his, slipping and teasing, while she moved toward him, pressing her body against his.

His kiss softened as she responded. He teased her lips with his own, licking along her lower lip before leaving her mouth to trail soft kisses across her cheek. She shivered once again, astonished by how sensitive the skin covering her cheek was. Never had she suspected that a man's kiss might feel so hot or that she would shudder with delight. He found her neck and pressed more kisses along its delicate surface. Her hands slid up and over his chest, discovering the ridges of muscles that she'd seen in the moonlight.

"You are sweet, Shannon, too damned sweet, and I have spent too many nights thinking about ye since we parted."

She was suddenly free, with the path to the door clear. Torin stepped back and reached for the tie holding his claymore at his right shoulder. His fingers yanked on the leather ties with sharp motions, betraying just how agitated he was. She could see his emotions flaring in his eyes. A muscle twitched along the side of his jaw as he fought the urge to pull her back against him.

"Leave me, before I tumble ye while I stink like a horse."

Her pride reared its head in the face of his arrogance.

But he yanked the tie in his hand clear in two with one hard motion of his hand, the leather snapping with a sharp sound. Warning flashed from his eyes, and she felt it deep in her belly. It was not something that her pride felt; it was something that the woman inside her recognized. A sure understanding that he'd do exactly what he promised and that she would not resist for long. The reason was simple—she wanted him. Wanted to be tumbled, and she didn't much care if he did smell like a horse.

She turned but froze in the door frame when he spoke again.

"Baeth seems to think ye wish to celebrate May morn."

Shannon peeked back at him over her shoulder. A roguish grin decorated his lips now, the claymore held securely in one of his large hands. She couldn't keep her gaze from dropping to that hand.

She had enjoyed what his grip felt like on the back of her head when he was kissing her.

A husky chuckle broke through her musings. Torin set the weapon down on a table and walked toward her. She had to force her feet to remain in place.

He reached up and ran a finger along her face again. Sensation rippled across her skin and down her neck in response.

"If joining the May revelers is what ye want, you have my permission to leave the castle."

"You trust me to return?" Part of her wanted him to. She suddenly realized how much she missed being trusted. That was a part of freedom that she hadn't valued until it was missing.

"I trust in the fact that if ye go dancing around the maypole with yer hair flowing behind ye, I'll be the first man who tries to take ye into the woods for more celebrating." His hand reached her hair, and he tugged gently on a few curls that had escaped her braid. Little ripples of anticipation washed down her body, touching off more sparks. "The only man."

"I said nothing about going into the woods."

His lips curved higher with arrogance. "Yer kiss sure enough did, lass."

His smug tone drew a gasp from her. She flattened her hand against his chest and pushed him away from her. It was a mistake, for he instantly captured her hand, holding it prisoner in his larger one. Beneath her fingertips, his heart beat steady and strong. It was hypnotic, drawing her toward him.

She tugged on her hand but might as well have saved her strength.

"Release me. I can assure ye that I'm no' interested in celebrating May morn with you."

His thumb rubbed over the tender skin of her inner wrist. He pushed right past the cuff of her underrobe to find the spot where her pulse was throbbing frantically. Victory lit his eyes, his lips thinning into an expression that sent a twist of excitement through her belly, because there on his face, she could see that he knew what turmoil she felt. He understood because it was something they shared. Sensation rippled across her skin, and her nipples contracted beneath her gowns.

"Yer heart rate says otherwise, and be very sure that I will nae allow another man near ye." He lifted her wrist up and placed a hot kiss against it. She gasped, unable to hold the sound inside her. Indeed, it felt impossible to contain all the sensation that his touch solicited. Her clothing felt as if it would smother her.

"That's a promise, sweet Shannon."

He offered her a wolfish grin before releasing her. He turned so that she could see his bed behind him. One dark eyebrow rose in mocking question.

She hissed at him and his presumption. Excitement or not, she would be the master of her choices.

"You are a brute."

"Is that so?" His face darkened. "Yer face was nae marked from my hand, lass, when I found ye. It seems to me that yer life is better for the fact that I brought ye north."

"I am not afeard of my sire." She stood straight and tall before Torin and tossed her head in the face of his arrogance. "Ye're a prideful fool to assume that I want to go out on May morn because I intend to take a lover."

"Take *me* as yer lover, ye mean."

One of his dark eyebrows rose, along with a smirk appearing on his lips. Saying the word "lover" out loud was being interpreted by the man as surrender. His eyes sparkled with anticipation. Of course, she had to expect such from a Highlander, especially the one who had stolen her.

"I've barely felt the sun on my face this last month, by your order. That man of yers trails me to church and back, making sure I don't linger outside. Of course I want to go outside these walls, and May Day celebrating has nothing to do with it. What I want is to be free of this confinement. Go chase yer own women through the woods if it's a tumble ye crave. I want some fresh air, ye daft man."

Grabbing a handful of her skirts, she turned her back on him but had to suffer the sound of his deep chuckling while she made her way down the stairs.

Connor Lindsey was leaning against the wall when she gained the bottom floor. Shannon didn't give the man time to torment her with a knowing look. She skirted past him quickly, refusing to lock stares with him. He'd no doubt take the same arrogant attitude that Torin had: that women found men irresistible.

She muttered beneath her breath. All right! Connor Lindsey was assuming that she found Torin McLeren irresistible.

Which wasn't true; she simply needed to focus more on ignoring the man.

And his kisses.

Even if she were battling the urge to do exactly as Torin said, she had no intention of making it known. With a huff, she headed toward the kitchens and some sort of work that would take her mind off her feelings. Maybe there was laundry yet to do. Plunging her hands into hot water would keep her from thinking about how much she enjoyed the man's kisses.

But the longing gnawing at her insides persisted. It tormented her for the rest of the day, growing stronger as the sun sank. Her chamber felt colder and lonelier than before. The dress she'd enjoyed sewing in the evenings didn't draw her interest tonight. Instead her stitches were slow, and she had to pick out as many as she put in, because they were sloppy.

She finally surrendered and placed the project back on the small table. Her mind was alert, and sleep didn't call to her in the least. With a frustrated sound, she turned to stare at the closed shutters.

Was Torin bathing in the loch again?

That idea tantalized her, tempting her to cast a look out the window. It would be so simple to watch him. Shannon snorted at her thoughts. There would nothing simple about it. She'd burn even more if she caught sight of his bare form again. Mayhap even worse than that; maybe she'd simply give into her longings and join him.

He wanted her…

All her life she had been raised to think of such a thing as sinful, but tonight it felt like a compliment, one that was more sincere than any she had ever been given. She'd seen the hunger flickering in his eyes just as clearly as the flame of the candle on the tabletop.

Just as she burned…

It was neither good nor bad. It was simply a fact, and it followed her into bed and kept sleep from taking her away. She noticed how much better it was to be covered in only a thin chemise. But she also took note of how chilly the sheets were compared to her memory of Torin's touch. She longed to discover what it felt like to be pressed completely against him.

To discover what it was like to be his lover.

⤜⧫⤏

Torin growled and sent his fist into the mattress of his bed. Shannon haunted his chamber like a ghost instead of the living and breathing woman who he knew damned well was only a few hundred feet away. He stared at the wall, hating the stones that lay between him and her.

Sweet Christ, he'd gone daft. His mind was nothing but softness now.

A few sweet kisses and he was like an untried lad who still believed a hard cock meant love everlasting.

Turning over, he lay on his back, despising the way his mind reminded him that May was only one more day away. His cock hardened with the idea, rising up in demand. The thing that drew a heated curse from his lips was the fact that the only woman he seemed to want soothing his hard flesh was Shannon McBoyd.

He was a bastard to want her. A man who wasn't strong enough to overcome his lust in favor of remaining honorable was less than civilized. She was his captive, and only a marauding savage took advantage of a lass he'd stolen. He didn't care if the world around him was filled with men who would label him soft for thinking such. He'd not use his lairdship to take what he wanted because the clansmen followed him and would not speak against him even when he was wrong.

That left him with a swollen cock and no way to ease it. There were women aplenty who would eagerly warm his bed, but they would come to him out of greed for his position.

A sarcastic grin twisted his lips; there was a reason to explain his fascination with Shannon. The woman was not interested in easing her life by spreading her thighs for him. That was an all-too-rare thing for a laird. She had good reason to attempt to charm him, and yet she refused.

Spirit. She had something burning inside of her that fascinated him with its pure brilliance. Even the fact that her life might be in jeopardy didn't send her to him to secure a protector.

He wasn't sure he'd be able to turn her away if she did.

She was drawn to him just as surely as he was to her. His grin faded, and his cock hardened further. Their personalities were like flint and iron; when they met, sparks flew. It was as alluring as it was annoying. But it was also exciting in a way that he'd never experienced.

Which only made him crave her more.

Seven

"TOMORROW WILL BE A GRAND DAY."

Baeth smiled at her. Shannon watched the older woman suspiciously. There was nothing about her smile; it was measured carefully, giving nothing away. The head of house pointed toward the open doors of the great hall.

"They've raised the maypole this morning; ye can see it from the steps."

Shannon stepped forward and sighed when the afternoon sun touched her face. Spring had arrived fully; she could smell the rosemary on the breeze and the heather. The stale smell of winter was gone, leaving behind a sense of hope that made her want to smile in spite of the McLeren plaids in sight. Her McBoyd arisaid set her apart. She fingered the edge of the wool while looking through the open gate to see the maypole. It stood tall and proud against the blue sky, with lengths of thin, brightly colored cloth hanging from its top. A crown of new spring greenery was already set on top of it so that the celebrating might begin as soon as the sun rose. There had been much work to do today in the kitchens. The villagers had brought up freshly felled game for the feast that would be offered the next day. Meat pies and fruit tarts were being made, while the younger girls all whispered about what delights they hoped to sample on the morrow.

The clergy had preached against May Day that morning, but their urging to ignore the festival day was falling on deaf ears. The traditions went back further than anyone recalled, and the maypole standing so tall in the afternoon light confirmed that the McLerens would be carrying on with welcoming in the spring. No one wanted to tempt fate to turn her disfavor on them. It was fabled that May Day drove winter away so that crops would flourish. Any baby conceived on the morrow would be a welcome sign that fate, along with all her minions, was pleased and in the mood to bestow the gift of a good harvest.

"You should sit down and make yerself a wreath. I hear the laird gave ye permission to go out tomorrow; you do nae want to be missing that."

Now she understood what Baeth was nudging her toward. There was a knowing look in her eye that made Shannon snort. Torin had been busy with his captains and his fellow laird all morning, which was a blessing. She'd tossed and turned most of the night, gaining little rest. Her mood was sour indeed. Baeth's insinuation gained a soft hiss from her.

"That does nae mean I plan to wear a wreath or unbraid my hair. I just want to take a walk on something other than hard flooring."

Baeth clicked her tongue. There was a wealth of knowledge in her eyes. Denying her attraction to

Torin gained Shannon nothing with Baeth. The older woman was too wise to be fooled.

"Your tone is sharp for such a lighthearted topic. You younger ones have a way of not cherishing the brighter moments of life. Trust me, girl. They are too few and far between to toss aside so carelessly. Think on that before you say nay. Only fate knows if ye shall ever have another chance to choose whom ye would like to lie with. Many a lass must wed for more practical reasons, leaving her only a few short moments to enjoy a man she truly desires."

Baeth's words were blunt, but Shannon could not stomach the truth in them, so she walked down the steps. Baeth was wise, even if that knowledge chafed. It seemed such a short time ago that she'd feared her life was going to end at the point of Torin's dagger. She'd wished for more time to taste the things she never had and those that she knew were sweet. All the things that brought warm happiness to the heart and a smile to her lips. She should make a wreath, sit down, and enjoy the feel of the greenery between her fingers while the scent of rosemary and heather filled her nose.

Who knew if she'd see next spring? If Atholl was condemned, it wasn't too far-fetched an idea that her father might be next. Just because she was born a daughter didn't mean she'd be spared. Not when one considered that she'd been on the road to wed into Atholl's family. The Douglas had wiped out entire families before.

Was that why Torin had kissed her again? Because he'd just witnessed how easily life might end? Or rather, she should say… unjustly. Even if the scriptures did say the son was guilty of the father's sins, she had to admit that in her heart she did not agree that it was always so. She was not guilty of her father's murdering raid on the McLeren.

Had his kiss been a chance to touch that part of life that was sweetest? Baeth's words echoed in her thoughts as her body recalled just how much she did enjoy being pressed against the McLeren laird. Only it wasn't his position that she found attractive. It was the man he was. Her father and his friends were lairds, but they were not the same; there was no honor in them. At least not the sort that she felt in Torin. It drew her to him, making his kiss something she couldn't resist even though she knew she should, if only for the principle of the matter. She was his captive. Despising him was expected, but her life at Donan Tower was better than it had been in her father's home. She could not hate him without cause, which made it impossible to ignore how much she wanted to discover what came after kissing.

For once Brockton was not in sight. Shannon let out a sigh of relief. With his laird returned, the man had no doubt run as quickly as possible away from the duty of guarding her. She finished descending the steps and found no one watching her. The men on the walls had become used to her—that, or they considered her broken.

She wasn't sure if she cared just why they didn't turn to stare at her, only that they offered her some peace. The yard was busy. Two wheeled carts came through the raised gate, their beds crowded with goods like peat for burning in the hearths or freshly cut hay for the horses. Younger boys were taking instruction with their wooden swords on one side of the yard. She stared at the number of them. There were more than fifty, and there were older lads whom she could see beyond the bridge working on their riding skills. Young girls followed their mothers to learn the art of making a home. The shutters were open, allowing her to see the workrooms with their spinning wheels and looms. Herbs were being hung from the ceilings now to dry before they would be stored away for the winter months.

Donan Tower was bristling with activity and growing excitement for the celebration day coming on the morrow. People walked just a bit faster while they hurried to finish chores so that they might begin making merry. There was happiness in the air, an excitement that drew her out into the open. If that was a pagan idea, so be it. The hall behind her was suddenly so dreary she didn't think she could bear forcing her feet to carry her back inside.

She'd practically forgotten what earth felt like beneath her feet.

A shadow fell across her, and the sound of horses' hooves filled her ears. She tipped her head back to look up at the huge stallion that was pulled to a halt but a few feet in front of her. Torin held the reins in a gloved hand, almost as if he'd sensed she was thinking about him and his kisses.

Sure command was reflected on his face, even as the animal pranced slightly. Torin moved in unison with the stallion, his thighs clasping the saddle. All the strength that she'd noticed in him was on display now.

The trews he'd worn before were gone now, and she could see his bare thighs where the folds of his kilt were flipped aside.

"You have spent too many hours indoors, Shannon; yer skin is pasty. I'll take ye outside the walls if ye have the courage to ride out on the back of my horse." He extended his free hand toward her. She chewed on her lower lip because the invitation was too tempting. The warning in the back of her mind wasn't able to compete with the desire to feel the sun on her skin. There was a hint of challenge on his face too, but that only made her want to go with him even more.

Who knew if she'd get the chance again?

To have the choice to mount that horse was too much power to resist. Her hand landed in his before she bothered contemplating whether it was wise to accept an invitation from a man whom she craved so much. All that seemed to matter was the delight that sprang up inside her when his fingers closed around her wrist.

"Hold on to me, lass."

His voice was husky and tempting. Her arms went around him without any pulling or rope. She wanted to touch him too much, but the soft sound that came from his lips surprised her. She felt it vibrating through his chest with her arms more than she heard it.

The moment her hands closed around him, he pressed his heels against the belly of the horse. The stallion surged forward, making for the raised gate. Excitement rose inside her; there was no stopping it. The number of eyes on her was unable to affect her joy. The moment they crossed onto the bridge, she felt as if she could breathe again. Like there had been a belt strapped too tightly around her chest, making her struggle for every breath she'd drawn since being brought inside the curtain wall.

She suddenly noticed how green the hills were and how strong the man she clung to was. His scent filled her senses, touching off heat that spread rapidly over her skin. Her heart accelerated, and she felt his heart beating against her cheek, where it lay against his back. Her hips moved in unison with the horse, and she suddenly realized how intimate the motion was.

But that only sent a bolt of heat through her. Torin made for the woods that grew above the village. His horse was clearly used to such ventures, for the beast never hesitated. The new leaves on the trees blocked out some of the sunlight. Looking up, Shannon watched it sparkling through the openings in the branches. It was cooler in the forest, but her skin was still warm, and the man she clung to even more so.

"I know I promised you some sun, but I want to show you how grand the Highlands can be. 'Tis a fine place to call home."

He lowered her to the ground and swung his leg over the neck of his horse almost in the same moment. But he didn't release her hand. He clasped it firmly and tugged her toward the edge of a cliff. The trees didn't grow along the edge of it, and that allowed for a spectacular view. Out in front of her were hills green and rich with newly blooming heather. The scent of it was carried on the wind. Water flowed down from some loch hidden within the hills, while large rocks broke through the earth. The sky was deepest blue above it all, with fluffy clouds that looked so close she might raise her hand and touch them. Below her was a fall that would be deadly if one were foolish enough to go too close to the edge, but she was too absorbed with the wonder around her to be afraid.

"Ye see there, lass? The Highlands have beauty, no' just savages." His hand was still holding hers, and he had her arm pulled down straight to keep her beside his body. "Even if I did act like one when I brought ye here."

His voice was soft. It was almost an apology, something she'd not expected from him. She wasn't sure how to deal with this side of him. He was suddenly likable, and that removed the last barrier between them.

He was pulling on her hand, and she looked down to where his fingers were wrapped around her own. Her flesh was very happy, enjoying the security of that hold. But he released her, sending a soft lament through her body.

"It is a very nice view." Polite and sweet, her words were as close as she might come to thanking him for taking her outside the castle. Moving away from him, she discovered herself shuffling her steps because she truly didn't want to part from him.

No, she wanted to have him for her lover…

There was no denying the thought. It flowed into her mind like warm honey, thick and sweet, to fill all her senses. A blush began to stain her cheeks, but she turned her attention back to Torin and gasped softly when she met his eyes.

Hunger shone in those dark orbs. It was startling to see it in the light of day, and yet somehow expected.

She realized she'd have been disappointed if he didn't look at her with passion now that they were away from every set of eyes that wanted to critique them.

"Why did you bring me out here?" The question crossed her lips before she thought about it. He looked surprised but shrugged, his wide shoulders moving easily beneath his shirt. Her eyes were drawn to where his collar lay open, the ties dangling down to lie against his chest. Creamy skin, lightly bronzed by the sun, was open to her gaze where the edges of his shirt parted.

"I wanted to see if we might try just being a man and a woman. Without the colors of our clans between us."

"We are still on McLeren land."

He tilted his head slightly. "Well, there's only so far I can take ye before my ability to protect ye is jeopardized."

Yet he'd made the effort, which he didn't have to do. It was a gift that she could not overlook easily, unless she wanted to be disagreeable simply because of who he was. But the scorn she'd felt her first night at Donan Tower kept her from that; hating anyone for the family they were born into was wrong. She would not treat others to that unjust fate. She recalled the sting too well.

"I understand."

His mouth curved into a grin. "But are ye pleased?"

Her own lips twitched, and she turned away to hide it. She shuffled her feet once more as she walked back into the trees and wove slowly between their trunks. She could feel him behind her, following her every step. She was suddenly shy, unsure of how to answer him. But she liked knowing that he was watching her and following her. There was something seductive about it. She felt it deep inside her belly, and it flowed toward the top of her sex. It was shocking to become so aware of that part of her body.

"That shouldn't matter to you."

Her words were sharper than she'd intended. Turning around, she looked back to discover what expression crossed his face first.

"Yer father should nae have contracted ye into a marriage with the only purpose being to overthrow the rightful king." Torin stood still, watching her from behind an expression that told her little. His eyes glittered with frustration, and his lips were pressed into a hard line. He suddenly blew out a harsh breath.

"Yet he did, and I do care if ye are pleased today. I do nae care for the manner in which I brought ye to my home. Donan Tower is not a prison."

"There are Highlanders who do not share yer hesitation about making their homes into fortresses that keep their enemies locked away."

There were stories of people who had never been seen again once they were captured.

"Not on McLeren land; not while I am laird."

Pride edged his words, and she witnessed it on his face. He leaned back against a thick tree trunk. The relaxed pose drew her closer to him. She had never seen him so at ease; it was hypnotic, because it made him far more human. He lifted one hand and curled his finger to beckon her toward him.

"Come here, Shannon."

"Why?" It was a foolish question, for the look on his face told her what he was wanting. Yet he didn't look at her with disdain or superiority for asking. His expression lacked any smugness at all. What was there was something that she longed for: it was the look of a man who wanted her, just for herself.

"I want ye to come to me because I caught you both times I've kissed ye. So today I'm asking ye to come to me and offer me yer sweet lips."

Her cheeks heated, but her lips tingled with anticipation. She leaned around a tree, remaining behind it while staring at the laird asking her for a kiss. He was a handsome devil, now that he was taking the time to charm her. "And if I tell ye nay?"

"Well then, I've heard it said the third time's the charm."

He abandoned his lazy stance, pushing away from the tree he leaned on incredibly quickly. There was no darkness to hide him now, and it was startling to see how fast he closed the distance between them. Determination was etched into his face, and his eyes full of anticipation.

A soft shriek crossed her lips as she straightened up. That proved to be an error, for it placed her in the open, making her an easy target. A grin curved his lips up before he opened his arms wide and bent his knees. He looked every inch the Highlander about to capture his chosen prey. Torin scooped her up, picking her right up and off her feet without a single hesitation. His arms closed around her, satisfying the longing she'd struggled against. Delight filled her senses as she felt his strength truly surrounding her. It was more pleasurable than she'd imagined, more sensual than any imagining ever could be.

"Since I've caught you, I will claim my prize."

There was no doubt about what he wanted from her. His hand captured her thick braid, but she lifted her chin before he began pulling on her hair to gain her compliance. She craved his kiss and could not deny it. In fact, she didn't want to resist the urge anymore. She felt fate breathing down her neck with the promise that soon Douglas would arrive to pass sentence on her family.

Torin's embrace was a haven from that dark reality. His arms were unyielding and capable of giving her every bit of support she needed. Pleasure flowed from his touch, but she wasn't close enough yet. She angled her head so that he could press a kiss against her mouth. Sweet and bold, he licked across her lower lip before sealing his mouth over hers.

It was not a delicate kiss. He demanded complete possession, pressing her mouth open while his hand retained a hard hold on her braid. He wrapped the rope of her hair around his hand to keep her captive to his will.

Yet she was a willing prisoner. In truth, she was eager to embrace the man who held her. All those who had forbidden her to touch and be touched were too far away now to impose their will on her. Freedom was as intoxicating as whisky.

Her hands reached for him, seeking out the open collar of his shirt and the bare skin that had teased her. The first touch of her fingertips against his skin drew a shudder from him. Shannon gasped, the small sound breaking through their kiss momentarily. All her fingertips felt abnormally sensitive. She was aware of each one as they made contact with him. He was so strong, and yet his skin was smooth and soft. She sent her hands farther into the open shirt until she found his collarbones and then the warm column of his throat. A soft male sound rumbled up from his chest. It was only a tone-on-tone sound without structure, but it conveyed his enjoyment. That bit of knowledge intoxicated her further, to know that her touch gave him cause to make sounds of pleasure, just as his did to her. It placed them on an equal footing, a position that she had never expected to be in.

He lifted his head away from hers. A soft sound of disappointment crossed her lips, but he didn't heed it. He broke away from her grasp completely, leaving her body quivering with the loss. There was a sharp snap and pop as he pulled on the tie that held his claymore against his back. Hard purpose was etched into his expression. The look should have frightened her, but it didn't. Instead she stared at him in fascination and slight disbelief.

For the first time in her life, she truly felt pretty. No words might have convinced her, only the look on his face. It was hard and taut, not soft or gentle as a song might have her expect. Yet that suited her far more, because it was his strength that drew her to him.

He swung the sword off his back in a fluid motion of his large arms. His eyes stared straight into hers in challenge. She stood still, her breath frozen in her lungs while he set the weapon aside. Understanding was plain. There were few reasons why a man such as he would put his sword aside. Not for a quick tumble, and not for a woman who he'd forget the moment his kilt dropped back down over his spent cock.

He reached toward her, doing it slowly now to gauge her response. It was another challenge, and it drew a twist of excitement from her belly, the anticipation building to an almost-unbearable level. She shivered when his fingers made contact with her. He stepped close in response, startling her with how intensely aware he was of her every response.

Truly, she had not understood what intimacy was before. It was becoming harder to know where he began and she ended.

"Kiss me."

His voice was deep and husky but still edged with authority. It was that commanding edge that gained her attention. The impulse to tease him returned.

She rose up onto her toes and tilted her head. Excitement lit his eyes, but she pressed her lips against his jawline and sank back down.

He frowned at her, but there was a twinkle in his dark eyes that betrayed his enjoyment.

"I see that I will have to be more detailed in my requests." His fingers tugged on the ties that drew her overgown into shape around her body. "That could be most interesting."

Her outer gown loosened. She felt the giving of her garment like a splash of cold water against her bare skin. His fingers captured the fabric and drew it over her head before she finished gasping.

Whatever she'd considered saying about his removing her clothing died when she looked at his expression. His gaze had dropped to her chest, his dark eyes fixated on the points of her nipples where they raised the soft fabric of her undergown. Her overgarment fluttered toward the ground, completely forgotten. Torin reached for her but not too eagerly. His hands spanned her waist, gently grasping her body once again.

"Come here, Shannon. I've spent too many hours dreaming of having you in my embrace."

He didn't want to move slowly. A muscle was twitching along the side of his jaw, telling her how much self-discipline he was employing not to grab her.

There was another thing she had not expected. No woman did, for it was a man's nature to take what he wanted. Torin wanted her; desire flickered in his eyes, while his hands smoothed a path across her ribs and onto her breasts.

He cupped them both, closing his hands around the tender curves. She shivered with enjoyment. The sensation raced down her back and into her passage. Both of her nipples were drawn tight into hard nubs that throbbed softly. Hidden between the folds of her sex was another point that pulsed with the same racing beat as her heart. He gently teased each peak with his thumbs, rubbing back and forth over them while closing the last step between them.

His body brushed up against hers, restoring the sweet, intoxicating cloud over her senses again. She lifted her hand and pulled at the ties that kept his shirt closed. When she'd loosened it enough, he reached up and tugged the garment over his head. It fluttered to the ground behind him, but she lost interest in watching it.

His bare chest was much more to her liking.

Up close, he was more magnificent than he'd been, standing on the boulder.

"Touch me, Shannon, for I've seen in yer eyes that ye want to."

"That's true."

His command wasn't necessary, because she was hungry for life's pleasures. Nothing short of bindings on her wrists would have stopped her from reaching for him. She needed to touch him. Too many hours of thinking about it had left her desperate to discover what the reality felt like.

His eyes closed when she laid her hands on him. His expression became one of intense male satisfaction. It was fascinating, and it made her bold. Smoothing her hands along the hard ridges that covered his breast, she felt every bit of strength that she'd felt in his embrace.

"If I die right now, I'll go happily, for yer touch is perfection." He opened his eyes and pulled her against him with a solid arm around her waist. Her hands ended up trapped between their bodies, and there was something in his eyes that said he liked knowing that she was helpless in his hold for the moment. It was a subtle male need to show her his strength. What surprised her was the way she responded to it. Passion blossomed into full desire. She was suddenly aware of how much she craved having him press down on top of her. Carnal and wicked as it was, she could not deny how much she wanted to be taken.

He leaned down and pressed a hard kiss against her mouth. There was no teasing now. His tongue probed the seam between her lips, prodding her until she opened her jaw for him to thrust it down into her mouth. Her body craved the same penetration. Her hips flexed toward him without thought, instinct guiding her motions. Behind the pleated folds of his kilt, his cock was hard. Her entire being craved knowing what it would feel like inside her. Hunger clawed at her to stop teasing and rush toward what lay ahead.

Torin was done playing, it seemed. His kiss was full of demand, but he broke it off in order to strip her undergown from her. The afternoon air was suddenly not as warm as she'd thought. She felt the chill of it brushing along her bare legs and arms and across her belly and breasts. Hesitation gripped her, and her arms came up, trying to cover her nudity. One crossed over her breasts, and the other lay across her belly so that her hand might guard her sex from his keen gaze.

Torin scooped her up before she realized he meant to. Sweeping her feet off the ground, he turned before sinking to one knee. She shivered, but not in worry that he'd drop her. It was a ripple of sensation followed by another as she became aware of how good his bare skin felt against her own. Where his shirt was missing, he was warm, almost hot against her. The soft male hair coating his chest felt just harsh enough against her skin. He laid her down on top of their clothing, pressing her onto her back and following her until he was stretched out alongside her.

"It's nae May Day, but I refuse to spend another night waiting to claim ye."

"Claim me?"

His words were arrogant and edged with pride.

One hand boldly cupped her bare breast while his expression became tight with hunger again.

"Aye, lass, claim ye. I swear I'll be the only lover ye have."

She stiffened, disliking the chains his words tried to bind her with. Lifting her hands, she pushed at his wide chest.

"I never promised ye anything of the sort, Torin McLeren."

He refused to budge, stubbornly remaining exactly where he was, with her breast held in his grasp while she tried in vain to dislodge his larger body.

He leaned down until his warm breath teased her moist lips. "Of course ye haven't, lass. But I have nae had the chance to show ye just how good a lover I'll make yet. Once I do, ye'll have no desire for any other."

"Ye're an arrogant brute." Her words didn't sound sharp, but she still frowned at him.

He smirked at her. "Nay, lass, what I am is confident, and you'll learn to appreciate that facet of me personality."

Shannon hissed at him and pushed harder against his chest. "So you say."

His thumb brushed over her nipple, sending a hot shaft of desire through her. Her arms lost a great deal of their strength. His expression became less mocking and far more intense.

"'Tis something I'd far rather prove than mince words over."

She hoped so…

Hot and thick, passion beckoned to her. She didn't

want to think, didn't want to have to talk, because it drew her away from the sweet intoxication that allowed her to forget about everything beyond what her flesh craved.

Torin didn't disappoint her. He leaned down and sucked her nipple deeply between his lips. Her back arched, while a startled cry passed her lips. The heat was searing. But the pleasure was so intense, she could not remain still. It was like a living thing trapped inside her; she had to arch and reach out for him.

He pressed her onto her back, the pile of their shed clothing making for a comfortable spot to lie. His mouth teased her nipple, sucking hard on the tender point before the tip of his tongue began to worry it. The afternoon air was no longer chilly; it was a soothing coolness that eased the burning heat that was licking its way along her. Torin smoothed a hand down her body, teasing her belly for long moments before venturing lower. Her thighs closed, but he teased the curls that lay on top of her sex, toying with them while that spot that throbbed just beyond his reach begged her to spread wide so that he might ease the ache there.

He lifted his head from her breast, and the air was cold against the wet tip of her nipple. Hard and hungry, he stared at her.

"I am going to be yer lover, Shannon."

His hand moved lower, pressing her to relent and part her thighs.

"Only because I want ye to be. 'Tis my choice, Torin."

Sitting up, she reached for his head and held it

between her hands while she kissed him. Mimicking the motions he'd used, she pressed his lips apart to tease him with her tongue. He moved to support her with a hard arm across her back. But he only kissed her back, never taking the lead away. She thrust her tongue deeply into his mouth, sliding it along his own and shivering at the way it made her clit pulse. There was no way to keep her thighs together any longer. The folds of her sex felt too swollen to be crushed closed. Allowing her thighs to spread felt natural and correct.

"I'd not have ye any other way, Shannon."

He rolled over her, stopping on the other side of her body. Only now her thighs were held open by his body, one of her knees bent and raised so that her thigh lay beneath his waist. He propped his forearm near her head, trapping one of her arms behind his back.

So easily she was placed at his mercy. He watched her while his hand smoothed over her belly again, stroking her with delicate motions while his dark eyes glittered with approval.

She hadn't really been in control before, but it had felt like she was. A very clever deception to mask his strength and draw her toward him.

"Did ye mean what ye said?"

His hand had reached her mons again, making it far too difficult to think.

"That ye are here because ye choose to be?"

Her lower lip went dry when he fingered her slit. Just a slight touch of one fingertip against that so-forbidden place. She arched but could not move away.

"Did ye mean it, Shannon McBoyd?"

She narrowed her eyes. "I did, but I'm rethinking

the matter now that ye are throwing my last name at me."

"Use mine."

His finger had frozen, making no movement. Her body protested, urging her to arch toward him to gain friction against her clit. He leaned down, covering her body with his own. Bare chest to bare chest, she sighed with pleasure. Never had she suspected that her body might find so much enjoyment all at the same time. Torin pressed a soft kiss against the side of her neck and then another and a third. Little ripples of delight raced across her skin.

"Say my name, Shannon. If ye choose me for yer lover, call me by my name."

"Torin."

He lifted his head to stare into her eyes. She knew what he wanted, could see the demand shimmering in his dark eyes. But there was also hunger there; she could see him struggling to contain it.

"And that is the only name that I'm interested in taking for my lover. Torin and Shannon. If ye want the rest, get off me and we'll compare our colors, or ye may go and negotiate with my father for me."

"It is the first time ye have called me by name. Can I nae take a moment to savor the sound of it on yer lips?"

And he enjoyed it. Another bit of hidden power that she had not expected to wield. But it affected him deeply. Lifting her free hand, she gently stroked his face, smoothing her fingers over the hard line of his jaw to where the muscle began to tic once again.

"Kiss me, Torin."

He didn't hesitate. His mouth found hers, his lips

moving insistently over hers. His hand began seeking once more, this time delving between the folds of her sex until he found her clitoris. Fire and pleasure flashed through her, so intense, she gasped. Her head fell back, her eyes closing as the sensation became so blinding, there was nothing to do except allow it to consume her.

He rubbed gently at first but gained speed while she gasped beneath his touch. Time seemed to stop while her ears were filled with the sound of her blood rushing faster and faster. Her heart beat at a wild tempo, and her lungs struggled to keep pace. Her passage felt empty, so much so that it ached with need. Her hips arched upward, seeking to take his finger inside her. But he pinned her beneath his form, keeping her in place while his fingers continued to torment her.

Need and hunger became too much to bear. She cried out because there was no way to contain the boiling emotions. She needed something so badly, she jerked and arched in an attempt to gain it. Her belly was a knot of tension that was pulling tighter and tighter, until it suddenly burst in a fiery explosion of white-hot pleasure. It felt like she was falling, and she didn't care if she ended up dead when she reached the bottom of the abyss. There was too much pleasure. It flooded her, washing over her from her belly outward and then returning to her passage, where everything became a soft glow of contentment. She collapsed against the ground, opening her eyes to see the sky turning pink with sunset.

"That is the reward that lovers sneak away to gain, lass."

Torin pressed a hard kiss against her lips while

rolling completely over her. He pulled her knees right up to her waist to spread her body wide for his possession. The head of his cock nudged her open slit, stoking the fire that had been burning inside her.

"Are ye a virgin?"

His jaw was set tightly, the effort of holding still making his expression harsh. The muscle along his jaw twitched and his body shook, but his cock remained exactly where it was, only teasing the opening of her body with its hardness.

"I am." And she realized that she was proud of her purity.

He drew in a stiff breath, his eyes glowing with some emotion that surfaced from deep inside him.

"I should say that I'm sorry to cause ye pain, but I'm not." A fierce flash of enjoyment lit his eyes, and he pressed forward, thrusting his length into her. He felt too large, too hard, but her passage was slick, allowing him to penetrate her. Her body began stretching to accommodate the invasion, pain nipping along the area that he'd gained. He pulled free. Regret raced through her, a longing for more raking its claws across her.

Torin did not leave her wanting. He thrust smoothly back into her, ripping through the barrier that had blocked his path. Pain slammed into her, forcing the breath from her lungs. It was searing agony that ripped into the most tender part of her body. Every muscle drew taut, her body attempting to arch away from his. Torin held her solidly in place, his body resting on top of hers and pinning her, but he allowed only enough of his weight onto her to keep her still. The rest he supported on his forearms, which were braced on either side of her head. Her lungs began burning from lack of breath. After sucking in a deep one, she blew it out with a soft cry. The pain subsided, leaving only an ache where his hard flesh still stretched her.

Tears gathered in her eyes, making her vision glassy when she opened them. Torin watched her, his dark eyes glittering with satisfaction. She should have been annoyed to see him so pleased that she was a virgin, but her pride didn't allow her temper to rise. His fingers gently stroked the sides of her head, across her temple and along her hairline. The little soothing motions allowed her to draw another deep breath and blow it out slowly. She suddenly noticed that he was remaining still for her sake, and that needled her pride.

"Go on, then. I'm not that fragile."

And she wanted to know what was next. Her passage might ache, but the feeling of his hard flesh filling her was what she'd been craving. Hunger was still gnawing at her behind the ache.

"Aye, I've noticed that." He flexed his hips, pulling his cock out of her. The motion sent new sensations of enjoyment through her that chased away the memory of the hurt.

"But I'm intent on proving that I am no' a savage by nature. A lover does nae simply toss up the skirts of his partner and proceed with rutting her without a care for allowing her body to adjust."

He was having trouble concentrating on his words. Strain took command of his features, while his thick arms shook slightly. She hadn't realized that her nails had dug into his skin. Forcing her hands to relax, she watched his eyes fill with need.

"I'm well adjusted now, Torin." Her tone was husky. His slow thrusts renewed her enjoyment. It was more than enjoyment; pleasure filled her with every soft thrust. Her hips began lifting toward him, eager to take his length.

He offered her a soft growl in reply. But she enjoyed the raw male sound. Somehow it fit the moment. This wasn't the time for sweet words. She wanted to move, wanted to feel him thrusting faster and harder against her. All her senses were keener, making communicating with words unnecessary. She wanted to feel, not think. Her thighs grasped his hips, and her eyes closed.

Another soft growl vibrated through his chest. She felt it as much as she heard it, because he was still pressed against her. The soft mounds of her breasts were gently pressed down by the harder planes of his chest. Her neck arched back, and he leaned over her, his breathing becoming rough. His hands tangled in her hair, holding her tighter while his body answered her need for faster motion. He thrust deeply and hard now, every plunge sending equal amounts of need and enjoyment through her. It far surpassed the delight he'd given her with his hand. This was deeper and more intense. The feeling of his hard flesh inside her was satisfying the hunger that had begun with watching him swim. This was what she'd craved, this deep intimacy that unleashed so many sensations in her.

He felt it too. She could feel his body quivering, her fingers telling her that his muscles were drawing tight along with her own. Her hips rose to meet his, and she wasn't sure whose breath sounded rougher, only positive that they were both lost to the same need for each other. Her body twisted and strained toward his. Even being so close wasn't enough. She wanted him deeper, wanted his cock to fill her. There was nothing but the building hunger in her belly. It tightened further and further, until it broke in a shower of hot pleasure. Shannon strained upward as the delight rained down on her. Her breath froze, and she heard nothing but the blood rushing through her ears. The pleasure shook through her, demanding every last bit of attention. Torin snarled softly when she cried out, his hands holding her head tightly and his body plunging down to impale her with several hard thrusts. A harsh sound came from Torin a moment before he buried his length deep inside her and she felt his seed filling her. The hot spurt of fluid unleashed a second jolt of pleasure inside her, the walls of her passage contracting around his cock to milk every last drop from him. Her thighs locked around his hips, and his hands held her tightly.

Eight

SHANNON SUDDENLY HEARD THE WIND AGAIN. IT WAS whipping up with the onset of night. Her heart began to slow, and her body felt spent, unable to move except for the necessary rising of her chest to breathe. Her thoughts returned in a flurry of disorganized ideas, rushing in to tear at her.

Her eyes flew open as she realized that she might conceive. It was a startling idea, one that she'd not considered in all her musing. But the hot pulse of delight in her belly told her that nature had everything it needed now.

Firm fingers moved along her hairline, bringing her head down so that Torin could look into her eyes. She shied away from his gaze, ducking beneath his arm to avoid his seeing her thoughts. The man was too keen, too able to read her emotions. For all that she'd just given him her innocence, she was suddenly shy.

He grunted and rolled onto his back. But he didn't allow her to escape. One arm hooked her around her waist and brought her back against him.

"Do nae start with that yet, Shannon."

He pressed her head down on top of his chest. His thighs clamped around one of her legs to keep her near.

"Yer kilt scratches my skin."

He muttered something in Gaelic, his arms tightening around her, but he gave a snort and released her.

"That is nae the reason ye are restless." He rolled onto his feet in a fluid motion, lifting her up as well and setting her on her feet. His strength still astounded her. A tiny shiver rippled across her skin as she realized how easy it would have been for him to take his pleasure without regard for her pain. He was displeased with her now, his expression telling her that plainly. But the fingers curled around her arms never closed too harshly.

"What is? Regrets for lying with me?"

The evening breeze was chilly. It blew across her bare skin, making her shiver.

"I'm cold."

It was a truth, and it offered her an escape from meeting his eyes. Bending back down, she reached for her dress. But she stopped short when her gaze fell on her undergown. Made of a lighter-colored linen, it was marked clearly with blood. There would always be a stain on the garment too, because blood was impossible to remove completely once dried.

She shivered again, her body cooling down rapidly. There was a soft sound of frustration from Torin. In the next moment he scooped her off her feet and set her aside. He plucked her underrobe, holding it for a long moment while he stared at the stain. Shannon felt more exposed than she ever had, hugging herself with her arms to cover her nude body. Tears stung her eyes, and she stubbornly blinked them away.

She'd made her choice.

"Give it to me, Torin. I'm cold."

One corner of his mouth twitched. If he smiled, she didn't see it, because he gave her undergown a snap before setting it over her head. The fabric blocked out her view of him. Relief flooded her, and her cheeks turned pink with shame.

She was acting the fool but couldn't seem to control her feelings; they were whipping around inside of her just like the wind.

Struggling to put her hands through the sleeves, she wiggled until her gown fell into place. Torin was waiting with her outer dress, and he placed it over her head the moment she peeked past the first garment at him. It slithered down her body, feeling heavy and confining.

"Now tell me what yer worry is."

Torin stood, unconcerned about his bare chest being open to the evening air. Instead the man pegged her with a hard look that warned her he was not in the mood to be denied. She recognized the man who had told her he was taking her to the Highlands no matter what she thought about the idea.

Her chin rose, as did her need to stand her ground. "I was cold, and I do nae need to explain that. The sun is almost gone. Dusk has arrived."

And that was a blessing, because she welcomed its dark folds to hide her expression in. The church bell began tolling in the distance. Torin grunted.

"That is not what disturbed ye."

He spoke with a quiet voice that was full of authority. He was accustomed to gaining the answers he sought, and didn't care for her refusing him.

Shannon tossed her hair. "Even if it weren't, it is the only answer I am giving ye."

He crossed his arms over his chest. Without a shirt, she could see every muscle where it corded across his wide chest.

Being pressed against it had been perfection…

"Is that a fact?"

"It is."

He snorted before reaching down to yank his shirt off the ground. He shrugged into the garment with motions that strained its seams. Faint ripping sounds joined the birds whistling in the trees. Torin tucked the tail in with a few hard motions before he reached out and clamped his hand around her wrist.

"What are ye doing?"

He was already walking back to where his horse was standing, taking her along with him. His strides were long and quick, making her hurry to keep pace.

"Taking you back to Donan Tower." He dropped her wrist and untied the reins that he'd looped around a young tree trunk. A second later he turned and grasped her waist with a solid grip. He tossed her up onto the back of his horse with one soft grunt. The stallion shifted, prancing nervously. Shannon grasped the neck of the beast while staring at the distance to the ground. It seemed a lot farther from the top of the animal than it had standing beside the horse.

Torin swung up behind her, encircling her body with a hard arm that bound her against his body. She was sitting on the horse sideways, and he pressed up against her while gripping the reins in his right hand.

"I'm not finished talking to you about this, Shannon."

"Well, I'm finished."

He dug his heels into the stallion, and the beast took off with a toss of its head. With his arm around her, she felt as trapped as she had with her wrists tied.

He chuckled against her ear, and there was nothing kind about the sound. It was pure male promise. A soft quiver worked its way through her; he felt it. His grip opened, and his finger began soothing over the skin of her forearm instantly. The kindness in his gesture brought the tears back to her eyes.

Torin leaned down to whisper against her ear. "Then I'll have to try my hand at changing yer mind, Shannon McBoyd, for I'm going to know what soured your disposition toward me so that I can smash it into bits that will nae interfere with us again."

But how could she place a child in the same position she was in? That was irresponsible as well as selfish of her. Taking a lover was all well and fine if she had thought to take some precaution against conceiving. There were herbs that would keep it from happening, but she'd have to ask Baeth for them. Powerful plants such as the ones she was thinking about could be used to kill. They were used in medicines and kept locked away. The head of the house held those keys, her years of experience and proven trustworthiness a critical thing.

They emerged from the trees, and Shannon felt her belly tighten just as it had the first time she viewed Donan Tower. Yet her reasons for feeling

apprehension were different now. It was still imprison-
ment that she feared, but for a far different reason.

Being kept inside the gray walls meant being within
Torin's reach. She craved the man so much, she
doubted her ability not to act the fool and surrender
everything to him no matter the consequences. Out in
the forest was different. He could forget he was a laird
there, and she could forget she was the daughter of his
enemy. Out there, they were the same as peasant folk
who had sneaked away to enjoy each other.

Except that they weren't peasant folk. Any child
they created would be born the child of the enemy
because her father had raided Torin's land. Men did
not think of such things. A man could dally where he
would and no one would judge him for it. She would
bear that burden. It might be her willing choice to be
his lover, but a child had no choice and it would be
stained with her McBoyd blood. That was something
she understood too well.

The moment his horse took to the bridge, she felt eyes
on them. The curious watched from the village, and she
saw the men on the walls peering down toward them.
Her cheeks heated as they drew closer to the gate. Calls
went out to tell one and all that the laird was returning.
That drew even more attention to them. Boys looked
out of the stable windows, eager for a break from their
evening chores. Maids looked on from the open doors
of the great hall, their eyes widening when they saw her
seated on the front of Torin's horse.

He was their laird, and everyone took notice of
his return. Torin stopped in front of the hall, where
Brockton had stepped out to greet him on his return.

"Keep yer eye on her."

Shannon gasped and hit Torin's jaw with her head because she jerked around to glare at him. A soft exclamation brushed her ears, and then she was being lowered to the ground before getting a chance to shoot a displeased look into his eyes.

"Aye, Laird." Brockton stepped up beside her, reaching out to gently grip her upper arm.

Shannon shook his hold off with a violent twist of her body. "He said eyes, no' hands."

Brockton was startled by her action, his hand releasing her, but his eyebrows lowered, and his lips pressed into a hard line that told her he'd do exactly as his laird instructed in spite of her displeasure. She turned her temper on Torin.

"What means this?"

Torin remained in the saddle, his thighs gripping the stallion powerfully.

"Answer my question."

"Or ye will have me hounded by yer dog?"

Torin's expression darkened, but he nodded in a single, hard motion.

"Fine then. I'll suffer yer dog. Perhaps that's just the lesson I need." She tossed her head, feeling her braid snap behind her back.

"Enough." Torin spoke through gritted teeth. She could hear how much his control was being tested, but did not care. "I care if ye are here and no' tempting fate by attempting some foolish escape."

He turned and headed toward the stable. Her temper burned hot enough to keep the night chill from bothering her. Her throat was suddenly too tight, cutting off her ability to breathe. Lined up along the open doors of the great hall were too many maids to count; they were peeking over each other's shoulders to get a look at her. There were smirks and more than a few condemning expressions.

She was no coward.

Shannon held her chin steady. Aye, she was no coward. Grasping her skirts, she climbed the stairs and walked right through the parting crowd of onlookers. Let them stare; let their laird make a public display of her.

That did not make her his!

It did not.

⁘

"That was a wee bit harsh." Connor Lindsey was rubbing down his mount when Torin reached the stable.

"I thought ye were heading home."

His friend raised an eyebrow at his tone, and Torin cursed. He was grateful for the fact that he was at last in a place where he could speak his mind. His control was worn thin.

"I'm going as soon as the moon rises, but I'll admit that I'm thinking about taking Shannon McBoyd with me."

Torin slapped a hand on the rail between them. He did it with every bit of frustration that was bottled up inside him. The wood cracked with a splintering sound that made the horses snort nervously.

"Do nae jest about her, Connor."

"Why? Because ye have had her?"

Torin raised his head and glared at his friend. "Aye,

and I seem to have no humor in me when it comes to any man, even ye, talking about taking her."

Connor shrugged. "Ye have always been a one-lass man."

Torin drew in a stiff breath. Connor was correct. His affairs had been few, and he would rather sleep alone than with a woman for whom he did not have feelings.

"I need more than the tumble. My uncle used to say that I inherited that from my parents' love match."

His uncle had considered it a weakness and predicted it would cost Torin a good match someday, because he'd be too softhearted to marry for gain, exactly like his father.

"Well, ye have no bastards because of that habit. There's something to be said for that. I hear the Douglas has too many to count, and that's among the ones whom he cannae cast doubt upon."

"There's plenty who say my lack of bastards is because my seed has no life."

Torin didn't care who heard him, because he knew it was being whispered behind his back. His cousin Lundy was beginning to raise his voice now, telling one and all that he would be the next Laird McLeren.

"More likely, yer mistresses have repaid yer loyalty by making sure they didn't conceive. Women have their ways, but it is getting time for ye to wed and silence Lundy. The man is making my head ache."

"That's the first time ye have joined the crowd telling me to contract a wife."

Connor slipped a bridle over his horse's head. "This business with the king has me thinking. I need to consider what mess I'd leave behind if I died out on the hills beneath the moonlight I like to ride through so much." Connor turned a hard look on him. "I plan to marry before summer is finished, and I suggest ye think of doing the same. The pair of us both have several cousins all in line to inherit behind us, and there would be fighting if we left no heirs. We're no longer boys to be thinking our lives do nae affect others."

"Aye, we're grown, and that's a truth. It is time I took to courting a bride."

"Well I am nae sure about this strategy ye seem to be employing of setting a guard on the lass. That didna gain ye any of her favor. Ye'd better find another way to charm her."

"You think Shannon McBoyd would make a good bride for me?"

Connor offered him a smirk. "I think it will be amusing to watch ye try and slip a bridle onto her. That lass is not impressed with yer McLeren lairdship."

Torin muttered a profane word that drew a chuckle from his friend.

Connor pulled his stallion forward. His men were waiting in the courtyard for him. They preferred to ride at night. In spite of his light coloring, Connor was a man who embraced the shadows. It was the thing that Torin liked best about him.

Torin suddenly chuckled at the smirk sitting on Connor's lips.

"Do nae worry about how I'll gain her favor, just be very sure that I will."

Connor swung up onto his horse's back. The stallion wore no saddle, only a thick blanket secured with a wide length of leather. Connor Lindsey had been raised by a resentful aunt who never allowed him to forget the fact that his mother wasn't married on the day that she birthed him. He'd been denied things that were noble, such as saddles. He clung to some of those things to remind everyone that he was proud of who he was in spite of their opinions.

"Maybe ye will, and then again, maybe I'll have to return and run ye through because it's more Christian than watching ye suffer."

With a wolfish smile, his fellow laird took to the bridge. His men followed, and the gate lowered behind them. The sun was gone, night began to capture the last of the daylight. Torin watched his men light the torches set along the wall inside the yard to keep it lit. Along the walls there would be others who went without light so that they could see in the dark.

He could smell her.

Shannon's scent clung to his body, sweet and spicy. He battled the urge to confront her and turned to the task of caring for his horse instead. There was no point in arguing with her. She was his. If that required him to hold her captive, so be it. Connor's words were sounding more and more logical, but he admitted that it was more than logic behind his idea of wedding Shannon McBoyd. Part of him wanted a woman who didn't come to him by her father's command. His parents had loved each other, and it was something that too few in the world understood the value of. He craved that, longed for a woman who would take him and nothing else, even if his lairdship were stripped away at first light.

Someone like Shannon McBoyd, who accepted

him as her lover but lifted her nose at the sight of Laird McLeren and his commands.

He snorted. It was possible he'd found the most perfect woman in Scotland.

⁂

Baeth watched her bathe.

Shannon felt the weight of the woman's stare but kept at the task of cleaning Torin's scent from her skin. She forced herself to continue even as regret clawed at her. There was no other choice. She had been foolish to believe that taking a lover was a choice she might make. Her father had been right to keep her virgin. She'd have to begin praying that her sin did not bear fruit.

"Yer thoughts are too deep, lass."

Shannon jumped, and the water betrayed her by splashing up and over the rim of the tub. "I am simply tired."

Baeth raised an eyebrow at the tone Shannon used. The older woman moved further into the room. Shannon felt her heart freeze between beats as she realized what the older woman had draped over her arm.

It was a McLeren arisaid, and the head of house was intent on taking her McBoyd one.

"Stop."

Shannon stood up as Baeth was reaching for the wool set neatly on the top of a stool.

"Why, lass?" Baeth turned to look at her. "Is there something better waiting for ye back on yer father's land?" She reached down and pulled the soiled undergown off the stool, shaking it loose so that the dark stain was clearly exposed.

"Ye should take the place ye have earned."

Earned? The only place she had earned was that of a leman.

"Accepting anything would make me a whore."

Baeth clicked her tongue in reprimand. "You need to learn that life is nae so often a matter of black versus white, girl."

"In this case it is. If I take anything for my favors, 'tis a prostitute I am."

Baeth shook her head. But the head of house turned and left. It wasn't until she'd disappeared through the doorway that Shannon recalled that her undergown was still in the woman's possession. She felt the sting of tears once more and sat back down to finish rinsing the soap from her hair.

She wiped the water from her eyes when she heard Baeth's steps reentering the bathing room.

"You'll be using this and no argument, lass, or I shall fetch the laird to decide the matter."

A clean undergown was in her hands, and her expression was tight.

"Mine will be well with a good washing."

Baeth grunted. "Which will nae be happening tonight."

Shannon stood up and dried off her body before reaching for the garment Baeth held out toward her. She wanted to refuse it, but the idea of dealing with Torin was not to her liking. It was a fact that she had no resistance in her when it came to him. If ever she'd thought there were truly spells and magic in the world, her fascination with Torin McLeren proved that she'd become the victim of such dark forces. She donned the undergown in spite of her reluctance. Torin would consider it a challenge if she refused. She didn't have the will to battle with him so soon. Tomorrow would be different. Once the sun rose, the magic spells inhabiting the darkness would fade, leaving her able to think.

Baeth held out the McLeren arisaid.

"I am McBoyd. Donning McLeren colors will not temper anyone's opinion toward me."

Or her children. It was black-and-white, without any hint of anything else.

"What ye are is stubborn. Did ye not plan to be accepted by the family that ye were being sent to marry into?"

"I am not married." Shannon looked at the offered arisaid and shook her head. "Not even hand fasted. But I thank ye for being kind to me."

Baeth scoffed, disapproval clear on her face. The head of house shook her head.

"Stubborn. Far too stubborn."

～

Shannon watched dawn break on May morn. Sitting in her window with the shutters wide open, she stared at the horizon. Pink fingers of light appeared first, like a hand reaching over a ledge. More light pushed against the night, until the darkness evaporated in a golden flood.

Her hair was still contained in the long braid that trailed down her back. Tears stung the corners of her eyes, but she resisted the impulse to pull off the tie that held the strands.

Her impulses had already led her too far astray.

Below her window, she heard laughter. The girls of the McLeren clan began running toward the gate and the maypole in the village. Music drifted up from the pipers and drums. Men played at their instruments while walking among the merry girls.

She would not go.

It was settled.

She made her way down the stairs to the kitchens. Only a few women remained to tend the hearths, all of them married, and they looked at her with knowing eyes, the fact that they considered her claimed by their laird apparent. Maybe she wasn't wed, but when it came to a girl that was warming the laird's bed, the other men would be expected to ignore her.

Well, that was what embracing free will had gained her. She wasn't completely repentant. There was a part of her that had enjoyed it full well. Deep down inside her was a woman content in knowing what it was like to decide whom she gave her virginity to. Just like every other member of the clan, her body had been the property of the laird. Lads were expected to swear their loyalty and fight when needed, while the girls were expected to marry up and produce more loyal McBoyds. Being the laird's daughter only meant that she was expected to serve in a different manner; her body was to be traded for an alliance.

Well, that had not been the case yesterday.

Call her disloyal, fine; she would wear the label proudly. Because along with that went the feeling that she was a woman. She'd never expected it to mean so much to her, never really realized that she longed to make her own decision about who used her flesh. That was the reward for standing up to the looks being cast her way today, judgmental looks, narrowing of the eyes from the other women.

At least there was plenty to do. It kept everyone busy and their lips sealed. Brockton remained behind as well. The burly Scot appeared as unhappy about his posting as Shannon was. He was more diligent than before, only taking his eyes off her when another man appeared to take charge of her. His constant presence set her on edge. An ache formed in the center of her shoulders before noon, and it had naught to do with the work she was doing.

The day dragged on endlessly. Each hour felt like three, and the merriment drifting in on the breeze grated against her straining nerves.

Was Torin lying with another? A girl who wasn't refusing to dance about the maypole? He was the laird and expected to attend the merriment. She caught herself looking toward the maypole with a yearning that threatened to make her weep.

She was ready to weep with relief when the sun finally set and the last of the supper chores were finished. The chamber she'd been given had suddenly transformed from a prison into a sanctuary. At least it would offer her privacy and relief from the constant presence of Torin's guard.

She pushed the door shut a little too hard behind her, and it slammed. But that didn't keep her from leaning against it and sighing. She heard the guard walking away, his steps echoing on the stone steps. The window shutters were still wide open. Shannon stared at them, recognizing that the McLeren women had declined to do anything to ensure her comfort today. The maids closed all the shutters at sunset to conserve the heat inside the tower. A quick glance at the fireplace showed her a cold and dark pile of ashes that had not been shoveled out either.

She would not care about it. The spring evening was not bitter. Stars twinkled in the dark fabric of the night sky, beckoning her toward the open window to enjoy them. It was enchanting. Magical and hypnotizing, even the crispness of the air was alluring. It turned her cheeks cold, and when she breathed it deeply into her chest, it felt renewing, like a bath. It was strange the way the soul longed to frolic outside while logic told you to remain indoors where there was shelter.

She began to pull her braid free. The breeze tugged at the curls that had worked their way free during the day. She suddenly needed to feel her hair loose. Denying herself the privilege of wearing her hair down had been a strain, and her self-discipline was worn thin now. Reaching around to where her overgown was tied, she undid it and pulled off the thicker garment. Soon she'd happily wear her new spring dress because it was made of a thinner wool. Her undergown was free to billow away from her body now, the air teasing her legs. A tiny ripple of awareness moved along her legs and up to her sex. She was more aware of that spot than she'd ever been before. A slight soreness marked the passage of her innocence, but what captured her attention more was the certain knowledge of how much pleasure might be had when she surrendered.

When she surrendered to Torin, that was. There wasn't another man she'd ever met who made her body tingle with hunger. It was a blunt fact, but at least she might take solace in knowing that she was not a slut who sought tumbles with any man willing to entertain her.

Her father would certainly consider her attraction to Torin McLeren worse than being a slut, but she could not help the fact that she admired the man. He was kind when no one would blame him for being harsh, and he was a man of honor, not one who used the word when it suited him. She realized that she trusted him. That was something that she'd never had before, for every man wearing her father's colors would have done whatever her sire demanded. Torin McLeren would not be bending to anyone, but he didn't use that authority to take her against her will. That was what drew her to him; it was the reason she'd struggled against her urges to taste him again in spite of the irresponsibility of such an act. She wanted to be his lover, and there was no way to deny that. It sat gnawing away at her belly, flickering in the little nub at the top of her sex while the darkness sang to her of ages and ages of trysts that had happened beneath its velvet curtain. With only her undergown on, she felt her breasts hanging more naturally. A sense of her femininity seemed to wrap around her, and it brought a smile to her lips.

Picking up a comb, she began to work it through her hair. Below the window, the water of the loch slapped sharply against the boulders that rose above its surface. She continued to brush out her hair, leaving the shutters open. The sound of the water was inspiring, helping to drive away the hopelessness that was trying to sink into her thoughts again.

"There's something I was hoping to see this morning."

Shannon gasped, and the comb went clattering onto the floor. She whirled around to face the man she'd been thinking about most of the day. Torin was only two paces away, plenty close enough to reach out and grasp her if she started to fall out of the window yet again.

"You should nae…" Her words trailed off because the look on his face was captivating. She'd never considered herself a pretty woman, but the expression on Torin's face proclaimed her lovely.

"And ye should nae have hidden in the kitchen on May morn." His lips thinned. "You do nae know how many times I wanted to find ye and carry ye off over my shoulder, Shannon."

"Is that some sort of threat that I'm expected to heed?"

He shrugged. "It is the truth."

His gaze traced her hair, and his expression became one of pure male appreciation. He reached out, one of those large hands intent on touching her.

She stepped aside, edging along the wall. "Ye should go. I'm sure ye didna suffer any lack of invitations today." Her voice was low because she feared that he'd hear how weak she was when it came to him. Better to keep her shame private. Beneath her loose gown, her nipples beaded and clamored for his lips to taste them once again. She forced her feet to move away from him again because her belly was turning into a cauldron of hot need and she couldn't seem to halt the rise of desire.

"If ye had nae hidden here, ye would know that my people know that I am not a man who enjoys quick tumbles for the sake of satisfying my lust."

Torin turned and followed her with slow steps that kept the space between them exactly the same every time that she moved. The end of her bed brought her up short, her eyes widening when she realized she'd moved toward the very place that she did not want Torin to get her to.

"But I admit that part of me enjoys knowing ye hid from me inside me own tower."

She stiffened. "Ye made sure of that with yer guard set to watch my every step, Laird McLeren." She used his title because it would have been so easy to allow the look in his eyes to melt her resolve.

"Fault me if you like, Shannon, but I was nae willing to take the chance that ye would try and run. Because I am laird, I canno' keep my own eyes on ye the entire day long. I assure ye I would like nothing better."

He sounded sincere, and she was hungry for his embrace to shelter her from the harsher realities of life. But those arms would not be hers when dawn broke.

"It would be better if ye left."

Torin crossed his arms over his chest, his dark eyes considering her intently. They narrowed slightly, betraying the fact that he was not as calm as he appeared.

"Ye enjoyed my touch full well, Shannon."

Male satisfaction edged his words, but he did not grin at her. His face had taken on a hard look, one that she recognized from the night they'd met. The Highlander in him was not going to back down easily. But neither was she.

Her hands settled on her hips. "That does nae mean I plan to warm yer bed every night henceforth. If that were true, I'd be wearing yer colors to make it plain that I am yer leman. Baeth tried to give them to me."

He stiffened. "And ye refused my plaid after yielding yer purity to me?"

"I did."

Her tone drew an instant response from him. The muscle on the side of his jaw twitched, but she was only granted a moment to notice it. Torin moved as fast as lightning once again, reaching out for her and grasping her wrist. He lifted her arm up and leaned toward her while lowering his body down onto one knee. With a quick jerk on her hand, she tumbled toward him and over his broad shoulder. He surged back up to his full height, taking her with him. Her hair instantly fell down to wrap around her head and block her ability to see. Torin turned and only paused when he got to the door to her chamber. Without any hesitation, he took her right through the doorway and began climbing the stairs to the floor above, where his chamber was. He took the steps three at a time, his longer strides making it a simple matter. She clamped down on her urge to hiss an angry protest at him. The stairs were in a narrow corridor built out of stone, and every sound echoed along their length. Just as she could hear someone coming up the stairs, anyone on the other floors would hear her berating Torin for his current behavior.

Her restraint ended the moment he shoved the larger door to his chamber shut behind them.

"Put me down, you brute."

He complied instantly, although not in a manner that pleased her. Torin tossed her down in the center of his bed. Her hair was tangled around her, and her gown twisted up above her knees. The bed shook when she landed on it, making it a struggle to sit up and fix the man in her sights.

She froze when she got a look at him. Torin yanked his shirt off and threw it across the room.

"I am nae a brute, Shannon McBoyd, even if I'm tempted to act like one because ye have called me such."

"What do ye call carrying me in here, then? Gentle behavior? Are ye courting me? Is that it?"

His eyes flashed with warning. His hand moved to the wide belt holding his kilt around his waist, and she swallowed roughly. There was no hiding the excitement that twisted inside her. She wanted to see him, all of him, just as she had the night she'd arrived.

"I call carrying ye to my bed a better idea than the one ye had that would have seen both of us spending the night alone."

"Spending it together is nae such a grand idea either."

He pulled the tail of his belt back to release the double brass pins that held it secure. He held the belt up in one hand and caught his kilt in the other. Years of practice must have made it possible, because it looked like a clumsy task to her eyes. Torin managed it without any trouble; nothing but smooth motions of his hands, and his kilt was laid aside on a table in mere moments.

"If it is nae such a grand idea, why are you watching me like ye are, Shannon?"

He turned and caught her staring at him, his lips curving into a grin to confirm that he'd only been guessing that she was looking at him. His voice was coated in satisfaction with having caught her doing exactly that. "It appears to me that you like what ye see. A very great deal."

How could she not?

Everything about him drew her closer. Her lips had gone dry, and she ran her tongue across her lower one. A soft gasp became lodged in her throat when she noticed him staring at her mouth. Hunger shone in his eyes, and his lips thinned as he pressed his mouth into a tight line. He turned in a fluid motion that once again betrayed how much strength there was in it. It was more than his strength that captivated her; it was his sure command of that power. His body was honed to perfection.

And his cock stood hard and erect.

His soft male chuckle bounced around the chamber. She heard his steps on the floor, a mere whisper of a sound as he moved closer to her. His hand slid across her face and into her unbound hair. He combed it with his fingers while another soft male sound rumbled through his chest.

"Yer face says ye enjoy being right here." The hand in her hair cupped the back of her head, raising her face. "So do nae call me brute."

"You are a brute, Torin McLeren, and I do nae think ye are sorry for it."

His gaze lowered to her mouth, and her lips tingled.

"Aye, lass, ye have that bit correct." His hand tightened in her hair, and the bed moved as he placed one knee on it. "What I still don't understand is why you turned so cold yesterday." His eyes glittered with determination. "Tell me why ye hid in the kitchens today."

His demand was like a bucket of icy winter water being tossed at her. His scent was teasing her senses, but his question shattered her rising passion, souring it with harsh reality.

"It does nae matter why, only that I have made my choice." She extended one arm and pushed against his chest. "Ye should respect my decision."

One of his dark eyebrows rose. "Careful, lass, no brute would respect anything but what he wanted. A barbarian takes what he wishes. There is no gentle courting involved, only hard possession."

He was using her words against her, neatly trapping her between what she thought was right and what his touch made her seek out.

"You were acting the brute when ye tied me about ye and brought me here, but that is nae the man whom I went riding with yesterday."

His expression darkened before she finished speaking. The fingers resting on her nape tightened.

"I can be that man, lass. Didna I prove that to ye? That was no' ravishing that happened between us. Ye surrendered to me."

"I never accused ye of any wrongdoing."

His eyes flashed a warning at her. "Nay, ye only turned cold, pushing me away without sharing the reason. That is not the way of it between lovers, Shannon."

She'd wounded him by doing so; the proof was in his tone.

"Is that why ye set yer men to guarding me?"

Something flashed in his eyes that looked as formidable as it did exciting.

"Aye." His tone was gruff. "Call me brute if ye like, but I was nae going to take the chance that you might try to escape me before I had another chance to lie with you and work my way into yer affections."

"Why would ye care if I have affection for you?"

His eyes narrowed. "It does nae matter why, only that I do, and like the Highlander ye have called me, I will nae lose what I crave."

He leaned down and took her mouth, pressing a hard kiss against it while pushing her down into the bed. It was his bed, and the feeling of it against her back sent a surge of anticipation through her. Her thoughts abandoned her as his mouth demanded that she part her lips for a deeper kiss.

She wanted to…

And desire was not far behind. His scent surrounded her, drowning her rational thinking in a flood of sensation. Sweet and pleasurable, her body eagerly reached for what she had forbidden it all day long. The endless hours had left her starving, and there was no refusing her appetite now that what she craved was within her grasp.

She opened her mouth, and his tongue thrust boldly inside. A welcome invader, she teased it with her own tongue. His bare chest was a delight for her hands. She slid her fingers and palms along the hard ridges that her eyes had enjoyed so much.

"Yer hair is beautiful, lass. A pure delight. Part of me is glad that ye saved it for my eyes alone."

Torin buried his head in the cloud that lay across his sheets. He drew in a deep breath, his chest vibrating with a sound of male enjoyment.

"But—"

"Leave me my imaginings, Shannon." He lifted his head out of her hair and looked at her. "If for nothing more than I have never left May Day for any woman like I did tonight for ye."

"Ye left?"

One eyebrow rose. "I couldn't bear the thought of ye undressing without me there to enjoy it."

"But... surely there were others…"

"I want ye, Shannon. It has never been my way to tumble many lasses, only to tumble the one lass whom I consider mine, very often."

He suddenly sat back on his knees with his thighs spread on either side of her body. Her breath lodged in her throat because he looked so powerful. He was once again cast in shadow, with only a teasing of scarlet coming from the coals gently glowing in the fireplace across the chamber. Determination was etched into his face. He reached down and grasped her gown in both hands. With a hard tug, he pulled her undergown up her body. She sat up with the motion and ended up flopping back down onto the bed in a cloud of her own hair. The night air brushed her newly bared skin. She felt so completely at his mercy, with nothing to shield her at all.

"And now I shall enjoy my barbarian stolen prize."

Her pride rebelled, needed to somehow even things between them. She reached out and grasped his erect length with one hand. It was bold and possibly wicked, but she could not resist the urge to touch him as boldly he had done to her. All the whispers she'd heard from other girls swirled around inside her head like a storm, pushing her frail protests off balance. He sucked in a harsh breath that whistled through his clenched teeth.

"Do you like this?" She worked her hand down the length of his cock. "Because if you do, ye had better notice that I am nae acting like a stolen prize." She slid her hand up and down his erection, marveling at the way his face drew taut. The strain pulled his lips until they were thin, baring his teeth slightly. But she could see the intense enjoyment in his expression. It was primal, and it drew a flicker of desire from her own body.

"I am happy to be corrected."

She chuckled at his words. His voice was husky with need, a need that she was building. Confidence surged into her, making it easy to continue to moving her hand along his length. She teased the slit on the head, her thumb slipping through a drop of fluid that had appeared there. Pulling her legs up, she rolled onto one hip so that she was lying across the width of the bed. The position was much more to her liking.

"Happy, ye say…"

His breath grew rapid. "Yer touch makes me far more than happy, lass."

Sharply edged, his tone was laced with passion, not soft and flowery like a sonnet, but as hard as the flesh in her hand. She preferred it that way; there was nothing about sweet words that she craved.

But she would not give in to those cravings yet. Her pride wanted to have its way, wanted to prove that she was no prize to be consumed at his will. She planned to give as good as she received.

Leaning down, she blew a soft breath over the ruby head of his cock.

"Sweet Christ."

Torin spoke through gritted teeth. She could see the muscles along the column of his neck, corded and tight. Yet he did not move away. Instead he looked down at her, anticipation glimmering in his eyes. He was waiting on her. Power surged into her and washed away the last traces of hesitation.

Torin cursed in Gaelic when she closed her lips around his cock. His hands tangled in her hair while she tasted him for the first time. There was nothing unpleasant about it. Her senses were filled with his scent, and his skin was smooth inside her mouth. Moving her tongue around the crown on the top of his cock, she heard him gasp. It was a deep male sound of enjoyment. Opening her mouth wider, she took more of his length inside. Another drop of fluid was resting in the slit on top of the head. It was salty against her tongue when she licked it away. His hips jerked, thrusting his cock toward her face. It slid deeper into her mouth, but she remained relaxed, allowing it to penetrate.

Torin growled.

The sound was praise. She soaked it up while returning to teasing him with her tongue. She flicked it over the head and across the skin beneath the ridge of flesh that encircled it. His hips thrust in a short, jerky motion toward her, the hands in her hair gently gripping to keep her in place. More drops of fluid appeared at the slit, and she sucked them away the instant she tasted them. Sending her hand back down his length, she teased the twin sacs hanging from the base.

"Enough, lass, else I'll lose my seed in yer mouth."

He pulled his cock from her mouth, keeping her from following him by his grasp on her hair. Frustration bit into her.

"I hear some men prefer it that way."

He reached down and hooked an arm around her body, beneath her arms. With one powerful motion, he lifted her up until she was on her knees just as he was. The arm remained, looping lower across her waist to bind her against his body.

"Some women prefer to climax beneath the tongue of their lover too. Shall we discover if ye are one of them?"

"What?" Her voice was a ghost of a whisper, shock holding her in a tight grasp. But hidden between the folds of her sex, her bud began to throb in earnest. She'd only heard of such a thing once, and she'd doubted that it was true.

Torin chuckled and scooped her off her knees. He didn't seem to have any difficulty lifting her and laying her down on her back. He rose up above her, looking every inch like a legend once again. Moonlight glittered off his torso, illuminating the ridges of muscles packed onto his chest.

"If ye knew to take my member between yer sweet lips, ye must have heard that a man can repay the favor."

"I did nae believe it…"

He chuckled, but it was not a happy sound. Instead it was full of wicked intent. He lowered his body to cover hers, his hands cupping each of her breasts. She felt his breath against her lips while he teased her nipples with his thumbs.

"I will be more happy to give you reason to believe."

"Torin—"

He pressed a hard kiss against her mouth, trapping her words of protest. This was no gentle kiss. Torin took her mouth with a hunger that stole her breath. His cock was hard and pressed against her thigh. Feeling that ridged flesh made her yearn to be filled. She was eager for it, her hands slipping down the sides of his body to grasp his hips.

"Nae yet, my sweet. The night is young, and we've plenty of time to sample each other."

He slid down her body, sending a rush of sensation through her as his warm male skin lay against her own. His hands parted her thighs, pushing them apart and up on either side of her hips. Anticipation spiked into her, making it nearly impossible to draw breath.

He toyed with the curls on her mons for a moment, pulling on the strands with delicate motions before venturing lower to touch the skin guarding her passage. She jerked, that first touch too much to remain still for.

She gained another husky chuckle from him.

"Amazing, isn't it? The amount of pleasure yer body can feel from so slight a touch."

His fingers played over her folds, stroking each side before he trailed one fingertip down the center. She shivered, her body arching toward that touch while she feared that the level of intensity might leave her insane.

"Torin—"

"Shh, my sweet. I enjoyed yer lips around my cock, and it is a selfish man who fails to repay his lover."

Her eyes widened at the determination in his tone. His fingers returned to stroking the seam between her folds, slipping between them with the aid of her arousal.

"I see yer body is receptive to my ideas, even if yer mind needs a bit of convincing." Even in the dark she saw his eyes flash. "A task I will be most happy to apply myself to, sweet Shannon.

He leaned down, and she felt his breath against her wet folds. Another shiver shook her, this one almost violently. Her hands grasped at the bedding beneath her as he opened his mouth and pressed a soft kiss against her sex.

"*Torin, you cannot.*"

"Oh but I can, lass. This little pearl is the center of yer pleasure, and it is a wise man who learns to stroke it correctly."

She suddenly frowned. "Ye've practiced? A great many times?"

"No' with as many women as ye are thinking, Shannon." His eyes glittered with something hard. "I've had a few mistresses, but I've nae bastards that I know of, because I kept to each one of them without straying."

It was an uncommon thing, and something she never might have thought of him. "But ye're laird now…"

"Aye, and there is even more reason for me to make sure where I place my seed. Connor was a bastard, and it is no' an easy life."

Shannon turned over and heard him make a frustrated sound beneath his breath, but he allowed her to move away from him.

"Then I should nae make any mistakes that might change the fact that ye have no bastards."

"Ye need to trust that I'll nae simply take my pleasure and discard ye the moment I'm spent between yer thighs."

Torin crossed the distance between them, his hands diving into her hair and holding her face for a kiss. He smoothed his hands down her back and cupped each side of her hips before he lifted her up and lay back down on the bed, settling his shoulders against the bedding.

"What are ye doing, Torin McLeren?"

"Gaining a better view." He held her above him for a moment before settling her over his lower body. Her thighs spread as she descended, and her knees pressed into the bed on either side of his hips. Trapped between them was his erect cock, taunting her with how hard it was.

"I've felt ye beneath me, lass. Now I want to know if ye have the courage to ride what yer passion craves."

"Ride?"

"Aye." His voice had become raspy again. He grasped her hips, lifting her up enough so that his cock sprang up, standing rigidly beneath her opening.

His words suddenly made perfect sense, and the image they produced sparked excitement in her. That same urge that had seen her wrapping her lips around his cock rose to the challenge of being the one to set the pace of their coupling.

He began to lower her onto his length, the head of his cock burrowing easily into the wet sheath above it. A soft moan crossed her lips, satisfaction at last rippling through her as he lowered her until his member was fully lodged inside her. She took him in this time with only a twinge of discomfort.

"Show me what ye crave, Shannon. Ride me."

"I will."

There was determination in her tone, and she spoke too loudly, because her words bounced off the chamber wall. Torin didn't seem to mind. His hands gripped her hips, beginning to raise her, but Shannon lifted her body up with her thighs, all the way until only the head of his cock remained inside her. Then she allowed her body to lower, taking his cock back inside her with the motion. His face tightened, betraying how much he enjoyed her actions. Shannon lifted herself once again, watching his expression, allowing it to fill her with confidence. She craved him for more than the pleasure his body gave hers; this was the only place that she had ever felt his equal. For the moment, there was only the pair of them, and neither was superior to the other. They fit together like two halves of something that was stronger when united.

For the moment she dominated him, setting the pace. Pleasure rekindled inside her, growing with every downward motion. But Torin wasn't still; he rose off the bed to meet her each time she came down onto his length. The sound of their breath growing labored filled the bedchamber, but she was most fascinated by the look on his face.

He was enjoying the view. Harsh and primal, his gaze roamed over her body. Moving from her face to her breasts, watching them bounce with each downward plunge. But his attention didn't remain there; it slid lower, until his dark eyes were focused on her mons, watching his cock disappear inside her.

"Sweet Christ, I could die here and never regret it."

He reached out and sent a finger between the folds of her sex toward her pearl. Her thighs quivered, breaking her rhythm when he found that sensitive nub. A soft chuckle rumbled up from his chest. Shannon bit her lower lip and continued riding him. His eyes glittered with challenge, one she was eager to meet.

But it became a battle of wills. He fingered her, sending intense sensation spiking through her. She increased her pace, rising and falling faster. His cock felt like it was growing even harder, and a muscle began to twitch along the side of his jaw too. But his eyes locked with hers, each of them intent on pushing the other into climax first. A moan rose from her throat, and the intense burning his finger was coaxing from her flesh consumed her. Coupled with his hard member filling her, a burst of pleasure loomed closer and closer, refusing to be resisted. She gripped his hips tighter between her thighs and moved faster, pumping her body quicker. His nostrils flared and his lips thinned, until his teeth flashed at her.

"Ye have too much instinct and use it too well, Shannon."

For all that he looked like he was at her mercy, Torin was anything but. He surged up, clamping his arms around her to bind her to his body. The bed shook violently as he turned and they both landed back on its surface. Only now, he was on top of her, his length still buried deep inside her. His hands moved to her hair, threading through the strands until he framed her face.

"Too well, for I have exhausted my restraint."

The bed shook again. Torin took command of their pace with a fury. His hips moved in hard, rapid thrusts that drove the breath from her. Shannon heard her cries but could not even think to bite them back. There was too much pleasure coursing through her, too much enjoyment of every hard plunge to contain it. The only thing to do was meet him on every thrust and clasp his hips between her thighs. Rapture broke through her, deeper and stronger than it had the first time. It ripped through her belly, the walls of her passage tightening around the hard flesh tunneling into it. Torin stiffened, his body bucking frantically for a moment before she felt him begin to spill his seed deep inside her. She actually felt the hot spurt of his release, and it caused another tremor to move through her womb. She lost the ability to think, her mind shutting down while her lover collapsed on top of her.

Her eyelids lifted later, but she wasn't sure how much time had passed.

Somehow, in spite of the night chill, Shannon discovered her skin coated in sweat. Every muscle she had felt too exhausted to move, even a little bit. The bed was a welcome support against her back, and her eyelids wanted to flutter closed while she waited for her heart to slow down.

She could hear Torin's rough breathing in the dark, just a mere whisper, but with her heart slowing, her ears detected the soft, raspy sound. A shiver rippled across her skin. She realized that the shutters were still open, allowing the night breeze to brush across her bare skin. It also allowed the moonlight inside. The silver glitter illuminated one shoulder and leg of her partner. A soft sigh passed her lips as she relived that first night she had watched him.

He suddenly rose up, propping an elbow against the bed and placing his head in his open hand.

"Come here, Shannon."

He didn't wait for her to comply but slipped one arm beneath her waist and pulled her toward him. Another little muttered sound of enjoyment escaped her lips because he felt so good against her. His skin was warm, and he hugged her close against his body, pressing his front against her back.

"No."

He made a soft sound of frustration, his arm tightening around her waist. While his arm was around her waist, his elbow was bent, allowing his hand to cup one breast. His fingers teased the nipple, toying with it while he nuzzled against her neck.

"I will sleep in my own chamber."

His feet closed around hers, locking them in place.

"Torin—"

"I enjoy the sound of my name on yer lips." His hand left her breast to brush down across her belly to the curls on the top of her mons.

"Torin, stop."

His fingers remained in the silky hair, petting the curls but venturing no lower. She heard him grunt with disapproval.

"Do not deny that ye enjoyed my touch now."

She squirmed but gained no distance from him. "I wish to sleep in my own bed."

"Yet it is not yer bed, but another one that I own, so what is the difference?"

Shannon sent her elbow backward, but all she gained was a chuckle.

"The difference is that I wish to sleep alone."

"Humm…" His lips pressed a soft kiss against her neck and then another. A shiver raced down her body, and her bottom wiggled ever so slightly against his hips, where his cock was still half erect. It was pure reaction, something her body did without consent from her logical thoughts.

"Release me, Torin."

"I think no'."

She wiggled, arching against his hold only to have him sigh against her ear.

"Lovers do more than couple, Shannon."

She froze because there was a note of tenderness in his voice that enticed her. It combined with the warmth of his body, making it impossible to resist. His fingers stroked across her belly on their way back to her breast once more.

"Lovers enjoy lying with one another, sharing their warmth." He cupped her breast once more, sending another shiver of enjoyment down her body. "There are too many nights that we must suffer cold, lonely beds. Why be in a hurry to experience that?"

His voice was sultry, tempting her to do exactly as he said. Her will to argue was crumbling like a riverbank during a spring flood, the ground giving way to the force of the water. His chest rumbled behind her as he chuckled.

"Ye shouldn't be amused by me." And she shouldn't sound so wounded, yet she did. Her emotions were suddenly so tender, it hurt to think. All she wanted to do was sink down into the night with his arms cradling her and savor the feeling of his arms around her. She hadn't realized that she was as lonely as she was in her own bed. Now that she had a comparison, she understood, and the difference was stark.

"Can I nae find enjoyment in yer company as well as yer flesh, sweet Shannon? Would that not be kinder than releasing ye to seek out a bed that is cold, with regrets for the passion we just shared?"

"Perhaps it is best if both of us recognized that the passion between us is wrong."

His fingers began pulling on her nipple once more. The sensitive tip was soft now, and he gently tugged it out, milking the soft skin. A gasp lodged in her throat as delight bled over the tender peak and into her core.

"It feels very right to me."

Her body agreed, the nipple growing hard between his fingers. She could feel his cock hardening against her bottom too.

"What is yer worry, Shannon? Do ye hate my blood so much?"

"Nay." She answered too quickly, knocking her head against his jaw as her body erupted with denial. He tightened his arms about her, while a harsh sound came from his lips.

"Then explain." His voice was muffled in her hair. She heard him inhale against the loose strands and sigh. That little sound defeated her. Lying with him was a delight, and one that she knew the opposite of all too well.

The chamber down the stairs would be cold. It would be more than the chill of the night too. It would be the loneliness that would be so difficult to bear. Here, there was the warmth of her lover. In spite of her fears, she could not reject the kindness. The reason was simple: Torin didn't have to hold her. He'd had what she'd always heard men wanted from women, and yet he wanted her to linger in his bed. His cock was erect now, pressed up against her bottom, and he did nothing to gain entry to her. Instead he nuzzled against her hair some more before blowing out a long breath.

"I'll not be forgetting, Shannon, yet I suppose I need understand that trust is not something that grows quickly. I'll wait for ye to tell me."

His words brought tears to her eyes. Becoming his lover hadn't meant that she expected him to care how she felt, not in her heart, anyway. It was too tempting to sink down into the moment and allow it to surround her.

Tomorrow would be soon enough to worry about the rougher edges of life.

Nine

SHANNON AWOKE ALONE IN TORIN'S BED. SHE TRIED to leave the bed quickly but discovered herself pinned by the heavy coverlet. It was tucked beneath the mattress and her body, like a mother would tuck a blanket about a child. Her own body weight made it hard to loosen.

The man truly was part night specter, for he moved too silently and too gracefully. She should have awakened when he left the bed. A soft snarl crossed her lips when she made it out of the bed. It was a huge one, with large posts that supported the frame. Each of those posts was carved like a lion's foot. She couldn't help but admire the craftsmanship. Her father didn't have anything so fine.

The shutters were still open, and the morning air blew across her bare body. Her undergown was lain over a chair, and she reached for it, eager to cover her nudity. It wouldn't be so simple to banish the other signs of her tumble into passion again.

Yet she would deal with her guilt once she was away from the chamber.

The stairs were mercifully empty when she peeked out of the chamber door. Her bare feet made no sound as she hurried toward her own chamber. Reaching for her comb, she began the process of bringing order to her hair. She craved a bath but refused to walk below looking like she had just been tumbled.

Even if that was the truth.

Her hand shook and tears stung her eyes because she could not deceive herself. She lacked the resolve to ignore Torin. Her well-thought-out reasons crumbled when he touched her.

Finishing with her hair, she dressed without stopping to consider what she'd done last night. The sun was rising along with her new thinking. If she could not resist the man, she'd have to see to her worry in another manner.

"There ye are." Baeth looked slightly flustered, which was a surprise, for the head of house always seemed so sure of herself.

"The laird is waiting on ye."

"Why?"

Baeth fixed her with a narrowed stare for answering her summons with a question. When the laird called, no one questioned his command. "I'm his head of house, nae his mother, lass. Come, and hurry."

Torin was waiting for her on the front steps. Several of his retainers stood nearby. A smile curved his lips when she appeared, and he stretched out a hand toward her.

"There is still much merriment in the village. Let's go and enjoy the music before spring becomes full of planting and chores."

She hadn't expected the invitation, certainly hadn't expected the laird to spend his day with her.

"Ye don't have to... to..."

"I want to, lass, so I hope ye'll take a chance and see if ye enjoy my company as well." He mounted his stallion and held out a hand for her. He lifted her easily up behind him.

"Besides, lass, I confess to enjoying the feeling of ye clinging to me, and this was the only way I could think to gain it again before nightfall."

She smiled against his shoulder, unable to resist being charmed by the moment. His men followed them out of the courtyard, the clatter of the horses' hooves on the bridge a happy one for a change. She held on to Torin and felt his heartbeat. She moved in unison with him and the stallion. In the distance, the maypole was still standing tall in the morning air. The bright streamers were interlaced from the top to the bottom of the pole; she suddenly felt a stab of regret for what she had missed yesterday.

But Torin had told the truth. There was still a bustling fair clustered about the maypole. Music and laughter drifted to her ears. There were scents of roasting meat in the air. A cheer went up when Torin rode closer, his people lifting their hands in welcome.

Torin pulled his horse up and patted the animal on the side of its neck. The horse lowered its head, obviously understanding what his master wanted. Torin swung his leg over the lowered head of the beast. He landed on the ground in almost the same moment, offering her a smile of enjoyment when he lifted his face toward her. He reached up and placed a hand on either side of her waist to lift her down.

"The ale is good, Laird!"

The music was louder here, and it was indeed merry. The pipers kept a lively rhythm while a couple of boys worked their hand drums. There was dancing around the maypole, with young and old all taking the time to enjoy the music. The girls still wore their hair loose and decorated with new spring greens. Even the boys had wreaths crowning their heads to welcome spring. The girls danced with enough passion to raise their skirts, and their partners happily encouraged them to dance even more.

"Here now, Shannon. It is not springtime without a bit of ale." Torin sounded more relaxed than she could recall him being outside of his bed.

"Whisky!"

It was his retainers who shouted for stronger drink than ale. Torin lifted one eyebrow before tossing a coin toward them.

"If that's what it takes to get ye to leave me alone with a pretty lass, so be it."

His men laughed before walking off toward a tent with a table and chairs where the merchant was selling whisky. A pretty girl was bringing the strong liquor to the men, and Torin's retainers sat down with grins on their faces. The girl offered them a saucy wink along with the whisky.

"That should give us an hour of peace." He shrugged and rolled his shoulders.

"But I wonder if they will not be more vexing when they have drained their whisky cups."

He began laughing. "Ye seem to be understanding McLerens, Shannon McBoyd."

Two women nearby turned abruptly at the mention of her last name. Torin jerked his head around to stare at them, and they went back to what they'd been doing.

"Ye don't need to do that." Shannon kept her voice low. "I expect it."

"I disagree."

"Well, obviously ye do…" Shannon clamped her mouth shut. Her voice was rising, and Torin was enjoying it. He captured her hand and pulled her along the row of tents that housed merchants selling food and whisky. People nodded toward him with pleasant greetings, most of them reaching up to tug on the corner of their knit bonnets or inclining their heads.

They all looked at her with curiosity, but Torin kept her close. She couldn't help but enjoy the moment. He was placing a great deal at risk by making it known that he sheltered her. Clan fighting was remembered for generations, yet he boldly strode through the market fair with her hand locked in his.

Just like everything the man did, he was attacking something he viewed as an obstacle.

"Ye have to be the only woman in Scotland who becomes annoyed when a man tries to share a bit of ale with her." Torin lowered himself onto a bench and patted the spot next to him. "Come, Shannon. I dare ye to sit beside me."

She was in the seat before she thought about it. Torin laughed at her, his chuckles drawing looks from those around them. Her lips twitched up because she couldn't ignore the humor in the moment.

"Laugh if you like, but being the daughter of a laird has its price too. I was nae allowed to drink ale with men, and I'd think yer own sisters would be raised with the same rules to safeguard their virtue for marriages that would benefit the clan."

Torin nodded, but there was a flash of something in his eyes that looked like compassion. "Aye, the world is demanding of a laird's family, no question about that. We're more alike than ye think, Shannon."

Maybe... She couldn't help but agree with him, at least silently, but she lowered her eyelashes because it felt as though the man were reading her thoughts.

A set of dice sat on the table, and she reached for them.

"At last, a chance to best ye," Shannon announced.

Amusement suddenly surrounded her as men turned and pulled their chairs up to join them at the table. Two mugs of ale were delivered by an apple-cheeked girl while the newcomers rubbed their palms together. Shannon bit her lip, the dice frozen in her hand. Each person near her now had silver to bet on their roll, but she had nothing to wager.

"Go on, lass; let's see if ye know anything about tossing dice."

Torin tossed some silver on the tabletop, and the men eagerly chuckled.

It wasn't her coin, but everyone was waiting on her to begin the game. She suddenly forced the lump in her throat down and rolled the dice. If she won, the money would be Torin's, that was all.

The game began with fury. Women leaned in to see who was winning, cheering for their choice. But the dice played a wicked game with them all, bestowing victory once before moving on to another player the next throw. It kept the money evenly flowing around the table, with no one gaining too much over another. That set a jovial mood that took control of them all. Shannon never realized when she finished off the ale brought to her, or when it was replaced with a second measure.

"Enough, lass! I've shared ye long enough, and now I'm feeling selfish." Torin scooped up their silver and dumped it back into his pouch before reaching for her hand.

She eagerly took it, no hesitation at all. They were suddenly just people intent on enjoying one another. Torin pulled her toward the dancing.

"Did ye ever dance at spring festival, lass?"

He didn't wait for her reply but pulled her into the group of laughing couples around the maypole.

"How did ye know I went to festival?"

Torin hooked his arm with hers and spun her around to the beat of the drums. A bolt of excitement tore through her belly when they reversed direction, and her gowns flared out to show her ankles and calves for just a moment before she was moving back in the opposite direction to the beat of the music.

"I heard."

She couldn't keep track of the conversation because Torin grasped her hips and tossed her up into the air. It was called hefting, and all around her there was cheering as the men tossed their partners skyward. The dance ended with them clutching at one another while Torin turned backward in a tight circle and spun her around and around until she squealed.

"Enough, Torin! I beg ye."

He stopped, but her gowns didn't. The fabric wrapped around his legs while the longer pleats of his kilt hit her legs. For one wild moment they were a tangle of clothing and clung to one another breathlessly.

"Ye do nae need to beg, lass; I'll take ye shopping happily."

He was already pulling her toward the other side of the fair where fabric was displayed. In the sun there were colors that shimmered like jewels, thick winter wools and light summer weaves. There was the softest linen for undergowns and rare metal buttons. There were also tools for sewing, pins and needles. Such wares were normally the most exciting part of spring festival for her. It might be autumn before the chance to buy more cloth was hers.

If she were still alive in the fall.

That morbid thought sliced through the bubble of joy that she'd somehow become caught inside of.

"Baeth claims yer father sent ye out shamefully lacking. Find something ye like."

That wouldn't be hard. The merchant nearest her held up a bundle of soft linen that would make a fine undergown, one just perfect for the warming weather. Her fingers reached for it without thinking.

"I have no coin."

Torin reached for the fabric and brought it toward her. "Ye won at the dice, so ye do."

"But with yer coin, so nothing is mine but the enjoyment of playing, for which I thank ye."

He wanted to argue with her but froze when her words of gratitude hit him. For a moment something flickered in his dark eyes that looked like happiness.

"Laird, ye must see my grandchild." An old man had lifted his hand and was waving at Torin. His hair was silver with age, but his steps still had life in them. He led a girl forward.

"This is Malcolm, an elder of the clan."

Malcolm inclined his head in greeting before waving the girl forward. "And this is my daughter, Amanda, she was our May queen last year. But look here, Laird; look at the fine little babe she ripened with."

Malcolm looked proud enough to burst. His daughter held up her baby, just three months old but bright eyed. The child was wearing a robe that was decorated with fancy stitching in rich, costly thread. It looked as if every woman in the village had taken a turn, which only made sense. When the May queen conceived, it was considered good luck for the coming year. Somewhere there was a current May queen, and everyone would be watching her belly in the coming weeks to see if she grew round with child.

"And this here is my new son-in-law."

Malcolm slapped the young lad on the back with more strength than Shannon would have suspected the elder had in him. It made a smacking sound that sent his new relation forward a half step. Malcolm chuckled.

"Got them married yesterday before the May dancing began."

"Ye have my congratulations and my envy, Malcolm." Torin offered his hand, and Malcolm clasped forearms with him.

"Would ye hold my babe, Miss? 'Twould be a blessing for him."

The girl was already handing the baby to Shannon.

She took him gently, because it was a delight to hold a baby. The infant stuck his fist into his mouth and sucked loudly. Those watching suddenly cheered, startling the baby. His face turned red, the fist popping out of his mouth as he began to wail.

"Would ye listen to that. Ye young men don't know when to hush." Malcolm grumbled as his daughter took her child and soothed him against her bosom. The baby hiccupped a final time before returning to sucking on his fist. Malcolm eyed Shannon with wrinkle-edged eyes.

"Ye look good with a babe in yer arms, lass."

Shannon felt the color drain from her face. The bell in the church began to toll in the same moment, and Malcolm frowned.

"I guess there's something that needs yer attention, Laird. I'm sorry to hear that bell."

But it continued to ring insistently, and Torin's retainers made their way through the crowd toward them. Torin sighed.

"I'm sorry, Shannon, but they'd only ring that bell if it were important."

He was sorry, too. That touched her with a tenderness that shocked her.

"Of course."

She choked out the words and felt herself fluttering her eyelashes as though they had been courting. Torin gripped her hand again and led her toward the horses. His people waved to him, for which Shannon discovered herself grateful. She turned to look back at the baby, still feeling his delicate body in her arms.

A baby. Such was not so unusual a result of having a

lover. Thinking about the possibility was not the same as holding him in her arms. She suddenly felt sick with the possibility that she might blacken someone else with her father's sin.

Torin deserved better than that.

❧

It was the only correct thing to do.

Shannon watched the other McLeren women through her eyelashes, waiting for them to move away from the stillroom door frame. She moved her hands more slowly than usual, washing the dishes left from the morning meal. The other women cast her long looks but decided to leave her to the chore. Their footsteps receded up the stairs and into the great hall.

Shannon pulled her hands from the water and dried them on a length of toweling while moving toward the stillroom. She knew what she needed and didn't want any other woman seeing her getting it. Every woman knew what certain herbs were used for, even if most of the men in the castle might not.

There were ways to fend off conception, ways that were passed down from generation to generation. The church forbid such knowledge, but it still remained. Even being kept a virgin under her father's roof had not prevented her from hearing the methods employed by other girls to keep their bellies from swelling after a night of unbridled passion.

She had sampled that well and truly. Her belly had been tender this morning, and bathing the scent of her lover off her skin wouldn't remove his seed from her womb. So she would have to mix up something to keep that seed from taking root. There wouldn't be any proud father showing off her child next spring.

The stillroom held all the herbs. New green ones hung from the roof to dry, but there were many more bundles of dark brown ones that had been carefully gathered during the last spring. These would see the inhabitants of Donan Tower through sickness and aches. There were also herbs for seasoning and others for the making of soap, but what she sought were the more potent ones that could force her woman's courses to come. Those herbs were kept at the far end of the room, where no one might take them by mistake. They were higher up so that younger girls would have to fetch a stool to stand on if they intended to touch them. They were even tied up in cloth to keep any small amount from dropping onto the worktable.

"There's a danger to taking that witch weed, girl."

Shannon turned too quickly, her gowns flaring out and betraying her guilt. Baeth stood in the door frame, her lips pressed into a disapproving line.

"Take that and ye might bleed too much. I've seen it; it is nae an easy death." Baeth moved into the stillroom. "Leave it be. A babe is a blessing that ye should nae be in a hurry to reject."

Shannon bit into her lower lip, indecision tearing at her. Baeth was the closest thing to a friend that she had at Donan Tower, but the woman owed her allegiance to Torin.

Baeth waved a hand at her. "I said come away. Do nae make me fetch Brockton."

Shannon stiffened. "Ye would do that?"

Baeth considered her for a long moment.

"It's a woman's matter, not something for yer son to learn about. I'm preventing a problem. I'd think ye, of all women here, would be happy to see that I do nae plan to bind yer laird to me."

The head of house shook her head. "Nay, lass, ye are wrong."

Frustration made Shannon's tone sharper. "Wrong? Bringing a child into this mess is what would be wrong. Will it cling to my skirts while I continue to roam this kitchen like an outcast without a place? Or worse still, will it be raised without a mother when a sentence is handed down on my father?"

"It would be the child of the laird, and it is time he had a child."

"His bastard."

Baeth snorted. "The laird is nae wed, nor is he contracted, so that is nae a certainty. Ye would nae be the first lass who gained marriage through birthing a son."

"Yet the possibility is nae something I can ignore. No child should suffer being bastard born." Shannon swallowed her pride. "Please, Baeth, turn yer back. I would nae stain a child with my own sin."

The head of house snorted. "I'll do nothing of the sort. Ye'll take yerself away from that poison and stay away from this room, lass. That's my word on the matter."

"Baeth—"

"Get ye gone and do some thinking. Ye're no' so young that ye can argue with fate about when she blesses ye with a babe. There's a reason ye and the laird are drawn to each other."

Shannon laughed. "The reason is that fate is cruel.

Taunting me with a captor whom I lack the discipline to stay away from."

A hint of a smile curved Baeth's lips. "Well, at least ye're honest and no' set to accuse the laird of forcing ye."

Shannon stiffened. "I do nae lie."

"Which is why I like ye. Now do nae be changing my thinking with this bit of nonsense."

"It is prudent, nae nonsense."

Baeth blew out a long breath that sounded somewhat like a growl. She lifted one hand and pointed a weathered finger at her.

"This talking has nae changed me mind. There will be no unchristian use of these herbs. Get ye to the upper floor, where there is work to be done."

There was the ring of authority in Baeth's voice now. Shannon felt bitterness rising up to choke her, but she turned toward the doorway.

"Do nae think me too harsh, lass; the laird has no children, and that is a shame, something that makes every McLeren worry about the future."

"That does nae mean my child would be good for the McLeren. My father is a traitor."

Baeth's face became set as hard as stone. "Aye, but that is none of yer doing. Mark my words, if his seed is meant to take root in ye, I'll set my son to making sure ye do naught to interfere."

❧

Harsh? Shannon did think the head of house an unrelenting woman. Brockton appeared and dodged her steps for the remainder of the day. The hours dragged on endlessly, but it wasn't the time that bothered her; it was the loneliness. Baeth had been the closest thing to a friend she had. The woman's displeasure sat heavy upon her shoulders. That made her miss Torin. Which was ridiculous, because men and women did not console one another. They were set apart by their genders; everyone knew that.

But he'd been so tender during the night… and he took her to festival…

Her mind took her back to those hours when Torin had pulled her close and kept her there. He seemed to like to stroke her, his hands moving over her in long motions that sent soft pleasure through her. She'd have said such was absurd too, except that she had experienced it. Torin was in contradiction with everything she knew of men.

Baeth kept her busy, but it was far past the normal time for remaking the bed in Torin's chamber when the sheets were finally given to her. It was late afternoon, but Shannon took them, wanting to be above stairs so late in the day. Torin's men had begun to filter in from the yard, their hair slick with sweat from training. Most of them would bathe before the evening meal, and their laird did the same.

Climbing the stairs, Shannon took a glance over her shoulder to see where Brockton was, but there was no sign of him. At least Baeth had not altered the privacy Shannon gained by being above stairs.

Relief flooded her. She suddenly noticed how much her neck ached. Rolling her head, she tried to loosen the muscles before taking a deep breath and forcing herself to walk into Torin's chamber. It wasn't that she dreaded the place; quite the oppo-site. She'd found such comfort here that she feared becoming too dependent on it. Torin was laird. He would be expected to marry. If her father were branded a traitor, she would not be a candidate for that position.

She might remain his leman. The idea was not unpleasant, but her pride refused. There would be plenty who would tell her that becoming Torin's lesser woman would be a higher station than any other she might hope to gain, being the daughter of a traitor, but even knowing that did not soften her resolve.

All the shutters were open now, the breeze blowing through the chamber and making it fresh. The bed curtains were tied up around each thick bedpost so that she might remake the bed. Shannon shook out the first sheet and walked around the bed, tucking it in. She stopped once it was finished, a snapping sound from the window gaining her attention.

Turning her head, she looked toward the open window. The sound persisted, drawing her toward the opening in the wall. Just a hint of ivory linen was peeking up at the corners where the hinges were set into the stone. One more step and she could see that whatever was snapping in the wind was hanging down the outside of the tower.

Since she had the sheets, it could not be one of them set out to air, and the piece she could see was too thin to be a blanket. One last step and she was able to peer outside.

A startled gasp broke through her lips. In the fading sun, her underrobe was lying against the lighter stone of the tower, the dark bloodstain clear as a mark of shame. Shock held her still for only a moment before she reached for one corner.

A hard hand captured her wrist, preventing her from grasping the garment.

"Leave it." Torin had appeared without a sound, sending another bolt of surprise through her, but it was not enough to keep her from hearing the snap of the undergown in the breeze. The sound cut into her ears like a knife.

"I will nae." Shannon struggled against Torin. "Ye have no right to shame me in such a fashion."

His grip never gave, not even a tiny amount. "Ye gifted me with yer purity, Shannon. Ye have the right to be honored for that. I told Baeth to hang it there."

"Ye… ye…" She sputtered, unable to pull enough breath into her lungs to complete her thought. "I am not yer wife."

But he'd taken her through the village on his arm, sure enough. As laird, she belonged to him now. At least his people would see it that way.

One of his dark eyebrows rose. "'Tis a simple enough matter to change, woman."

Shannon felt the color drain from her face. She froze, ceasing to pull against the hold he had on her wrist. Torin allowed her to be loose but stood in front of the window, blocking the path to her undergown.

"Ye do nae care for that, sweet Shannon? Why is that? Because I am McLeren?" He chuckled, but it was not a nice sound. It was dark and edged with warning such as she recalled from their first meeting.

He stepped toward her, looming large and forbidding once again. "You lay with me of yer own free will. It will nae take more than that admission to get the priest to wed us."

"Yer people will hate us both for it."

Her voice was quiet because she didn't want him to hear the disappointment in it. The emotion threatened to send tears into her eyes, and she fought against them. She didn't want to admit how much she longed to have him and have the sweet knowledge that there was hope in her future of something other than ending up with her throat slit in retaliation for her father's deeds.

"That is my worry, and this morning they didna hate it. They will adjust."

Shannon lifted her chin. "I disagree. A marriage is a union of two names. My children would be sneered at for their McBoyd blood. For the sin of their... grandfather." Her voice did falter, bringing color to her cheeks in shame. But she kept her chin steady, refusing to duck her head. "Besides, ye are not interested in wedding me for anything more than yer sense of honor. I care nae for the pity. That has never been something I sought."

"So ye would risk yer life to make sure my seed does nae take root in ye?" His face darkened with rage. "I swear to heaven I do want to wed ye, if for no other reason than I'll have the right to spank yer arse for thinking to take such a risk, Shannon McBoyd."

"*Ye would nae dare.*"

She didn't care if the priests in the church heard her screeching. She refused to care that the church said a husband had the right to spank his wife. No man was going to lay his hand across her bottom.

"Oh, I'd dare, Shannon McBoyd. Ye should know that, since I tied ye around me and brought ye here like the barbarian that ye said I am. I assure ye, I will dare to do what I please with ye."

"Quit with yer excuse that my words are the ones that make ye act like a brute. You behave as ye please, Torin McLeren. So unless ye are a coward, stop saying I am the one who prompts ye to action." She tossed her head and propped her hands onto her hips. His eyes flashed with challenge a moment before he snatched her clean off her feet. His arms closed around her, imprisoning her when she tried to push her way to freedom. He tossed her across his bed, and her gowns fluttered up in wild disarray. Shannon bounced in a tangle of fabric and limbs. Her face brightened even more when she realized that her bottom was facing up. With a sputter, she jerked her head off the surface of the bed and pushed her hands against the soft bedding beneath her.

Her actions came too slowly. Torin caught the ties at the back of her overgown and leaned over her to keep her in place while he worked the knot loose. Her skirts were already raised above her knees, and once he'd finished with the tie, he pulled both garments straight up her body.

Shannon snarled with outrage, but she was dropped back onto the bed in nothing but her stockings and shoes.

"Brute. Highland barbarian."

He laughed at her. Shannon flipped over, curling

upward to launch herself at him. Torin caught her easily, clamping her squirming body against his.

"And ye are a Lowland wildcat in need of taming. A task I'm finding I have an appetite for."

He bent his face toward her, but she flattened one hand against his mouth.

"I am no shrew. I was ever a gentle daughter, obedient as the church tells me to be, and look what that gained me."

He shook his head, gaining freedom from her hand. A moment later they both landed on the bed, but he caught his weight on his hands, controlling the amount that pressed her down onto her back beneath him.

"It brought you to me, Shannon. Something I am happy about, which is why I will nae see ye taking a risk with yer life. Promise me ye'll take what fate gives ye without complaint."

Torin didn't give her the opportunity to agree or argue. He pressed his mouth down on top of hers, forcing a hard kiss on her. Yet she lacked the will to truly resist. Her lips parted for his demand, moving beneath his and welcoming the sure thrust of his tongue. Hunger swept aside her anger, transforming it into a passion that refused to be quiet or submissive. She pulled on his shirt, seeking the ties that secured it at the front. Torin refused to lift his head away from hers, kissing her while she struggled to rid him of his shirt. She was acutely aware of the fabric between them, and it annoyed her. Her skin longed to be free.

She strained against his hold, determined to find the last tie on his shirt. A deep rumble of male approval was her response.

"If that's what ye crave, sweet Shannon, I will be happy to give it to ye." His voice dipped down into a low tone that made her shiver. "Very happy indeed."

The bed rocked, and she was suddenly alone. Torin stood next to the bed, pulling his shirt over his head with one powerful motion. His eyes glittered with hunger when she could look into them once more, but her attention didn't remain on his face. It slid down his bare torso, across the ridges of hard muscle, to where he yanked back the end of his wide leather belt until the metal prong holding it secure about his waist popped free. The folds of his kilt slithered down, unveiling his lean hips and thighs. His cock sprang up into view, the head ruby and swollen. Her mouth went dry, instantly this time. There was no building of desire. Her body felt like it was suspended over a fire, and all she could do was twist while the flames licked at her flesh.

Torin watched her, studying her with his dark eyes. "I enjoy the sight of ye in my bed."

His tone was dark with need, even if there was still sunlight illuminating the chamber. She enjoyed being able to see him but suddenly felt too much on display herself. Her thighs closed, trying to keep that most intimate part of her concealed.

"Do nae hide from me, Shannon. The sight of ye is more pleasing than I can say."

He lay down beside her, his warm skin soothing her when it pressed against her own. It felt so very right, nothing between them but the desire to share the pleasures their bodies might give one another. His hands smoothed along her sides and up to cup each of her breasts.

"I swear I cannae stand the sight of ye doing anything but being eager while in my bed."

"I am eager." Her voice had somehow become husky. She shivered as his thumbs began to toy with her nipples. Each one was drawn into a hard peak that was more sensitive, more needy of his touch.

"Not nearly enough for my taste."

There was dark promise in his tone. He leaned down to capture one nipple between his lips. Hot pulses raced down her, raising gooseflesh across her skin. Delight rippled through her, and she reached for him, her fingers hungry for the touch of his skin. Torin sent the tip of his tongue over the top of her nipple while his lips drew on it. The heat licking over her made her squirm as soft little sounds of enjoyment escaped from her parted lips, gaining her another deep chuckle from her lover.

"Better."

His hand left her breast to trail down the center of her body, his fingers touching off more delight as they stroked their way toward her mons. Her pearl throbbed with anticipation, her passage suddenly feeling even emptier as she felt him teasing her damp curls.

"Still, ye might yet be more eager."

He whispered against her ear, his breath making her shiver. Or perhaps it was his words coupled with the feeling of his fingers beginning to penetrate the folds of her sex. She whimpered, the anticipation becoming too intense. Torin made a soft male sound that drew her eyes to his. Hard need glittered in his dark eyes, but his lips were set into a smile.

"I enjoy knowing that I can make ye more willing for my cock."

Shannon gasped. "Ye shouldn't say such things."

One dark eyebrow rose, but her attention was snared by the first touch of his finger against her pearl. It slipped easily over the sensitive bud, threatening to drive her insane.

"Shouldn't speak the blunt truth that I can feel how slick yer sex is and that it excites me to know ye'll take my cock easily, even readily?"

"Words like that aren't meant to be spoken." But her tone was husky and rough with excitement. Hearing him say such things in his deep voice made her more keenly aware of how much she wanted them. The images played across her mind, tightening the sensation inside her belly. Beneath his finger, her flesh throbbed more insistently, her hips jerking upward without any thought. She was too tantalized by his words to resist any longer.

He leaned down until the crisp hair on his chest teased her nipples and the soft skin of her breasts.

"But lovers say such things, just as a lover has the right to ride atop instead of lying docile on her back." He rubbed her little passion pearl harder, drawing a deep moan from her lips.

"But I admit that at the moment, I like ye on yer back." He rolled over her, pressing his knee between her thighs. He pressed his hands on either side of her body and rose above her.

"Spread yer thighs for me, sweet lover. I've a craving to be buried deep inside ye that will nae wait."

His words were wicked, but she adored the sound

of them. Somehow she did not feel submissive while complying either. His attention was completely on her. He sat back on his haunches while she pressed her elbows into the bed and leaned on them.

"But am I eager enough for ye?" Her tone was still husky, and it added to her teasing. There was a deep intimacy to the moment, something else that she was beginning to crave from him.

"Yer hard nipples tell me ye are."

He hooked his hands under each of her knees and lifted them, obviously finished with waiting for her to spread her legs for him. His eyes flashed with triumph as she felt the folds of her slit opening wide.

"But I will have to make very sure, else ye'll label me a brute for rutting on ye before I've stoked yer passions." His eyes hardened. "We cannae be having that."

"What of yer reputation as a Highlander?"

His fingers began teasing her sex, slipping easily along the slick folds.

He smiled large and arrogantly, with his finger, began teasing her sex once again. "That is exactly what I am thinking of, lass. A Highlander is known for his way at winning the favors of his lovers. Those English lords have naught but their weeping brides because they lack the skill to stroke their sweet flesh just right."

He slid his fingers down to the opening of her body, fingering the entire entrance before thrusting deep inside her. Pleasure spiked through her, sending her back onto the bed as she lost the will to toy with him. Her body demanded more than that finger. He was too far away, and she sat up again, reaching for him.

"Aye, lass, ye have the right idea."

He growled his words through clenched teeth, his body easily coming with her demanding hands, falling down to cover her while the head of his cock pressed against the opening of her passage.

He didn't make her wait but thrust hard and smoothly into her. A hard grunt teased her ear as his hands captured the sides of her face.

"Sweet Christ…"

His words echoed her feelings. Being filled by his hard flesh sent her mind into a state of bliss. There was no thought outside of the need to lift her hips so that she might capture every last bit of his length. He pulled loose but sent his cock back into her with a powerful motion that sent a moan up and out of her body. Pleasure was tightening deep in her belly already, refusing to wait another moment. His cock was so hard, too large to resist allowing it to push her over the edge of reason and into rapture. Torin snarled something next to her ear that made no sense because she was caught in the grip of a pleasure so intense, it ruled her completely.

There was only one thing she wanted to notice, and that was the hard thrusting of her partner, the feeling of his length plunging deep inside her over and over, until his body went rigid and she felt the hot spurt of his seed against her womb again. He unleashed another burst of pleasure in her, this one deeper and longer than the first. Her hips curled up, determined to keep every last drop inside her.

Ten

"MY HAIR IS IMPOSSIBLE. YE SHOULD LEAVE IT BRAIDED."
Shannon was too relaxed to care that she was lying
with her back exposed. At some point, Torin had
rolled off her and she'd turned onto her belly. Her
body was so relaxed, she remained even when she felt
Torin move and prop his head into the palm of one
hand so that he might study her. She'd never had a
man look at her bare body before, and she nibbled her
lower lip with nervousness. But the memory of the
way he seemed to enjoy looking at her kept her from
trying to cover up. It was the truth that he made her
feel pretty without any words at all; it was there in
his eyes when he was studying her. It was something
that she discovered she enjoyed. Possibly too much,
but that idea wasn't enough to get her to move; she
wanted to linger in the moment and savor it.

Torin didn't heed her warning. He plucked at
the tie holding her braid and began to thread his
fingers through the sections until he had it all free.
His eyes narrowed and his lips thinned, but there
was no mistaking the enjoyment etched into his

expression while he slid his fingers down the length of her hair.

"Yer hair is magnificent. If I were nae worried ye'd catch it on fire, I'd forbid ye to bind it."

He reached for a silver comb that sat on the table near the bed and began to pull it along the length of her hair. She was amazed to see his larger male hands holding the delicate silver comb. It seemed tender, his acting the maid for her. It felt too good to really argue against, but the urge to tease him was too great to resist.

"Except that ye are nae my husband, so ye cannae forbid me such. Or I should say, I'd nae be bound to obey ye."

The comb paused, and there was a low rumble from him. "Careful, lass. Yer bottom is tempting me."

He reached over and rubbed a hand across her bare backside. "I could teach ye to respect my word."

"All spanking me would do is teach me to fear yer strength and the fact that ye would nae hesitate to cause me pain in order to bend my will. I know ye are stronger than me." Shannon shifted and looked at him over one shoulder. "Do ye wish for a woman who will shiver in this bed out of fear?"

It was a bold question, for the church preached that a woman was bound by heaven's law to obey her father first and then her husband. Most men wouldn't even tolerate a woman's asking. They expected women to learn such as girls and accept their place. Shannon stared straight at Torin, unafraid of pinching his ego. Part of her needed to know what he thought of her boldness, because it was the part of her that she had always hidden.

His lips twisted with distaste, but his eyes held a frustrated look. "What I'd like is to hear yer promise that ye will nae try that witch weed. It is a risk no woman should be taking. Especially ye."

Shannon chewed on her lower lip, studying him for a long moment. "I would have thought that you would be grateful that I was nae of the mind to bind ye to me with a child."

Yet he was not. She witnessed it flash across his eyes, only a momentary glimpse before he hid his true feelings by looking at the length of her hair that he was running the comb along. A heavy silence fell over them; she actually heard the comb moving through her hair. Another snap came from the window, reminding her that the undergown was still flapping in the evening breeze.

"Take my gown out of the window."

"Nay." Firm and unbendable, his tone drew a soft hiss from her.

"Ye have no right to announce anything to yer clan." Shannon sat up, taking her hair away from his reach. "It was between us. Lovers do not share their relationship with others."

"I am laird here, Shannon. Privacy is not something I have a great deal of." Each word was edged in the same steel that she recalled from the first night she met him. The fact that he was bare as a newborn didn't seem to have any impact on the man. He expected his authority to be recognized.

"Ye are nae my laird."

His face darkened, displeasure glittering in his eyes. "Ye are on my land, lass, which means ye answer to my law. The undergown remains where it is."

She snarled at him and rolled over the opposite side of the bed to escape. Her feet had barely touched the floor when someone used the heavy brass door knocker to announce his arrival. Her eyes widened, but Torin reached across the bed and hooked one large arm around her waist. He lifted her off her feet and pulled her back onto the bed. With another soft grunt, the man tossed the coverlet over her, folding it over to conceal her nudity.

But her face was still visible when Baeth entered the room. Three other maids lowered themselves in courtesy before carrying trays and a large pitcher toward the table. They began to set the table for supper, laying out plates. Baeth watched the maids with a practiced eye before her attention was captured by someone else at the doorway. Another girl entered the room and offered a quick courtesy before bringing something to Baeth. The maid shook it out to reveal a dressing gown.

"Up with ye, Shannon, before supper goes cold."

Baeth waited with the dressing gown held up for her to slip into, as if Shannon were the mistress of the house.

Her face flamed hotly. What she was, everyone from the lowest stable lad knew, thanks to the under-gown hanging from the window. Since the only thing that she might control was whether she looked like a coward, she slipped over the edge of the bed and onto her feet. The maid took the dressing gown and brought it forward before easing one side of it up her arm until it rested on top of her shoulder. The maid took up the weight of the garment while she passed behind her and brought the other sleeve up for her bare arm. Shannon reached for the tie, but the maid never allowed her the chance to grasp it. The girl overlapped the edges of the dressing gown and secured it with nimble hands. She lowered herself before quitting the room.

Shannon had to catch her lower jaw, else it would have dropped open. Maids did not lower themselves before her. As a McBoyd, she was beneath every one of them.

Baeth snapped her fingers. "Come in now."

Two lads appeared in the doorway, each of them holding a large tray. They inclined their heads respectfully before carrying the tray toward the table.

"Thank you, Baeth." Torin's voice was firm and without a hint of regret. Satisfaction showed on his face while he watched Shannon.

"Enjoy yer supper, Laird."

The head of house motioned the lads out the door with a quick wave of her hand. They went silently, but their eyes darted toward Shannon until the door frame cut off their view.

"Was it truly necessary to make my position so public?"

The dressing gown was warm and comfortable, a true luxury, but her cheeks brightened with shame.

"Is it really so important to ye to keep our relationship secret? Ye are the one who used the word 'lover,' sweet Shannon."

"Do not mock me with those words." She discovered that she could not bear it. Tears stung the corners of her eyes, taking her by surprise because she hadn't realized how much she treasured the endearment. She looked at the floor, trying to regain her composure.

A warm hand cupped her chin and raised her face.

"Ye're right, lass. Those words do not belong in our quarrel." His eyes held tenderness for a long moment.

"Yet the answer to yer question is yes." He walked back across the chamber until he reached one of the chairs at the table, then he pulled it back and looked at her.

"Ye will nae refuse to admit that we are lovers."

Pride flashed from his eyes and determination as though she'd slighted him.

"I meant no insult." Her words were edged with her rising temper. "But I do nae have any wish to polish yer ego by announcing to one and all that I haven't the discipline to—"

"To resist me?" Now his lips curved up in roguish delight.

"Don't tease me."

He shrugged and crossed the floor back toward her. Sensation rippled across her skin, an awareness that happened instantly just because he was near once more. He reached up and trailed the tips of his fingers across her cheek. It was tender, and she felt it so deeply, her eyes filled once more with unshed tears.

"I think that is exactly what needs doing, Shannon. A wee bit of teasing. Our time together has been too full of things that neither of us can control. In another time, we could have met at a spring festival and enjoyed teasing one another."

She sighed. The image his words conjured up was a feast for her starving soul. But he suddenly dipped down and scooped her off her feet. He cradled her against his chest, her weight doing nothing to tax him at all. In fact, there was a look of satisfaction on his face while he looked down at her.

"I am starving, woman, and our supper is growing cold."

Shannon swatted at one of his large shoulders. "Put me down, Torin. I can walk very well."

He cradled her effortlessly and only smiled at her frown.

"There is a certain comfort in knowing that I can move ye where I please, sweet Shannon. Maybe I'll share a few of my ideas with ye after we've eaten. I believe we'll need our strength for where my thoughts will lead us."

She gasped, but it was not in outrage. Anticipation began to flicker in her belly as he deposited her in the chair. He slid it back close to the edge of the table without any strain.

"Ye are a wicked man. I believe I should fear for my soul for the effect ye have on me."

Torin sat down across from her and reached for the linens that covered the trays. Steam rose up when he pulled them off, and the scent of hot meat filled her nose. Her belly rumbled low and long in response. Torin laughed at her.

"Wicked I might be, but ye are my co-conspirator, madam. Ye don't fear my insanity; ye welcome it because it pleases ye." He looked up at her. "Greatly."

That single word, uttered in his brassy tone, sent a quiver down her limbs. It was the tone that he used when he was deep inside her, the sound that she heard when pleasure was about to consume her.

Her belly growled again, interrupting her thoughts. Torin chuckled.

"We'll have to be returning to that idea ye were just thinking about, my sweet."

He began using a large knife to move thick slices of meat off the center tray and onto the plates; the enjoyment showing in his eyes made her laugh softly. One dark eyebrow rose in response.

"There is a boy inside ye sometimes."

"Aye, and he wants to take ye out to roll in the new spring heather."

Shannon waved a single finger back and forth. "That is not something a boy would be thinking about."

Torin swallowed what he'd been chewing and offered her a roguish smile. "Well now, lass, the boy is stuck inside the body of a man, so ye would be getting the best of both. The toying and the rolling as well as whatever else I can entice ye into doing."

She couldn't resist the urge to smile, and her eyelashes fluttered too. A soft blush stained her cheeks in spite of the fact that he had already had her. Somehow she'd thought that gentle seduction was only for maidens. Torin grinned at her before ripping a round of bread in half and offering her one side. At her father's home, she had never eaten alone, always taken her meals in the crowded hall. Tonight the simple act of taking bread from another's hand felt intimate. She noticed the way his fingers held it, and the way her eyelashes fluttered once again when she took it from him.

"I find that I like the combination quite well." She lifted her eyelashes to stare into his dark eyes. "The one of boy and man."

He liked her compliment. Enjoyment flickered in his eyes while he ate. Her hearing became more sensitive, her ears noticing every sound. She was focused on her company, watching him in a manner that she seemed to want to only do with Torin. She finished eating before he did, and sat back in her chair with her hands wrapped around a goblet of rich wine. Shannon sipped at it slowly but felt heat moving through her veins anyway. It wasn't the wine that sent fire flickering across her skin; it was the certain knowledge that Torin wanted her near. He'd had her and still longed for her company. Teasing, he'd said. Now that sent the sweetest rush of delight through her. It soaked into more than her flesh; it filled her heart, because it was more than lust. This went beyond the passionate needs of the body. Maybe there were no words, but in a way that was what made her notice her feelings all that much more.

It was startling, making it impossible to remain so still. Standing up, she left the wine behind. She was intoxicated enough on just her company. The sun had set, but the night was clear, allowing the stars to twinkle in the velvet of the dark sky. She leaned out of the window to enjoy the view. The candles died behind her, casting the room into darkness.

Torin wrapped his arm around her, cutting the chill with his body heat. The scent of fresh bread clung slightly to him, but what she noticed more than anything was the scent of his skin. Clean and masculine in spite of the fact that she would have been hard-pressed to explain what made it masculine. He smelled strong and capable, and she found it deeply attractive.

Her heart began to beat faster, and her lungs filled more quickly to keep pace. That drew more of his scent into her senses, doubling her awareness of him. He lifted one finger and pointed toward a boulder that was sticking up above the surface of the water.

"I like to swim out to that rock and stand there with nothing but the night surrounding me." His arm tightened around her, and she felt the press of his cock against her bottom through her thin dressing gown. "But ye know that, don't ye, Shannon?" His voice was a dark whisper against her ear. She shivered as passion began to lick its way across her skin. She rubbed her bottom against his cock, gently teasing him in return.

"I thought ye were the manifestation of legend, all washed in moonlight."

"I will happily play the part ye wish, my lady."

He scooped her off her feet once again, cradling her against his body so that she could feel his heart beating against her side. The moonlight painted the floor in silvery waves, across which Torin carried her his way toward the bed.

He placed her on her feet and tugged off the dressing gown. The air was soothing against her skin. She enjoyed being nude, and she climbed up onto the bed before Torin finished tossing the garment over a chair.

She froze there, poised on all fours. Torin made a soft sound that was more of a growl than anything else, but it struck her as praise.

"Ye could demand that I get on my knees, and I swear I'd do it so long as ye promised to remain just like that, lass. Bare and welcoming in me bed."

She should have felt awkward. Her breasts hung

down, and the moonlight illuminated her like an animal roaming the dark. Maybe she was more beast than human, for it was true that she was seeking what she craved.

"I cannae picture ye on yer knees, Torin McLeren."

He reached out and cupped one of her breasts. It was a soft touch, gentle and smooth, but she shivered in response, her nipple contracting into a tight peak.

"Then watch me."

He climbed onto the bed and knelt in front of her, his powerful body poised, his chest a mass of ridges that rippled down to where his cock stood up. The head was crowned with a thick ridge that she recalled tasting.

"Seeing ye on yer knees is suddenly much more appealing."

"Is that so, lass?"

She stared at him in the dark, their gazes locking while she felt her heart accelerating yet again. She could hear her blood rushing in her ears, but her senses were also keen enough to hear the slap of the water against the stones in the loch.

More than anything she was aware of the man waiting for her touch, so still, but only because he wanted her to reach for him. It would be simple for him to take her. But that was not what drew her to him. This desire to have her come to him summoned her forward, crawling toward him across the surface of the bed. His hands curled, but he remained in place, waiting on her whim.

Her attention lowered to the hard flesh standing so tall between his thighs. Lowering her body until she rested on her belly with his knees on either side of her shoulders, she reached out to walk her fingertips up the length of his cock. He sucked in a breath that whistled between his set teeth.

"Humm…" There didn't seem to need to be an actual word, only a sound that communicated her playful mood. She paused on the soft skin that sat just beneath the head of his cock. Playing with the spot, she listened to his breathing become rough.

"Be careful who ye call wicked, woman. At the moment ye qualify for the title more than I."

"Possibly… but is that a complaint or a compliment?"

"I've nae yet made up my mind on the matter."

His tone was edged with challenge. Shannon rose to it, leaning down to allow her tongue to travel the same path that her fingers had. He jerked, the hard muscles moving in a snap of reflex in response to her actions. A curse sailed over her head in a rough tone that was almost too deep to understand.

But she comprehended the reason behind it.

She was driving him toward the same insanity he so often did to her, unleashing sensations so intense, holding still became a battle of will against flesh.

It was the greatest compliment she'd ever received from a man. She could not recall any praise that impacted her more deeply.

Wrapping her hand all the way around his staff, she opened her mouth and closed her lips around the head. Her tongue began to play across the smooth skin, licking through the slit to taste the small drop of salty seed that had already arisen there. She cupped his sac with her free hand, rolling it gently while her tongue continued to flick around the crown of his cock. She relaxed her mouth and took more of his length inside. A large hand captured the back of her head, and his hips thrust gently toward her, driving even more inside. But it didn't bother her, she was absorbed in the sounds of male pleasure her touch wrung from him.

"Enough, lass."

Torin wasn't going to leave the matter up to her. He pulled her head away from his cock, and she looked up to see his face drawn tight. She continued to finger the spot under the head of his cock, and a tic appeared along the side of his jaw. Determination glittered in his eyes.

"Two may play at that game, sweet Shannon."

"What game is that?"

Her thumb slipped easily over the wet skin of his cock, drawing another harsh sound from his lips. His hips gave a short thrust toward her, and he growled with frustration.

"The game of seeing who might outlast the other. The battle of temptation."

She pushed her hands against the surface of the bed and rose up onto her knees. His expression softened, turning to one of hunger. His gaze traveled to her breasts, and he reached for them, cupping each tender globe in a gentle grasp. He passed his thumbs across the hard tips, back and forth, sending ripples of delight down her body to her pearl. The small point pulsed, keeping the same tempo as her heart.

"I dinna want to play games, Torin."

All she wanted was to be closer to him. Agreement

flickered in his eyes, and he slid his hands down her sides and toward the twin halves of her bottom.

"Aye, lass, I share that same desire."

He pulled her forward, lifting her up so that he might impale her. Her knees slid easily onto either side of his hips, and his cock pressed deep into her passage as he controlled her descent onto it. Shannon wrapped her arms around his neck, gasping as his flesh stretched her wide once more. So hard and yet so satisfying. His hands remained around her bottom, lifting her up so that his cock slid free up to the tip, and then he allowed her to sink back down until he was buried inside her to the hilt.

She moaned, unable to contain the rapture.

"Sometimes, slow is better."

Torin wrapped his arms tightly around her, binding her to his body with his length contained inside her. He pushed up off his knees and placed her back against the bed.

"But I need to feel ye beneath me."

She shivered, her flesh enjoying the idea his words sparked in her mind. There was no way to explain it, but she wanted to feel his strength on top of her. His body covered hers, wider, harder, and more powerful. It reduced her to a state of pure sensation. There was nothing but the feeling of their skin pressing together, nothing but the way she could feel his heart beating on top of her own. But most of all, there was the steady thrusting of his hips, driving his cock deeply into her body. He didn't hurry but kept his pace even. Her body wanted to quicken the motion, but Torin refused her that, keeping to his steady rhythm. It kept her poised on the edge of pleasure, neither fulfilled nor disappointed. Each thrust slid across her throbbing pearl, drawing the need inside her tighter.

"Torin… I can take no more…"

Her voice was unrecognizable, husky and hungry for release.

"Aye, lass."

He gripped her hair, holding her tightly in place, and gave her what she craved. His body thrust faster, driving her easily over the edge into the rapture that she sought. It swirled up around her, drowning out everything but the driving hips of her lover. His cock swelled and burst against the mouth of her womb, spurting his hot seed into her. Pleasure raced from her belly out to every point of her body and then back once more. The fingers in her hair curled tightly while Torin pressed his hips toward her, and the bed kept her still for the last drops of his seed.

Their hearts beat frantically against each other, separated only by skin and bone. Torin rolled onto his back but pulled her along with him, binding her against his body.

"Ye will share my bed, Shannon, the entire night."

"A lover has to ask, not demand."

He toyed with her hair, running his fingers through it before grunting.

"If ye have any strength left to try and leave my bed, I will be happy to ask ye to make love again, sweet Shannon."

"That was no' what I meant, Torin."

He pressed her head back against his shoulder when

she tried to raise her face. The effort was too great, so she let him have his wish.

"But it is what I meant, lass. Move away from me if ye have the strength, and I will chase ye."

"Brute."

He chuckled, and her eyelids slid shut. Her lips were curved into a soft smile, contentment glowing around her like the light of a candle in a black room. She was suddenly free of her cares, and her body took the opportunity to sink down into slumber, where there was nothing save for the warm arms holding her.

It was perfection.

Eleven

"Good morning."

Shannon opened her eyes and blinked. She turned her head toward the window that had never been covered last night to see the horizon turning gold. Torin reached toward her and placed his hand in her hair.

"I adore yer hair. It is more radiant than any crown."

Shannon groaned. She sat up and reached for her hair, wincing when she pulled it over her shoulder. It was a true mess from her having slept with it unbound.

"Do nae worry. Baeth will have someone set it right. I wish I had the time to do it myself, but the day holds work that needs doing."

Shannon jerked her head about to look at Torin. The man was already dressed, just pulling his plaid over his shoulder.

"I dinna want people waiting upon me because I shared yer bed. That would make me a whore."

His face darkened. He drew in a hard breath before caging her with his arms set into the bed on either side of her.

"A man does nae cuddle with a whore. He fucks her up against a wall or over a tabletop and tosses his coin on her the second his cock is spent."

She gasped. "Ye needn't be so crude."

"And ye need to stop rejecting what fate has given us. Do ye think such passion is common?"

"Lust is common and a deadly sin."

Torin pulled her from the bed, allowing her feet to touch the ground. He looped one arm around her body, holding her against him. The scent of his skin filled her, and her heart accelerated in response.

"Lust is common, but it does nae cause yer heart to race." He placed his hand over her chest, his fingers seeking out proof to support his words. She watched his expression transform when he gained what he wanted. His eyes narrowed, and his lips curved up. It made her throat tighten and tears threaten to fall down her cheeks. No one had ever looked at her tenderly. He suddenly took her hand and flattened it over his own chest. Beneath his doublet and shirt, she still felt the palpitations of his heart, and there was no missing the fact that it was faster than normal.

"Ye see, Shannon? That is nae something that comes along often. I wanted ye in my bed last night for more than the coupling." He raised her hand to his lips and pressed a kiss against the delicate skin of her inner wrist. A moment later he was moving toward the door. He paused before opening it, looking back to stare at her.

"I want ye back tonight, Shannon, and I hope ye'll think the matter through, because I swear that ye are a fool if you keep tossing happiness aside. The Douglas will arrive soon enough with a battle that we'll both have to pray we win." His expression returned to being harsh. "'Tis a battle I swear I will nae lose, and ye will nae tell me that ye do nae want my protection."

He closed the door behind him to keep her from replying.

That was a kindness, because her knees quivered. She sat down on the bed surprised by the fear that suddenly rose up to attack her.

Why did it matter now?

The reason was not hard to discover. It was right there in her chest, just as Torin had noticed. Her heart was full of new feelings; ones that she had never suspected might be so powerful. She wanted to live, but not just for herself. There were suddenly so many things that she needed to do before life left her.

Like having a child.

Her hands covered her belly, wondering if there was a tiny flicker of life inside.

It suddenly sickened her to think that she might have snuffed out that life before she was even aware of it. Such a selfish thing, to deny life to anyone just because the road might be rough. She would love her babe.

"Well, ye are a picture this morning."

Baeth opened the door without knocking. Shannon let out a startled sound and grabbed at the bedding to pull it over her bare body.

"Come now, lass. Ye have nothing that I do nae have myself."

Two more maids followed the head of the house. One of them bore a fresh undergown that Shannon was grateful to raise her hands for.

"Well, yer hair does have life of its own."

Baeth pointed at the mess her hair was, and one of the maids began working the comb through it. Before it was restored to order, both girls were needed to work the tangles from it.

But Baeth did not give her an overgown. Instead the woman pulled a measuring ribbon from her apron.

"Ye need some clothing that fits. I've never seen a more shameful trunk with a bride-to-be. Yer father is deplorable. A true miser."

"He taught me to be strong by having me make do just as others do."

Baeth began taking her measurements and writing them on a small piece of parchment. She placed an inkwell on the table, carefully pulling the stopper from it so that no ink might drip and ruin anything. She dipped a quill into the well to make her notations.

"I suppose that is a good thing, but sending ye out in shoes instead of boots was neglectful at best. Ye will be off to see the cobbler as soon as I am finished with ye."

"I do nae need boots. It is spring, and the weather fine."

Baeth snapped her fingers, her face becoming an expression of authority.

"This is the Highlands, lass. It rains more here than where ye grew up. Ye need boots, and ye shall be measured for them, or I'll have Brockton take ye to the cobbler."

Shannon pushed her lower lip out. "I do nae want a guard. It is insulting. Yer son must have plenty of other things more worthy of his attention. I detest wasting his time as much as I hate being distrusted."

"Well now, if there is trust between ye and the laird, I agree." Baeth wrote down the last measurement and put the stopper back into the inkwell. "But that is something ye shall have to discuss with the laird. He set Brockton to watching ye, and only the laird can undo that. But I would think yer own stepmother is looked after by McBoyd men."

"Well, that is expected. She is married to a laird and must be protected, else someone might steal her away and demand a ransom."

Baeth watched her with a serious look that Shannon shook her head in the face of.

"Torin has nae offered to wed…" Her words trailed off, because Torin *had* suggested that they marry. The gown hanging from the window was his way of proclaiming to all that he considered himself bound to her.

Baeth held up her McBoyd arisaid. "Ye might begin by having done with wearing this, lass, if ye have not come to terms with anything else concerning yer future."

Shannon felt the girls freeze behind her, and tension filled the room. She stared at her father's colors, the scarlet and blue that she had worn since the day she could walk. They looked so foreign to her now.

"I have, Baeth, but do nae burn it. They are my father's colors. That is unchangeable. I'd be a poor daughter to burn my sire's plaid."

But she would not wear them any longer. Her future lay in a different direction.

"Just leave it here. I'll see McBoyd colors only at night from now on."

"In this chamber?"

Baeth's voice was low but solid, seeking an admission that Shannon realized she was skirting.

Torin was not hiding their relationship, and it would no doubt gain him the anger of many of his own people. She was being very selfish not to do the same. His parting words rose from her memory, and she realized that he was very correct. The time they had together was short, for the Douglas would not forget her.

"Yes, Baeth, in this chamber."

Baeth nodded approval. "I'm going to have the girls make up a new undergown for ye out of the fabric the laird bought for ye."

"What fabric?"

One of the girls brought forward a bundle of soft linen, and Shannon instantly recognized it from the festival. She reached out to finger it, feeling tears sting her eyes. Torin did treat her better than a whore, and she was a fool to keep sniping at him. She drew in a deep breath, wondering why her pride was so swollen. There was much to be happy about. Sometimes being content was only a matter of looking at the good instead of the woes. Perfection was only found in heaven.

Or in the embrace of a man whom she loved.

"Aye, such a grand gift does make one misty-eyed." Baeth blew across the ink to help it dry faster. "Ye are wise to notice that the laird has affection for ye."

"I do nae feel wise."

But she did feel the tenderness, and it shocked her to think that she had lived life until now without knowing love. Stroking the fabric once more, she felt a lump lodge in her throat. It was a surprise to discover that a man might be so caring, even when he was being so stubborn when it came to setting his man to watch her. Like a velvet-covered iron gauntlet. Her feelings were a tangled mess that defied her understanding.

She felt very unwise indeed.

～✦～

The moment her foot touched the lower floor, Shannon felt eyes upon her. It was different than the night she had arrived. Now curious looks were aimed her way, and even several approving ones. Most of the tables were still in use, the younger boys all watching her while they sat in front of bowls of hot cereal.

Brockton inclined his head when her gaze touched on him. He fell into step behind her when she made her way toward the hearth. A bowl was handed to her with a smile this morning.

Shannon resisted the urge to be annoyed. Allowing her temper to rise would be to say she preferred to be hated. Her belly rumbled, so she sat down to eat. A moment later another girl sat down next to her.

"I am Isa. My mother told me to sit with ye because no one should have to eat alone." The girl had a dusting of freckles across both cheeks, and her eyes danced with merriment. "But truthfully I am dying to know if the rumor is true, and to my mother's shame and my father's delight, I'm bold enough to ask ye straight."

"If what rumor is true?"

Isa smiled and leaned close. "Did it take four men to bring ye down?" The girl's eyes had gone wide with her question, and she looked as though she was holding her breath while waiting on the answer. "Tera told me so. She's sister to Devyn, who was one of the four the laird sent after ye. He claimed it was four, but I still have to hear it from yer own lips."

The girl chattered faster than a spring river ran, but there was something irresistible in being included in conversations again, especially ones that were about nothing important but made you feel like you were at home.

Shannon suddenly smiled, because no matter what colors they wore, Scots liked their legends. Apparently she had become a bit of one herself.

"Well… I did have a horse… and the night to shield me…"

❧

"The laird has guests arriving. The Cameron and the Lindsey."

Baeth began issuing orders for the cook and maids, but her eyes kept straying to Shannon. It was clear that the other Highlanders were arriving to discuss the murder of the king and what her fate would be.

"Laird Lindsey asked that ye bring him up a pitcher of water." Baeth paused with a frown on her lips. "But 'tis the first time I've ever heard that man asking for water."

Shannon felt her cheeks turn hot, and it was most definitely due to her temper. Connor Lindsey might just get his pitcher of water poured over his arrogant head. She followed Baeth through the hall and toward the smaller tower. This one was the oldest, and the construction was very basic. Sound echoed more because there were no tapestries hung on the walls to absorb it. Built in a round fashion, the stones were light gray, with mortar holding them together. On the main floor sat large tables pulled together to form a triangle. Torin sat at one with his captains, and Connor Lindsey was at another. The third man in the room wore a plaid that was yellow, orange, and black. He had dark hair, and even sitting down, she couldn't miss the fact that he was a large man. Secretaries were sitting behind their lairds, a slight scratching coming from their quills. Shannon felt the muscles across her back tighten. The tension in the room was thick enough to cut.

She followed Baeth toward the cupboard. It was nothing more than a long table behind the main tables. It was where the young boys stood with their masters' cups, each lad assigned the task of ensuring that no one had the chance to slip poison into the vessel that he was guarding. When one of the men at the main tables lifted his hand, the boy tending to him would move forward with his cup, but the lad would return the cup to the cupboard, because there were parchments on the tables and paper was very expensive.

More than one man turned to look at her. Shannon refused to tuck her chin, and that gained her more than one approving grin. Baeth snapped her fingers, and the sound drew Shannon toward the doorway along with the other women, but she hesitated in the hallway, wanting to remain and hear what was being said. Whatever those lairds and captains decided, it would affect her more than anyone. But her gender set her apart from them.

It also protected her.

She shivered, suddenly realizing that if she were a son, she would no doubt be dead now.

"Come along, lass. There is nothing to gain by standing here worrying."

"Ye're right."

But that did not make it any easier to pick up her feet.

⊷

It rained in the afternoon. There was much to be done, and a crack of thunder across the sky surprised all of them. Shannon raced around the tower with the rest of the McLeren women to rescue the drying laundry pinned to ropes that ran up the stone face of the tower. The storm did not come in gently but shook the ground with thunder that echoed between the hills. Lightning split open the dark clouds, and rain pelted them while they tried to pull in the laundry. Shannon filled a basket and ran for the doorway, her own clothing plastered against her skin. Her shoes slipped on the stone floor once she was inside. Her basket flew into the air as she tumbled toward the floor.

But she never hit it. A pair of strong arms caught her, pulling her away from what promised to be a painful landing.

"And Baeth says ye argued about going to see the cobbler."

Torin didn't put her down but held her as though she weighed nothing. He frowned at her. "I told ye that shoes are foolish in the Highlands, lass."

"I went to the cobbler."

One dark eyebrow rose, but his lips also curved with arrogant satisfaction. Shannon pressed a hand against his chest.

"Go gloat somewhere else."

He allowed her feet to drop but held onto one wrist. His eyes flickered with something else now, and she stared at it, mesmerized by the heat.

"But I came in to steal a few moments with ye, sweet Shannon. And why can I nae be pleased that ye will be comfortable in my tower? Those shoes are meant for summer."

His fingers clasped her hand, and he pulled her along behind him, away from the bustle of the women crowding into the kitchens with their loads. Their chatter faded as Torin tugged her farther into the maze of hallways. He finally stopped and looked both ways before ducking behind a large weapons stand. There were only a few feet of space behind the huge wooden stand used for long bows and spears.

Torin pressed her up against the stone wall.

"Ahh, just what a stormy afternoon was truly made for. Trysting in dark corners." He leaned down and pressed a hard kiss against her mouth. There was water on her cheeks, but that didn't stop him from claiming her lips and pressing them open for his tongue. Passion began to burn inside her, her passage clamoring for attention.

"Torin…"

He didn't give heed to her tone but reached for the sides of her gowns.

"Someone will come upon us."

He pulled her garment up, baring her ankles and knees. "I shouldn't have told ye about fucking up against walls. I haven't been able to get the idea out of me head since the words crossed my lips."

She slapped at him, but he grinned at her and pulled her gowns higher. He slipped his hands beneath the fabric and onto the backs of her thighs. A shiver shook her, delight racing down her legs as he gently smoothed his warm hands over her.

"Do ye like this, Shannon? My stroking yer thighs?"

He was whispering against her neck, intensifying the pleasure his touch produced with his words.

"Ye… ye shouldn't talk about it…" Her voice shook, but a soft moan escaped her lips as those warm hands continued to slide and massage her thighs. He bent his knees so that he might cover the area between her knees and bottom.

"Haven't ye ever enjoyed hearing a story told to ye?"

"This is nae a story."

His hands slipped between her legs to stroke her inner thighs. Sensation rushed through her, igniting a need that was very receptive to his moods.

"Why can it nae be a story? Just because it is about trysting and passion?" He laughed low and deep. "Well, I've heard more than one tale of that."

"Is that so?"

He laughed again, this time soothing her with another kiss. It wasn't as hard as the first, which made it intoxicating. She moved her lips beneath his, kissing him back because she just didn't want to ignore the moment. It was wicked to be sure, but it was also exhilarating to know he'd come looking for her when there were no doubt plenty of his own clan who would ease his lust.

Torin wanted her.

She flattened her hands against his neck and smoothed them up to where his hair began, mimicking the motions of his hands. A soft groan came from his lips, so slight, she felt the vibration more than heard it. She was suddenly eager for each stolen touch, savoring the forbidden moment. Baeth's words echoed in her memory. She reached down, moving his kilt aside. His cock was hard and swollen, and he didn't waste any time. He lifted her up, her knees parting so that he might step between them. He did press her back against the wall, using his strength to keep her there. The head of his cock nudged her folds, testing how receptive she was. His breath hit her neck, and she wrapped her arms around his.

She felt too hot, longing for privacy that would allow them to shed their clothing. But the hard press of his cock against her passage was too delightful to postpone enjoying. Her body longed to be possessed right then, and she allowed more of her weight to press down onto that hard flesh.

A soft grunt teased her ear, and Torin surged upward, his hard length filling her completely. She whimpered, unable to contain all the pleasure flooding her.

"I see I am not the only one thinking of the other." Torin meant to tease her, but his voice was harsh with need. His hips thrust back and forth, pushing her closer to the point where she would not be able to hold in her pleasure.

It was deep pleasure too. Hot and shearing, urging her to move faster because she could not bear to wait.

She craved him, craved the pleasure that would soon be hers.

"More."

Her voice was a mere whisper, but Torin heard her. He bit her neck, a sharp yet intensely pleasurable sting that raced down her body to join the boiling need threatening to have her whimpering loudly enough for anyone to hear.

Torin pressed a hard kiss against her lips, sealing both their cries inside her mouth. Every muscle strained, pulling taut while rapture broke deep inside her belly. The sides of her passage clasped his length tighter to pull his seed from him. She didn't have to wait very long. Torin strained toward her, lodging his cock deep inside her while his seed flooded her.

Shannon lost track of time. Her fingers toyed with Torin's hair, and she wondered why she had never played with it before. He remained deep inside her, his chest rising and falling rapidly against her own. They were both wet, but neither of them was chilled.

"Sweet Shannon, I'm becoming yer slave."

His words pleased her too much. Dread wrapped around her heart as the future stretched out with its shadows of plots that neither of them might prevent.

Yet at the same time they were completely hidden away, with no one and nothing to interrupt them. Torin allowed her legs to come down, and her gowns fell to cover her once more, but he wrapped his arms around her, turning her away from him before pulling her tighter against him and binding her firmly to him. The thunder rumbled, echoing along the hallways, but Shannon discovered herself listening to Torin's heart more.

"Ye should be wearing an arisaid, but there is a part of me that enjoys seeing that ye have set yer old one aside." She realized why he was in back of her now; the man was hiding his expression from her. But trying to move proved impossible. Torin sighed and nuzzled her neck.

"It would please me greatly to see ye in my colors, Shannon."

It was an admission, one that she doubted many lairds would make. He was setting aside his pride for her, and she did not miss that fact. It would be simple for him to force his will on her, and once again she noticed that he didn't do so. He asked, which was a greater freedom than she had ever known.

"I thank ye for asking."

"So ye'll think on it?"

There was eagerness in his voice. Part of her wanted to say yes so badly, she struggled to keep it contained.

"And what of the widows that my father recently made among yer people? I do nae think they will be very pleased to see me in McLeren wool."

His hand moved on her shoulder, stroking it slowly. "Let me worry about that, Shannon. Ye would nae be the first daughter wed to the laird whom her father had been warring with. It is not an unknown way of settling things."

"Except that my father has pledged ye no peace. Ye would get nothing. Which means ye are pitying me once more."

She shook her head and pushed free of his embrace. Her pride noticed that he allowed her to turn and face him, but there was nothing she might do about how much stronger he was than she.

She enjoyed that strength far too much to complain about it.

"I shall not cling to ye, Torin McLeren, simply because ye are my lover. I am nae a coward."

"I know that." He delivered each word in a solid tone. "But ye are also a woman."

Shannon drew herself up stiffly. "That makes no difference to my way of thinking. I'll face what comes my way."

"Not alone, ye won't, and there is no point in trying to debate the matter with me. It is that spirit that has me trying to hold you next to me, lass. Besides, I stole ye, and a Highlander keeps what he brings home."

Shannon pressed her lips into a hard line.

"Ye're being stubborn, Torin McLeren."

"No more so than ye are, Shannon McBoyd, so that makes us a good match."

She snorted at him. "Enough, I'm going to bathe, since I'm half soaked."

She turned and began walking out from behind the weapons rack but jumped when a hard smack landed on her bottom.

"Torin McLeren!"

He caught her and kissed her in spite of her squirming. She finally gained her freedom and made it into the hallway, but his arrogant laughter followed her. Her bottom stung just a tiny amount from that smack. And part of her liked it. She smothered a word that she shouldn't know.

"Barbarian."

But one she enjoyed, so who was more uncivilized?

❧

"Ye shall eat at the high table tonight."

Shannon turned to glare at Baeth. She didn't care if it was the hardest look she'd ever sent toward the head of house or if it was disrespectful. Baeth did naught but lift one hand and point a single finger toward her.

"Ye will mind me, girl, because the laird is the one who told me to sit ye there, and the only way ye will be telling me what to do is if ye wed him and become mistress of this tower. For now, I am set above ye."

Shannon gasped. "Not you too."

"Not me, what?" Baeth shook her head. "Once again ye did nae know what to stop struggling against. I see the way the pair of ye look at each other. That is a rare gift, lass, too hard to come by to cast it aside. To be wed to a man ye love, now that is a precious gift indeed."

Was it true? Shannon turned to see Torin watching her. He was sitting at his high table with plenty of his own women trying to catch his eye, but he only looked at her. Her cheeks heated, and she began walking toward him without thinking. She had been thinking far too much. Her entire life, it seemed, had been nothing but thoughts and ponderings.

She was sick unto death of it. She wanted to touch and be touched in return. Torin's face transformed as she moved, becoming practically radiant. Approval shone in his eyes, and his lips curved into a smile that was full of joy. She felt that same joy filling her heart.

He stood up and offered her his hand. The hall quieted, heads turning in their direction. But it was the approving nods that made her quiver. She sat down and squirmed because so many still looked at her.

"This is Quinton Cameron, and ye have met Connor Lindsey."

Shannon offered the two men a respectful nod before sitting down. Connor offered her a silent kiss that earned him a glare that Quinton Cameron didn't miss.

"I believe I've come late to the gathering and missed something enjoyable."

"It was nae enjoyable." Shannon kept her tone sweet, and it gained her a smirk from Connor.

"I recall the moment differently."

Torin sent his fellow laird a hard look. Connor laughed, his amusement turning several heads toward them.

Cameron made a low sound. "Now I am truly envious." He turned toward Shannon and captured her hand before she realized that he intended to touch her. His hand was large, completely covering her own.

"Tell me ye did nae make a choice between these two pitiful excuses. I assure ye, I am a much better specimen for your consideration." He lifted her hand to his mouth and placed a kiss against the back of it.

"I assure ye, Laird Cameron, I was never in any doubt as to my feelings."

"I'm wounded," Connor announced.

Torin chuckled. "So I heard."

Connor didn't take offense; instead the man laughed, and Cameron pushed his lower lip out. "This is what becomes of spending too much time at court: I miss all the fun."

The meal continued, and Shannon found herself enjoying the banter of the men. They teased one another and laughed with honest emotion. But she was keenly aware of Torin beside her, her attention settling on his hands as he reached for his goblet. The skin on the backs of her thighs recalled exactly what those hands felt like against them. The sensation spread upward, until her breasts were warm and felt swollen behind her robe. Torin cut his gaze toward her, and her hands froze. In those dark orbs was a hunger that sent her thoughts away from the meal completely.

He pushed his chair back and stood up.

"Come, Shannon."

He offered her his hand, and she heard the hall grow silent once more. She didn't care. All that mattered was the invitation so close at hand. She placed her hand in his and felt someone pull her chair back when she stood up. Torin pulled her gently toward the stairs, and she felt his hand quiver.

Just a tiny amount, but it was dear. It proved that they were both drawn to one another and that Baeth was correct. It was too rare to struggle against. So she would not. She followed her lover to his chamber, unconcerned with the number of people who watched. What mattered was the privacy beckoning to her, that wonderful place where they might be only themselves.

❧

Torin was awake before dawn. Shannon lay against his side. He could smell her, the soft scent of her skin. He smiled as his fingers encountered the length of her hair, loose and curling against the sheets. He had never shared his bed with a woman, not this bed that belonged to the laird.

Shannon belonged in it. He'd heard other men talk of enjoying having a woman sleep next to them, but he had never believed it could feel so good. His fingers toyed with one curl while he listened to the sound of her breathing.

He would find a way to keep her. There had to be a solution, and he was not interested in hearing otherwise.

That single thought burned in his gut. It also churned up the dread that he'd been avoiding. There was no mistaking that time was running out. James II would have been crowned by now, leaving the way clear for the Earl of Douglas to cut down those who had stood with Atholl. There was no doubt in his mind that blood would be flowing soon. McBoyd blood. He looked over at the long table across his chamber. Shannon's arisaid sat there, neatly folded, a glaring reminder that she was the daughter of a known traitor.

There had to be a way. He just didn't know what exactly it was yet.

He eased out of his bed, tucking the covers around Shannon. He listened to the morning and heard the faint sounds of hooves on the bridge. It was slight because the gate was still down, so the horses would be standing still. He dressed quickly before he took his sword up from where it was still leaning against the wall near the bed and left the chamber.

He met Brockton halfway down the stairs.

"Messengers at the gate, Laird."

Torin nodded. "I've been expecting them."

Torin walked into the yard without a care for the limited light; his attention was on the messengers and the orders they would no doubt be giving him.

Brockton lifted one arm and waved toward the men waiting, poised above the heavy iron gate that kept Donan Tower secure by night. There was a groan as the men above the gate began to wind up the chains that moved it.

"Company so early?"

Connor Lindsey appeared, with his men following closely.

"Aye, messengers from Edinburgh."

Torin watched the men ride through the rising gate. They wore Douglas plaids and looked around the yard before entering it completely.

The man leading the messengers reached up and tugged on his bonnet when he met Torin's gaze. The man dismounted and crossed the space between them. "Archibald Douglas has been made lieutenant general."

Torin stiffened. "I expected as much."

"Aye." Connor added his voice to the moment.

"He's marched on the McBoyd."

Torin felt his teeth grind.

"Get to it, man. I'm no' a woman who needs gentling."

The messenger offered Connor a quick tug on his knit bonnet before reaching beneath his jerkin to remove a letter.

"The Douglas orders ye to McBoyd land." The messenger aimed a hard expression toward him. "Laird Lindsey is to ride with ye."

"Then we go."

Torin didn't waste any time. He covered the distance to his stable with long strides fueled by his need to see the last obstacle between him and Shannon removed. He returned to the yard a few moments later, while his men hurried to join him. It wouldn't take long; they were Highlanders well used to taking to the road whenever they needed to.

"Ye're not bringing the girl?" The messenger looked toward the steps that led into the tower.

"Nay. Whatever Douglas wants, he can have it from me. Highlanders do nae make war with women."

The Douglas messenger raised one eyebrow, but Torin shot him a deadly look.

"Shannon McBoyd is mine. I stole her, and a Highlander keeps what he steals."

Connor's horse rode up next to him, and his friend added a colorful word to the moment. "We want justice from men, no' women. I'd think the Douglas would understand that. Unless ye have been at court too long and listening to too many English."

Something flickered in the messenger's eyes, a brief glimpse of the uncivilized man inside him. "There are too many English at court."

Torin wrapped the reins around his fist and felt his stallion paw the ground with eagerness. "Then we go, and after justice has been satisfied, I will tell the new lieutenant general that I will nae give up Shannon McBoyd, no' even if he demands my life."

The messengers all grunted, but they were eager to be free of a stronghold that was not their clan's. They rode for the gate quickly, while Torin gave his retainers a few more seconds to kiss their wives and sweethearts.

"Are ye sure about that, Torin?" It was Connor who spoke, his voice low and his horse close.

Torin turned a hard look toward his friend. "Ye were the one that mentioned it was time for us both to consider what we might leave behind us. Shannon will make a fine wife, and wedding her will do something that the Douglas's marching on the McBoyd will nae achieve, and that's bring a sense of justice to my kin."

"Aye, I see what ye're thinking. If ye marry Shannon, there will be peace next season."

"It is no' all I am thinking."

Torin watched his friend consider him from narrowed eyes. Torin didn't care. He couldn't think of anything else save keeping Shannon in his life. Maybe his uncle had been correct about his inheriting his mother's common blood, because he wanted love along with his heirs. He wanted the tranquility that had been filling his chamber since Shannon had been sleeping in his bed. Even so short a time had branded the feelings into his heart.

"I will nae consider any other action." He kept his voice low and between Connor and himself. "I believe I love her, Connor."

His friend drew in a stiff breath. "Then I will ride at yer side and help ye keep her."

Twelve

Something was wrong.

Shannon didn't know how she knew it, only that she sensed it the moment she stepped on the main floor. The sounds of the morning meal were muted. She was not used to being greeted warmly, but somehow she had missed the fact that the McLerens had taken to her better in the last two weeks. She noticed today because many of them stared at their meals instead of looking at her when she entered the great hall.

"Cursed McBoyd."

The cause of the tension announced himself with a loud snort. Still wearing the dust from the road and their swords across their backs, these men wore the McLeren colors, but they ate only with one another.

"Why is this filth allowed in the hall?"

Shannon stared at the man insulting her. He looked a great deal like Torin, with the same features and strength, and yet she found him unpleasing. His face lacked anything she might consider attractive, because of the hate twisting his lips. He spit on the floor in front of her.

"Someone bind this traitor up as she deserves."

Shannon felt the blood drain from her face, but she lifted her chin, refusing to show her fear.

Where was Torin?

"She has been given the freedom of the tower by the laird." Brockton stood up, squaring his shoulders.

"Well, me cousin is nae here, so that makes my word law."

Snickers rose from the newcomers, and the sound sent a chill down her back.

"The laird's order stands. Just because he is no' here does nae mean his word is nae to be followed." Brockton refused to budge, even when Torin's kin advanced on him.

"Unless he manages to get himself killed, and then it will be me who is laird. Best remember who is set to inherit here, laddie, because I'll be recalling who cannae tell a traitor just because she happens to have a pair of tits." Torin's kin turned his attention toward her. "I'm Lundy McLeren, and don't think that I'm impressed with ye because ye warm me cousin's cock." He reached down and pulled a dirk from the top of his boot and sneered at her.

"In fact, I think I might just do me cousin the favor of slitting yer throat, since the man seems to lack the courage to do it."

The hall erupted into madness. Shannon didn't have time to become scared. Someone pulled her backward with enough force to see her feet sliding right across the floor without her moving a single muscle. Brockton barreled toward Lundy, clamping both hands around the one holding the dirk. Benches overturned and platters hit the floor, spilling their contents. Shannon lost sight of it in the mayhem as Torin's men pushed her behind them. They crowded in front of her, their wide shoulders making it impossible to see what was happening between Lundy and Brockton.

"Come with me, lass."

Shannon wasn't given a choice. Baeth grabbed her wrist with more strength than the woman looked like she had in her aged body. But it was Quinton Cameron who lifted her clean off her feet and placed her behind him. He blocked out her ability to see past him, and his men quickly moved her farther back so that they stood at their laird's back.

"Enough!" Quinton's voice bounced off the walls, and the shouting died down in response. "Lundy, ye are a pitiful man to pull a dirk on a woman."

"How dare ye insult me?" Lundy's voice rose in pitch until it sounded like a child's.

Quinton folded his arms across his chest. "How dare you pit McLeren against McLeren. The English do like to say that we Highlanders are uncivilized, but I, for one, do nae appreciate yer proving them correct."

Laughter echoed around the hall. It seemed to cut through the tension, and she heard the benches being righted.

"Enough! Do ye hear me? She is the daughter of a traitor! The only thing yer words are doing is making me even more sure that she needs to die before she follows her father's example and kills my cousin while he's sleeping like a besotted fool beside her."

"Shannon would nae do such a thing," Brockton snarled at Lundy. "And my laird is no fool when it comes to judging those he allows near."

"My blood is better than yers."

Lundy was furious. Rage colored his face scarlet, and he shook with it. Brockton still refused to move from the man's path, standing between the Cameron and Lundy. Baeth was still gripping Shannon's arm, and she began to pull her backward while Lundy screeched.

The Cameron lifted one finger and pointed at Baeth. "She stays with the Cameron since Torin is riding with the Douglas. There will be no blood flowing in this hall while Torin is away. I'm promising ye, Lundy, try it and I'll be the man who sets ye down, blue blood or nae."

"She is a traitor, and I'm here to take her to Archibald Douglas." Lundy seemed set on spilling her blood, and Shannon found herself disgusted by the man.

The Cameron shook his head. "Ye seem to be having troubling recalling that we were told to bring the girl to him alive."

Lundy spit on the floor once more, his eyes bright with rage.

Quinton stepped forward. "Or didn't ye think that I also received a message from the lieutenant general?" He reached inside his shirt and withdrew a letter. "He's wanted to see the girl… alive."

"She is a McBoyd. Scotland does nae need their like. I wager that the Earl of Douglas would be happy to have us do the deed for him. But if ye want the chore of taking her to the new lieutenant general, ye are welcome to it. I'll no' be wasting food on a traitor.

I'd like to slit her throat before she whelps another disloyal subject for the king to suffer."

"Ye are letting yer own agenda cloud yer thinking."

"I will nae have her giving my cousin a son with her tainted blood flowing through his veins."

The Cameron snorted. "Enough, Lundy. Ye have no right to try and make sure yer cousin remains childless. She's going to Holyrood alive. I've given my word on it, so that is what will be."

Lundy snarled something in Gaelic, but there were more Camerons in the hall. They clustered around their leader.

"I will nae be forgetting this, Quinton Cameron."

"Neither will I." There was a wealth of meaning in those words.

Quinton turned his back on Lundy and pointed Shannon toward the doors behind her. There was a clear warning in his eyes, but Shannon felt Baeth pulling on her arm too. There wasn't really any choice, except in the manner in which she would be leaving the hall. If she refused, she would be carried away.

Still, part of her wanted to hesitate, because she had learned to love being inside the tower. Leaving it was as bitter as she had feared it would be. But her time was spent, just as she knew it would be, and there was nothing to do but face the justice her father's actions demanded.

She'd do it with courage, so she turned and walked toward the yard.

The morning was brisk, but the sun was quickly burning it away. Shannon shivered without an arisaid to cut the chill. Or maybe she shivered because of the number of horses in the yard. There were nearly a hundred between Lundy's McLerens plaids and Cameron's colors. The men stared at each other, their clan loyalty strong and fierce. It wouldn't take much to spark a fight. It was suddenly clear why Lundy would think he'd be able to order her death; there were even numbers of his men and Cameron's. With a child sitting on the throne, it looked as if the regent and lieutenant general didn't trust anyone. That was the only reason both men would have been sent to fetch her.

"Do nae be worrying about Lundy, lass. I will nae be allowing him to harm ye." Quinton Cameron considered her for a long moment. "Is it possible ye might be carrying Torin's babe?"

Shannon drew herself up stiffly. "It is, but it is none of yer concern."

He was amused by her tone, a slight flicker of admiration appearing in his eyes. But it died when Lundy spoke up behind him.

"The slut has been warming McLeren's bed, even hung out a soiled sheet, from what I hear." Lundy appeared with several of his men, and there wasn't a kind look among them. "Obviously this McBoyd thinks to avoid justice by spreading her thighs."

"The laird ordered the sheet flown."

Baeth spoke up without hesitation. There was firm disapproval in her tone. She pointed at Lundy. "Take a good look at my face, for I want ye to remember it. I will nae be frightened into submission. The girl was pure, and the laird wanted to make sure everyone knew that he respects her."

"Fine, then. She will die a respected traitor." Lundy sneered at Baeth and made a motion toward her with one hand. Quinton Cameron stepped quickly between him and the head of the McLeren house.

"I have no argument that her father is a traitor, but a daughter has no say in what her father does. Ye will be saving yer accusations, Lundy. I'll nae see the lass terrorized by yer threats."

"It would take more than a blustering fool to frighten me."

Quinton smiled once again, amused by her. Lundy wasn't, and the man aimed a stare that was smoldering with hatred toward her.

"She needs to die. To wipe this threat to the king away forever."

"Enough." Cameron turned and lifted one hand. A portion of his men moved forward, one of them leading a powerful stallion.

"I said it before, Lundy. We were ordered to fetch the lass to Holyrood Palace, and that is all we were told to do." He stepped up to his horse and fitted one foot into the stirrup. He didn't linger but swung up onto the back of the animal with solid strength.

"She rides with my men because ye are far too eager to ensure ye inherit the McLeren title by making sure Torin remains childless. If he had a soiled sheet flown, that's good enough for me. They are hand fasted, to my way of thinking. Torin will wed her soon enough, mark my words. It's time he married, and that will settle this matter her father began so that it does nae become a feud. That is what we need, peace in the Highlands, nae another slit throat that will bring her kin marching to claim vengeance, and that will in turn see Torin having to repay that bloodletting. He's a wise man to think to wed to avoid all that killing."

Many men nodded in agreement, but Lundy became more enraged.

"The only thing that will satisfy me is the death of every McBoyd."

"I do nae care, Lundy, do ye hear me? The lass rides with me, and that's the end of it."

"No, the lieutenant general will be the one deciding what the end of it is." Lundy pointed a finger at her. "Ye will die with the rest of yer disloyal kin."

"I will like it better than licking yer boots." Maybe she should have remained silent. For certain her father would have raised his hand against her, in spite of her words being in his favor. Shannon didn't care. A sound of approval rippled through the Camerons, but Lundy's expression turned even darker.

"Lundy, man, that ambition is going to be yer downfall."

Quinton Cameron spoke quietly, but his words still drifted to some of his men. They held their thoughts behind stony expressions, but their eyes darted between her and Lundy, missing nothing.

Quinton let out a short whistle, and a mare was brought around for her. Baeth grabbed her arm and thrust something toward her. It was a McLeren arisaid, still warm from the head of house's body.

"Ye cannae go out onto the road without something to cut the chill. Take it, lass. There is no time for quibbles about the colors."

"Thank you, Baeth." Shannon didn't argue but hugged the length of wool to her chest. It was more than an arisaid, it was a symbol to every soul watching that Baeth approved of her. That was something that might never be bought. "For every kindness ye have shown me."

Baeth snorted. "Ye are worthy of them, and I will be waiting on yer return."

Brockton pushed his way to the front of those clustered on the steps. With a firm hand, he steadied her mare and offered her a hand in gaining the saddle.

"Stay with the Camerons, mistress. Lundy is a greedy man. He'll do exactly what he said in a moment if he gains the opportunity. Do nae give it to him."

She was on the back of the horse before her brain truly registered what Brockton muttered to her. He kept his voice low, so that his words remained between them. Tension rose in her throat so thick it threatened to choke her. The feeling was remarkably similar to how she had felt the first time she stood at the foot of the stairs leading into the tower.

Quinton Cameron watched her and raised one hand up the moment she was holding the reins of her mare.

"Ride."

He spoke the single word, and the men in the yard surged toward the gate in a rush of leather and hooves. Her mare followed without urging, and the Cameron men closed around her, making it impossible for any of Lundy's men to ride near her. It was not a simple matter. Lundy's men guided their horses too close, attempting to get the Cameron retainers to pull up, but they didn't. Instead the entire mass of horses and men surged through the gate and onto the bridge. Shannon wasn't given time to lament her departure from Donan Tower; she was swept along by the current of men.

She felt torn away from something that was dear. Pain raked across her heart, and she turned to look back at the place in which she had gotten to know the other side of her captor. The stark difference between Torin and Lundy made her want to retch. She was grateful that she had not broken her fast this morning, else she would have disgraced herself by emptying her stomach in the midst of so many.

They crossed the long bridge and made their way through the village without slowing down.

It would seem that fate was eager to claim another victim.

❧

The Cameron laird didn't call a halt until the horizon was a mere scarlet stain. His men dismounted and began to make camp quickly. Shannon sat for a moment watching Lundy search for her among the mass of men and horses. Even from the distance she could see a sneer curling his lips back.

"Allow me to help ye down, mistress."

Quinton Cameron held up a hand to her, but the man also reached for the bridle and secured it in a firm hand. Shannon stared at his hand for a long moment before sliding down the side of the mare without placing her hand into his. She heard a soft snort from him before he handed off the mare to one of his men.

"I can see what Torin likes about ye."

She doubted it but held her thoughts behind silence. Making an enemy of the only man standing between her and Lundy wasn't a wise idea. Here on the road, her body might never be found, not that being discovered mattered if she were long dead. What comfort was there in knowing that her bones rested in church ground? The clergy might argue that her soul was more important, but at the moment she was more interested in remaining alive.

"But that stubbornness must nae encourage ye to leave my sight." Quinton Cameron's voice was edged in warning that she didn't need to hear, because she felt it running down her neck and leaving the tiny hairs raised.

"Ye do nae seem to be allowing me any space to do so."

Cameron raised one eyebrow. "Any man who thinks himself undefeatable will shortly find himself nursing his injured pride. In yer case, I doubt there will be any need for nursing. Lundy will slay ye if he gets the chance."

Shannon lifted her chin. "I heard the man clear enough."

"Good. I hope ye do nae make the mistake of thinking ye can outrun us."

The warning flickering in his eyes annoyed her.

"Ye all seem to think that I am loath to travel to where this might all be settled."

Cameron offered her a skeptical look. "Are ye saying ye are content with going to Holyrood?"

Shannon pulled the McLeren arisaid up to cover her chilled neck. "Let us simply say that I am loath to continue on with this waiting. I am nae a coward to hide behind an honorable man like Torin McLeren."

"Torin is that, which is why I owe him the service of keeping Lundy from ye. If Torin took ye back to Donan Tower, I suspect there is a reason."

For all that Quinton Cameron seemed to be looking at her, the man was also remarkably aware of his surroundings. He suddenly looked past her and nodded.

"You will be staying within my reach."

He didn't allow for any resistance to his command either. He reached out and grasped her upper arm in a grip that promised pain if she tried to refuse. His men had raised a simple tent while they spoke, only two poles driven into the ground with a length of canvas secured to the tops before being pulled down at an angle to the ground. Other such shelters were being erected around them as flint was struck to small piles of wood. Conversation was low and subdued, dying completely when Cameron passed by with her in tow.

"Ye'll sleep in the back of my tent."

"With ye?"

The space was small, no bigger than the bed she'd shared with Torin. Flaps fell down on either side to make the space private and keep out the elements.

"Aye. Ye may relieve yerself in back of those rocks, and ye have only a few moments of light left to do it. Once it's dark, ye will be in the back of my tent, where I can be sure of where ye are."

She snarled softly, biting back the words she wanted to use to argue with him, but her body urged her to wait until she'd tended to her personal needs first.

Cameron didn't look as though he were open to negotiating how much time she had.

She returned just as night had fallen completely. Quinton pointed toward the tent.

"Go on, do nae make me put ye in there. It's the only solution that will ensure I complete my duty to see ye delivered to Archibald Douglas. Torin McLeren is a man I call friend. Ye'll not have any trouble from me, only my protection from Lundy there." Quinton Cameron suddenly winked at her. "I steal my own women."

Shannon growled softly but sank to her knees so that she might crawl into the back of the tent. There was a length of canvas spread out to form a floor. It kept the dirt from soiling her but did little to cut the chill. Most of Cameron's men had pulled their own tartans over their heads now too. Without the sun to warm them, the air grew cold. She went toward the far corner of the tent, seeking some space between her and the man guarding her. It forced her to lie down, but at least she gained what she wanted. Cameron was now separated from her by an arm's length. The man's back was wide and thick with muscle just as Torin's was, but she was not drawn to him. Her gaze didn't trace those shoulders with the same devotion that it did with Torin. It was very simple to look away. The man was talking to one of his retainers, ignoring her as easily.

But the moment she spread out, her belly growled low and long. He turned to look back toward her. Shannon frowned because she didn't want him thinking about her needs.

He held out a small pouch and skin, turning to face her more.

"I am well enough."

His eyes narrowed. "Ye are hungry, because I forgot to feed you. I suppose I'll have to be learning to remember that when I get to stealing myself a woman."

He winked at her, but Shannon frowned. "It is nae a good jest, that of stealing women."

"Ye looked rather happy last night by Torin's side, for a stolen woman."

Her cheeks heated slightly. "I was happy."

The pouch and skin landed near her head with a flick of his wrist. He turned his back on her once he had tossed them to resume talking to his captain. Their voices were low, and she only caught every other word, so she stopped trying to understand them. Her belly cramped and demanded she dispense with her pride. Where the mind might have been willing, the flesh still had needs. At least Cameron seemed willing to allow her to eat in private, or something close to it. His large body kept her out of sight for the most part. When she turned over and faced the end of the tent, she was able to relax her tight control over her expression. The low conversation drifting to her ears from Cameron gave her enough peace to keep her back turned to the rest of the group.

Inside the pouch was a small offering of nuts and dried meat. There were also hard baked biscuits in thin lengths like fingers. They were difficult to chew, but she had nothing else. The skin held water, and it was fresh and sweet, making the biscuits easier to swallow. For all their dryness, they filled her belly remarkably well. Once she drank from the skin, what she'd eaten felt like it was expanding inside her.

"I'll be telling the Douglas about the sheet."

Shannon gasped, choking on what was in her mouth. She forced it down before glaring back at Cameron. "That is between Torin and me. I never wanted him to fly that soiled gown."

Cameron looked amused. "So it was a gown, was it? Not a sheet? Very interesting to hear that bit."

"'Tis nae interesting. It is my private affair is what it is."

Quinton's face became pensive. He studied her for a long moment.

"Nay, lass, it is a matter for more than ye. In fact, that is the driving force behind Lundy's need to do ye harm. He fears that ye might conceive where all others have failed. Affection can have that effect on a couple."

Her neck tingled once again. "What do you mean?" She wanted to deny that she harbored affection for Torin, but it would have been a lie, and he deserved better than that. Besides, life was suddenly sweeter today, she could feel the sand running through the hourglass that was her time in this life. She needed to embrace every good moment, not shrug it off. There would be plenty of grief to contend with. Cameron leaned back on one elbow and smirked at her.

"I notice ye didna deny yer feelings for the man."

"That is—"

"None of my concern?" His voice was arrogant and mocking, annoying her greatly.

"I liked it better when yer back was to me." Shannon threw his pouch and skin back toward him. She rolled over onto her back and looked at the canvas above her.

"All right, lass. Ye made yer point rather well. Torin is a lucky man."

Shannon failed to rein in her curiosity and rolled back onto her side to look at the man. He was studying her once more, this time from beneath lowered eyebrows.

"Aye, ye heard me correctly. I said Torin was lucky because ye clearly do hold affection in yer heart for him. I believe Lundy might be justified in his worry. Ye might just be the one to give Torin a child." His face darkened, as did his tone. "That's something that is long past due. Torin McLeren is a good man."

"His mistresses were all good women if they didn't allow themselves to conceive."

And it also meant that Torin had told her the truth about his devotion to whichever woman he considered his at the time. That was something no wife might expect, but that every husband demanded. It made her heart ache for him even more.

"Aye, they were that." Quinton drew in a stiff breath. "But Lundy swears it is on account that *he's* meant to be laird of the McLerens. I think Torin deserves something else."

"He does."

"If he flew the proof of yer innocence from the window, ye are something important to him."

Shannon bit into her lower lip, trying to remain silent. Cameron laughed at her efforts.

"Some couples are favored with love. I envy Torin yers." Cameron leaned slightly toward her. "I see it in yer eyes and the way ye keep edging away from me."

He narrowed his eyes. "Ye'd be trying to cling to me if ye gave up yer purity to gain Torin's protection."

Shannon scoffed at Cameron's ideas. "Torin is an honorable man, and I am nae a coward. That explains why I am not interested in clinging to ye. Or to Lindsey, when he tried his hand at impressing me."

She rolled back onto her back to end the conversation. Cameron was correct about one thing: she wasn't interested in clinging to him, even if it meant facing Lundy. The man she longed for was not near, and she felt the separation keenly. The ones who peered toward the tents through the darkness made her neck tighten with tension. Some of them would kill her if they could. The night stretched out in an endless string of hours that just might be her last.

"I do nae mean to be rude. I appreciate ye keeping Lundy from me. Truly I do."

She heard Cameron snort and turned her head to look at him. Disgust thinned his lips. "That part ye do nae need to thank me for. It is the truth that I enjoy taunting Lundy. The man is too greedy, too eager to tell one and all that Torin has no children. That is nae something any man should be gleefully announcing. Life is a precious thing when it comes to children. I cannae respect a man who does nae have any humility when it comes to another's lack of children or the whim of fate when she is in the mood to be less than kind."

"Torin is nae an old man. He'll likely marry and have lots of babes."

"Maybe with ye."

"With any healthy woman, I'd say."

Quinton shook his head. "He flew that gown for

a reason, lass. He'll come for ye. I'd bet the harvest on it."

Shannon cast one final look at Quinton before rolling onto her side to give him her back. The man was too keen, and she needed to keep her thoughts private.

Come for her?

Sweet Christ... she prayed so!

She fought back tears and lost the battle. They eased from the corners of her eyes and left trails down her cheeks.

She did love him.

Quinton was correct about that. Shannon pulled the arisaid closer as she grew colder, but the chill came from inside her. The reason was simple; it was very possible that she would not see Torin again. Not in this life.

Which meant she would not be able to give him a child born from her love.

But the Douglas would not have taken her away from Torin while he was away if he intended for her to live. There was no way to ignore that bit of truth. It drilled deeply into her heart, making sleep impossible. She ached, and the pain was a torment that defied everything she had ever known.

So cruel. Fate was truly unkind.

☙

Holyrood Palace was an old abbey. James II had been born beneath its ceiling and crowned there as well. Shannon looked down on it, marveling at the activity that was clustered around it. There was a stream of people trying to enter the main gate, but it looked as though many were being turned away. When they rode closer, she could see that many of those denied entrance were dressed in their finery. Ladies wore overrobes of velvet with pearls and veils of transparent silk. Their faces were dusted with powder, and they looked out of the boxes they sat in by pulling back the curtains. Those seat boxes were held on long poles between two horses. Shannon had seen only a few when her new stepmothers arrived, because they were more suited to the road of a city than the rocky paths of the country. They were extreme luxuries, their only purpose to protect the costly garments the occupants wore and to transport those noble people in comfort. Some of the chairs even had iron boxes beneath the seats, where hot rocks might be placed.

Some of the men were dressed in costly overtunics, but there were far more kilts than not. Fancy hats with trimmed and curled feathers adorned their heads, but they clung to their clan colors. The number of people being denied entrance was growing and growing. They moved off to the side of the gate with frustration written on their faces.

"The Earl of Douglas is not taking chances with the young king he's been placed in charge of. The palace will be a quiet place for a long time to come."

"I can see the wisdom in that." Shannon could also see the advantage to the lieutenant general's wiping her entire family off the face of Scotland. Atholl had tried to claim the throne because he and James I had the same grandfather. The man had married twice, dissolving his first marriage. But there were those who didn't agree with the children of that first marriage being cut off from the inheritance of the crown.

Atholl had amassed all those who he could to his cause, and the only true way that James II would continue to rule was to make sure such a cause could not rise again. Atholl was gone, and with him the blood that threatened to topple the reigning monarch. Or more importantly, those who ruled in his stead like Archibald Douglas. The queen was also regent for her son, but she was English born and needed the powerful earl to help her keep her son on the throne.

Inside the palace there would be no mercy for anyone who had backed Atholl. Shannon felt that truth ripple across her skin as they rode toward the main gate. Their number was great enough to alarm the guards on the walls. She saw their arrows being notched against their bows when Cameron and Lundy rode forward without pausing. Unlike so many others, they passed through the double iron gates and into the lower courtyard. There they met the royal guard and the Douglas retainers. They were pouring out of the barracks and out into the yard to confront Cameron.

But Lundy spoke first. "I brought ye a McBoyd traitor."

There were snarls from the Douglas retainers. Metal slid against metal as many of them lent action to their opinions of her name. The Cameron men clustered about her.

"The man's daughter, so sheathe yer weapons, because the lieutenant general sent for her."

Eyes narrowed, and no one moved. Shannon felt as if the moment became an entire hour while she waited to feel those unsheathed swords pierce her flesh. She heard each of her heartbeats, an eternity between each one, because she was conscious that it might be one of her last.

"Aye, the lieutenant general did send for her. Make way."

The sea of angry faces parted to reveal the grand entrance to the palace. Two stories high, it was a curved opening framed in ivory. The palace itself was made of brown stone that looked almost golden where the sun shone on it. There were small windows, set with true glass panes, to testify that it was in fact the residence of a king, but what drew Shannon's interest were the thick walls built to be inescapable.

How many had come to this beautiful place to die?

She did not envy the king or his queen mother. She would not want to live in any place that sat over a dungeon where torture and death were an everyday occurrence. What joy was there in the expensive ivory edgings and glass windows when she knew that beneath it lay suffering?

Her opinion did not matter. She was swept inside between Cameron retainers, who buffeted her against the snarling Lundy ones and the brooding Douglas ones.

She drew in a deep breath and lifted her chin. Whatever lay in front of her, she would face it without cringing.

That was what she had always shown Torin, and today she would not be changing.

Thirteen

TORIN SAT LOOKING OVER ANOTHER SMOLDERING tower. Thin trails of black smoke rose above the stone tower, betraying the fact that it had been put to the torch. There was an unnatural silence, one that he noticed and felt lonely hearing. All around, the hills were green with flowers and the buds of new crops, but around the McBoyd tower there was nothing but death. From the front gate, four bodies hung. Those men would be McBoyd's captains, the same ones who had attacked White Hill.

Torin didn't feel any sense of victory. It was an ending, but there was nothing good about it. There were more widows now, and the color of their tartans didn't matter—not here, not to these people. The only place that it mattered was in a palace where a boy was being used as the justification for seizing control. It was not a unique battle; history was full of them.

"Why would the Douglas tell us to come here when he was clearly no' going to wait for us?" Connor asked the question with suspicion coating his voice.

"He didna need us." He never had. Torin cursed his lack of forethought. He wasn't used to thinking on the orders of his overlord; he did as commanded. Which was exactly what someone had counted on.

"I need to return to Donan Tower."

"Aye, that we do."

Connor spoke with passion and turned his horse in the same moment that Torin did. Their men fell in behind them, shaking the roofing thatch of the villagers' homes they passed. No one came out to see them; they hid inside their homes, fearing another round of justice. Torin leaned low over the neck of his stallion. He felt the prickle of urgency pushing him to go faster. The sun set and he pressed on, unwilling to rest.

Donan Tower was visible at dawn. Torin didn't slow down to greet the villagers who waved to him on his way toward the bridge. Dread was pounding through him, driving him forward. The gate began to grind upward before he was halfway across, but he still had to pull his horse up and wait while it rose high enough to allow him to ride beneath.

Baeth stood on the top step, and the pallor of her face sent his blood boiling.

"Where is Shannon?"

His head of house looked furious. "Lundy took her off to Edinburgh."

Torin roared. His rage shook the rafters and drew men and boys out from every corner of the castle. Brockton appeared with a scowl on his face.

"Cameron was with him, but they came with the authority of Archibald Douglas, the lieutenant general. We could nae hold her."

"Cameron is a fair man." Connor slid from his saddle, and his men followed. "We must rest the horses, or they'll die beneath us halfway to Edinburgh."

Torin wanted to argue, but his friend was correct. Two days of riding and his horse needed time to recover its strength. He dismounted in spite of every muscle resisting the urge.

"We will ride tonight." Connor's face was alight with anticipation in spite of the fatigue that was etched into his expression. Beneath his eyes there were dark smudges, but in his eyes there was no trace of that exhaustion.

"You may count on it, my friend. I will be honored to have yer company."

Connor grinned cocky and arrogantly. "Of course I am coming. We Highlanders must stick together. We keep what we steal."

"Ye have that correct, my friend. I will be keeping Shannon McBoyd, and woe be to the man who gets between me and what I consider mine."

❧

"I will bid ye farewell here, lass." Quinton Cameron shot her a serious look. They were being escorted down a long hallway that echoed with the booted steps of the Douglas retainers surrounding them. They paused for a moment outside a set of double doors. A chamberlain stood there, his hand wrapped around a thick staff. He listened to the captain for a moment before disappearing through a small side door.

"I wish ye the best of luck too."

"I doubt there is enough luck in the entire country."

Cameron smothered a short bark of amusement. "Well, if nae luck at least ye have plenty of spirit."

"And ye have an abundance of arrogance."

Quinton didn't bother to smother his laughter this time. It drew the disapproving looks of their escort. Shannon felt her lips twitching up too; if she were heading to her execution, there really was no reason not to enjoy what she might. If fate were going to be unkind, the least she might do is laugh at it.

The chamberlain appeared and walked back to his post. He cleared his throat before lifting the staff and striking the stone floor three times with it.

"His grace, the Earl of Douglas and lieutenant general, summons Shannon McBoyd."

His voice bounced off the stone walls. The doors opened, and the sound of the wood parting was like a cannon. Shannon drew in a deep breath while her escort began moving. She hesitated, her pride refusing to jump the moment that she was told to. Cameron reached out, but she struck his hand away.

"I'll take myself there."

He watched her with an expression that was bright with respect. Shannon stepped forward and discovered that the first one was the hardest. After that her feet moved faster, until she was even with her escort once more. They all lowered themselves to a knee and stayed there while the man sitting in the throne aimed his attention at her.

Archibald Douglas was a proud man. That was the thing she noticed most about him. He sat on a raised platform in an ornately carved chair that looked fit for a king. He wore an overrobe that was fine wool dyed a deep blue. It was a costly dye, which none used save to polish vanity. He stared at her, frowning when she did not lower herself to a knee. All she offered him was a deep curtsy. He snorted and waved his hand.

"Leave us. Cameron, ye have our gratitude."

Shannon straightened, stunned by the use of the word "our." Only monarchs spoke in such a way. Of course, the man was king in everything but name. His retainers quit the room with another round of boot heels hitting stone.

"Ye are either brazen or foolish to nae get on yer knees in front of me."

"I was taught to kneel in church and that I should not offer the same to any earthly person, else I diminish what I offer to God."

He tilted his head and pressed his lips together in a hard line.

"Ye are more opinionated than I care for in a female. A woman should know her place. Which is lower than a man's."

Shannon lowered herself again, this time slowly. It was a silent mockery of him and his ego, possibly a foolish thing to do, but she refused to coddle him. She suddenly understood why so many nobles walked willingly to their deaths; they refused to abandon their dignity by begging the monarch who signed their death petitions.

She felt the same way, undeniably, deep inside herself.

Douglas laughed at her, a short bark that hit the closed doors behind her.

"I see yer point, mistress, and I'm pleasantly

surprised to discover ye have enough spine to make it." His eyes narrowed. "There aren't many men who would test my good humor."

He sat forward and began rubbing his fingers against one another. His forehead furrowed while he contemplated her.

"Yer father and brothers have been condemned for their allegiance to Atholl and for raiding the McLeren."

He watched her to see her response. Shannon simply let out a short breath. It was practically a relief to have the matter at an end. The Earl of Douglas lifted one dark eyebrow.

"Ye have nothing to say?"

"Nothing that would change anything. My words will only further damn them. I watched them celebrate their raiding of the McLeren. It was disgusting."

The earl nodded. "Aye, I suppose I see the direction of yer thinking. Yer father sent ye to Atholl, and if ye told me that, it would seal his fate all that much more. I owe McLeren a debt for preventing yer wedding."

The earl stopped and fingered his chin while his gaze slid over her. From head to toe, he inspected her, every curve, even lingering over the apex of her thighs for a long moment. Her cheeks heated, but she bit back her scathing words. This man was powerful, and there was nothing she might say that would sway his opinion when it came to what he believed women were placed on earth for.

Torin did not treat her so…

The earl suddenly stiffened and drew in a harsh breath.

"I have nae decided what to do with ye, Shannon McBoyd. Not yet."

Relief flooded into her so quickly, she stepped back, a single step that she was helpless to prevent. Douglas snickered, amused by her show of emotion.

"So ye do understand that I hold yer life in my hands. I am impressed with yer courage. Ye may see yer father once, and I suggest ye do it soon, because he's nae going to see many more days."

"My father is here?"

The Earl of Douglas nodded, his expression grave. "Every clan that stood with Atholl will feel the weight of my fist for it. Every traitor will die."

He flicked his hand toward the door.

"Go on. See yer father, if ye please, and do nae give me a reason to sentence ye to the same fate. Ye will remain here and stay where I put ye until I've thought on the matter some more."

Shannon lowered herself into a curtsy once again.

Douglas leaned forward and rubbed his fingers against one another again.

"Ye look like ye meant it that time. Why? Because I spared yer life? I didna promise ye that yet."

"Ye said ye would think upon the matter more, which proves ye to be a reasonable man. That is something I can respect."

His face reflected shock, his hands closing around the ends of the armrests.

"I see why yer father has no affection for ye, Shannon McBoyd. Ye are nae the sort of ego-coddling creature he prefers his underlings to be. That is worth a bit of thinking on the matter of what is to be done with ye. I have no stomach for cowards, be they male or female."

His eyes narrowed, and she felt her throat tighten. The earl was a man who planned to rule, and that meant he could not afford subjects who refused to bend to him. That was where rebellions began. More than one king knew that to kill the leaders meant the rest would bend in submission.

"Go. I'll think on yer fate."

The door behind her opened, and two burly Douglas retainers moved up beside her. Turning her back on him, Shannon swept from the room.

But she couldn't help wondering if the retainers wouldn't be the same men who would later take her to her execution. Douglas might find it much easier to condemn her if he didn't have to look at her face while he did so.

Too easy.

❧

"She's a strong girl." Joan Beaufort moved out from behind the tapestry where she had been sitting. The widow of James I wore a simple overgown of wool to mark her mourning.

"She is a woman, which makes her more of a threat. I do nae need that sort of thing. Her blood alone is a good reason to send her to the gallows with her kin."

Joan shook her head. "Daughters do not decide their father's actions. They obey."

"That does nae mean her blood will not inspire further rebellion among her father's men." The Earl of Douglas stood up and faced her. "This is Scotland, madam. If ye want yer son to remain king, you will listen to me. Strength is respected here."

"And you believe it is different in England?" Joan kept her voice mild and smooth, just as pleasing as her face. "I saw plenty of executions as a girl there. In fact, there were times James was forced to watch them to remind him that he was a captive of the English king and subject to his will."

"Then why are ye arguing with me, madam? I am the man who will help ye keep yer only son sitting on the throne. If I fail to keep these lairds in check, what do ye think will become of ye and yer gaggle of daughters?"

Joan Beaufort, cousin to the king of England, held her tongue through years of practice. She had only one living son. His twin had died at birth, and fate had given her nothing else save for daughters. Her position was precarious. Her son's inheritance hung in the balance. The lairds of Scotland sneered at her English blood and the string of girl babies she'd produced. But James had loved every one of them, just as he'd loved her. Love was worth holding her tongue for, especially in the presence of a man who was too stupid to understand the treasure that love was. Douglas only looked at something if there was gain there for him. He was ruthless, but that was in her favor, because her son needed men like this one to help him remain king until he was a grown man. Once enough years had passed, Archibald Douglas would be given his due. She would wait silently until that day.

The Earl of Douglas took her silence as a sign of surrender to his will. "Ye need to keep yer mercy for yerself and yer children. Ye do nae have enough to spare."

"You said you owed Laird McLeren. I hear he has affection for Shannon McBoyd. Would it not be a good reward to give her to him? That would settle your dues and cost you nothing in the doing of it."

Douglas snickered. "He has lust for her, like any man. My own cock is hard after meeting her. She's a fresh bit of meat with spirit, and that is something no Scot ignores. Especially no' a Highlander."

Joan walked in a small circle, fighting against the urge to snap at the man who was so gleefully trying to impose his will on her. A woman's life was filled with tests of her resolve to outmaneuver the men surrounding her.

"I hear he flew a soiled sheet from his window after spending the night with her."

"I heard it was an undergown, which means he tumbled her when he caught her in a dark-enough place."

Joan drew in a deep breath to make certain her voice remained calm. Being queen had helped her refine her control in a manner that she had never thought possible.

"And yet Laird McLeren flew the proof of her virginity. I only thought to add that to your thinking. The man may well want her back. I hear your Highlanders consider what they take during raids to be theirs to keep. It is possible he will be most unhappy if you hang her."

Douglas grunted. "Aye, ye have that correctly. Which is why I need to think on the matter."

Joan Beaufort, queen of Scotland, lowered herself deeply and gracefully before the lieutenant general. She did it perfectly, and the man was vain enough to think her sincere. She was not. Inside, she was a cauldron of boiling discontent, but that must never be suspected. She was a mother, and all her energy must be directed at keeping her children in the positions to which their blood entitled them.

"I will await your decision."

Joan quit the room, craving a bit of solace to calm herself. She must always be careful of showing her feelings. The earl was correct about one thing; she didn't have enough friends to be worrying about other people's children.

And still Shannon McBoyd drew her interest. She did not care for the fact that it was most likely that Douglas would send the girl to the gallows. Such an action would make everyone rest easier, for it would wipe out the last of the traitor's blood and serve as a grisly example to those who might think about rising up against her son. Not only would they die, but their families would as well. It was one sure way to ensure that her son continued to wear the crown of Scotland.

But it would be innocent blood shed for the survival of her own innocent son.

It would also not be the first time such was needed. She could not say she was entirely against the idea.

Yet she could not set the matter aside either. Her conscience pestered her even as she tried to outwalk it.

❧

The dungeon reeked, a true stench that made Shannon want to retch.

It smelled of blood and rot and worse yet, of fear. The stench was enough to make a person's knees quiver.

Shannon followed the Douglas retainers down the rough stone steps toward the cell where her father was. The stone was uneven here and dirty. It smelled musty and dank from the lack of sunlight. She suddenly realized that she could smell the fresh springtime on her clothing; she noticed it because with each step the air became more stale and moldy. Every downward placement of her feet took her farther away from the light of day. It was like sinking into hell.

A soft whimpering touched her ears, and the grating of something against metal. They were forlorn sounds, almost too pitiful to endure. Candles flickered in their iron holders against the stone walls. There was a chill surrounding her that told her they were well underground now, where the earth was still frozen from winter. During the summer it must be like the mouth of hell, without a single breath of air to relieve the suffering.

Of course it was intended to be a place of suffering. The dungeon was where traitors went. She looked around at the black mold clinging to the stone walls and tried to recall the way her father had so gleefully celebrated slaughtering his neighbors. She couldn't dismiss the fact that they were a good fit for each other, murderer and dungeon.

Another whimper and a sob. This time they were louder. There was something familiar about them too. Two more steps and they reached the main floor of the dungeon. The flickering flames from the candles danced over the mold-splattered walls while leaving deep shadows in the corners. The scent of human filth was so strong, her stomach heaved.

"Shannon McBoyd! You must beg Douglas for mercy for me!"

Shannon jumped away from the iron bars near her. Fergus appeared, and his face told her she'd discovered the source of the whimpering. He still wore the clothing she'd met him in, and she could smell the scent of his unwashed skin. His eyes narrowed, and envy shone brightly. His fingers clasped the iron bars so tightly, they turned a ghostly white where they were not black with grime.

"You tell him… you tell him to have mercy on me." His voice broke, and another sob passed his lips. "He'll listen to a woman. Tell him that I am naught but an obedient servant, doing as he was commanded." His eyes brightened. "That's the way of it. Tell him how diligent I am to the will of my master… tell him I will serve him as well."

"Stupid weakling." One of the Douglas retainers aimed a jab at the secretary. "The only mercy ye can expect is a hanging, as opposed to some of the things a traitor might expect. Besides, the girl cannae help herself, much less anyone else. Spend yer time making yer peace with God so that ye are ready to meet him. It will be soon."

Fergus scooted back to avoid being hit, his sobbing becoming smothered behind one of his forearms. The retainer looked at her.

"Don't try the lieutenant general's patience by siding with traitors."

It was wise advice, especially when she considered that Fergus was guilty. But her heart still ached. Life was a precious thing, full of so many wonders.

Thinking that it was going to end was a misery beyond compare. She understood the lament surrounding her; it was plastered onto the walls with their thick wax drippings that had not been cleaned away. Beneath some of the candleholders, there was a full foot of wax dripped down the walls. Worse than that, where there were manacles set into the walls, the wax had been carefully molded into little sculptures of flowers and other things, like ships. Along the floor, she could see them scattered into the shadows, the hands that had formed them long gone. Scuff marks marred the floor, telling a horrible tale of prisoners who had been chained long enough to leave their marks in stone.

Her belly heaved again.

"McBoyd." The retainer hit the iron bars of a cell with his long spear, making them vibrate. "Ye have a visitor."

"Well now, is that a fact?" Her father rolled out of the bunk that stretched across one end of the cell. It wasn't even long enough for a man to fully stretch out on, and it took up the entire width of the cell. It was also only a stone shelf and not really a bunk at all.

"Have ye brought me a priest, lads? Better fetch the man a stool. My confession is going to take a good long time."

Her father peered through the dim gloom toward her. He began chuckling, continuing into full laughter.

"Ye brought me my daughter. The most useless thing God ever cursed me with! I suppose this is Douglas's attempt to torment me."

He stumbled toward the front of the cell, unable to straighten up because of the low roof.

"Well now, girl, look at this mess ye've gotten me into."

"Shannon?" Her oldest brother spoke from the cell next to her father's. "Shannon, ye must go to the earl and beg him for mercy for us."

"Aye, there's an idea." Her father suddenly raked her with cold eyes. "Offer yerself to him. A man will do a lot for his mistress. I hear Douglas has quite a hunger for female flesh. Maybe that's the reason God cursed me with a daughter."

He reached through the bars. "Go on, I tell ye. Get on yer knees, and tell him ye will please him any way he likes. I hear McLeren had ye, so ye should know yer way around a cock now. That should do the trick. Use everything ye learned in McLeren's bed to coax Douglas into freeing yer kin. Even the mighty lieutenant general is nae stronger than his lust."

"Aye, Shannon, Douglas likes his women on their knees, I hear." Her brother sounded hopeful. "Suck his cock…"

"Stop it! Enough scheming. Look what it has brought ye."

Her father snarled and reached through the bars too, but she was not close enough for his fingers to grasp. "Ye'll do as I command, Daughter! I am yer sire! God demands that ye obey me…"

"I will nae."

Shannon turned around because she just couldn't stand the pathetic sight any longer. Her father let out a strangled sound.

"A curse and blight upon ye, then! Do ye hear me, Daughter? *A curse upon ye…*"

"Yer blood is curse enough, traitor." One of the retainers tilted his head to the side and looked at her. "I suggest ye leave. There is nothing for ye here. At least the earl did nae say ye were to join this lot."

"Aye. A kindness, that."

She left the dungeon much faster than she had entered it. It felt like a blessing to emerge from the musty, stale air. The chill clung to her long after she smelled the change in the air. That was because it was coming from her heart. She scolded herself for becoming upset. Her sire had never seen her as anything but a burden.

"The lieutenant general has given orders that ye be kept in the south tower."

The Douglas retainer spoke almost kindly toward her. The man watched her through an expression that guarded his true thoughts. Living in the palace must make it a necessity to be able to hide what you were thinking.

"I am ready to go there."

The retainer nodded with approval. Shannon cringed as she realized that the man was not sure if she would do as her father instructed or not.

Was she wrong not to? Wasn't life worth more than her pride?

She followed the two men, her thoughts tearing at her. But she recalled the way Torin had looked at her when she was on her knees facing him, and her entire body rebelled against doing as her father commanded.

That wasn't pride; it was love. She couldn't offer herself to the earl, because she loved Torin. It might mean her death, but she could not change how she felt. It was too strong, filling her heart to the point of madness. That love had the power to drive the scent of the dungeon away. It was life, shining and shimmering with everything wonderful. She allowed it to fill her mind while she followed the Douglas retainers to her assigned chamber. It was a cell, but so much better than she had dared to hope for. She kept her mind on that, and it gave her the courage to keep placing one foot in front of the other.

She would not be dragged, and she would not whimper. At least, not until the door was shut and no one might witness her shame.

"Here it is. It's not so bad. I'll send some of the maids up this way." The older of the two men looked around the room and nodded. "Mind ye, ye will not be allowed out without escort. I'm going to leave young John at the door. Do nae be giving him any trouble while I'm fetching up some girls to tend ye. I dinna like to treat the lasses poorly, but I'll do what needs done, to make sure I follow my orders."

"I shall nae, and thank you."

The man tilted his head slightly. "Ye are a good lass. Shame about yer kin, though. Right nasty lot they are. Still, at least yer no' sharing the dungeon with them."

"Yes, that is a kindness. Please thank the earl for me."

Maybe the last she might expect. In truth, it was more than she had hoped for along the road, with Lundy aiming sneers her way. The door shut, leaving her to investigate her prison. It was certainly better than where she had just visited her family. The room was large enough for a bed and sitting area. It was an entire floor of the tower and had windows set into three sides of it. They were small windows, but the afternoon breeze blew through them with a whistling sound. She could smell the heather blooming in the hills, just a faint hint of it, but her senses were keen to it.

Life was most definitely sweeter now that she felt it slipping away from her.

Besides the bed, there were a table and two chairs. No fireplace to cut the chill, but there were curtains hung on the bed. The floor was bare, the wood marked in places. The wind whistled again, this time sounding lonely. There was a forlorn feeling in the chamber, the furniture seeming to hold so many tales yet unable to voice them. How many days could she last within the bare walls, with nothing to do save think, before her father's idea became palatable? She doubted she would be the first prisoner broken by the stone she stared at. What value did pride have when there was nothing to do, no one to listen to, absolutely nothing at all?

But she had her memories of Torin. Her lips curled up, and she walked in a slow circle while she allowed the images of him to fill her mind. Contained inside her mind were treasures of recollections too priceless to name. She happily allowed them to drown out everything else.

❧

Well after sunset someone knocked on the door. Shannon turned to watch one of the retainers arriving with more food. He set it down and left without a word. She stared at the food but was sure it would stick in her throat if she attempted to swallow any of it.

Was Torin coming for her?

She closed her eyes and felt as though she could see him riding that stallion of his.

But would that be enough?

Torin would be subject to the earl's will too. She paced around the chamber until the lack of light sent her into the bed. She might burn the candles, but there was something fitting about the darkness. It suited her dark thoughts, so she climbed into the bed and shivered, in spite of the blankets.

In her dreams she reached out for him, straining to make her fingertips reach him. Sometime in the darkest hours of the morning, she relaxed. There was no longer any reason to struggle. She could feel him near, feel his presence in the night. Smell his scent…

She turned her face toward that teasing hint that she was no longer alone. She sighed when she felt the warm slide of fingers along her jaw, the palm cupping her cheek. No one did that except Torin…

Her lover…

"Sweet Shannon… open yer eyes, lass."

Fourteen

SHE GASPED AND FOUGHT HER WAY FREE OF SLUMBER. She ended up sitting up too fast, startling her lover.

A curse split the darkness, and she was instantly wrapped in a steel grip, one that compressed her body, but she enjoyed it so greatly, she felt like shouting.

"Tor—" That hand that had been so dear a moment ago now sealed every last sound behind it. He pushed her back into the bed, his greater weight making it impossible to resist. Her mind was suddenly sharp and keen, the last of slumber evaporating as her back was pressed deeply against the bedding.

It was Torin...

Doubt surfaced to nip at her. The room was pitch-black because she had closed the shutters. She suddenly realized why Torin slept with his open, so that even when the coals died down there was light. A man like him wouldn't risk being blind, even when he slept.

"Hush, lass. I sneaked in here and don't want any company save yer own."

She made a soft sound that filtered through his hand. It wasn't really an attempt at speaking; she was too full of emotion for that.

"Aye, lass, and I'm happy to see ye as well."

He was gone a moment later, disappearing into the darkness as if he'd been summoned from her dreams. Shannon sat up, trying to force her eyes to find some trace of him, willing him to materialize once more.

"Torin?"

Her voice sounded too loud in the room, but she couldn't take not knowing if it had been a dream. Could she have wanted him there so badly, her mind convinced her that he was with her? Was her mind broken as she had feared it would become? If so, she would gladly place her hand into insanity's so long as it brought her back to Torin's embrace.

A thin sparkle of silver moonlight cut through the blackness. Just the width of her finger and then two and then her entire hand. The night was cloudy, but the light poured into the room in direct contrast to the blackness between the walls of the chamber. It illuminated the man from her dreams, showing him to her and drawing another whimper from her lips.

He made a slashing motion with his hand, and Shannon clamped her fingers across her lips. He opened the other side of the shutter before walking back toward her. He paused and listened for a long moment before untying his sheath and propping it next to the bed. He sat down, and the bed gave beneath his weight. That little confirmation of his realness set tears into her eyes. He leaned over, and she heard the snap of leather while he worked the lacings on his boots free. He stood back up and pulled the tail end of his belt free and tugged on it until she heard the metal prong that kept it secure pop free.

His kilt slithered down, but he caught it with a practiced motion and laid it on the table. Every step was silent. It was as if he truly were part of the night. He pulled his shirt over his head and stood perfectly at ease in nothing but his skin. He was the man she'd first seen standing atop the boulder in the loch, his hair resting on the back of his shoulders and the moonlight casting him in silver.

Shannon shivered. Not from fear or cold, but because she knew he was coming to bed to couple with her. Her gaze drifted down, seeking out the proof of what she suspected, and found his cock standing erect. She shuddered next, the motion too violent to be called a shiver. He watched her, silently observing her while she drank in the sight of him.

But he was too far away for how much she had longed for him.

Shannon rose onto her knees and tugged her undergown up and over her head. She tossed it toward the foot of the bed, caring little about where it landed. Her attention was on her lover. She lifted her arms in invitation, beckoning him toward her.

Torin moved the moment her hands stretched out toward him, his body flowing in motion that was the perfect blending of power and control. He caressed her face with the back of his hand before clasping the sides of her head. Her memories were poor substitutions for the way his touch actually felt. Her heart beat faster, and the night air became soothing instead of biting. Passion's flame licked along her skin to warm her, but her lover was warmer still, and she longed to press against him. The world was too ugly, the palace a horrible place. Torin was her sanctuary.

"Ye truly came."

He joined her on the bed, pressing tiny kisses on each cheek before pausing to inhale the scent of her hair. A shiver raced down her spine because no words of praise would ever convince her that she was attractive more than such actions did. It was in the way he touched her, his fingertips gliding across her skin, slowly and without rushing. He didn't hurry toward sinking his erection into her just because she had invited him into her arms. That was what made him her lover.

"I'm a Highland barbarian. I cannae be allowing anyone to take what I've already stolen."

She tried to bite one of his fingers in response. It was a slow motion, one that never had a hope of success. But Torin allowed her to sink her teeth into one hand, a light nip that sent his lips curving up.

"Ah, there is my Lowland wildcat."

She pressed a kiss against the spot she'd bitten and another and yet another, until she was making her way up his arm and across his wide shoulder. She kissed the hard ridges of muscle and then the firm column of his neck before touching her lips against his jaw. She slid her hands into his hair, conscious of the fact that he was waiting on her, remaining still when there was nothing to stop him from claiming her as he would. That made it all the more tender.

"Kiss me, Shannon, for it cost me a fortune to bribe the guard at yer door."

His voice was a bare whisper, but it fit the moment. Lifting herself up, she found his mouth with her own and did as he commanded. Torin followed, allowing her to lead the kiss. She pushed at his lips, and he opened his mouth. She sent the tip of her tongue out to lick along his bottom lip and felt him shudder.

His control broke. His arms pulled her against him and bound her in place. One hand threaded through her hair to cradle the back of her head, further imprisoning her.

Yet she was a willing captive, surrendering completely to his kiss. He demanded and she complied, moaning softly with delight as his mouth moved over hers. His tongue teased her lower lip before thrusting into her mouth. Pleasure flowed down her body until it reached her belly, where hunger began to burn.

Her hands were no longer content to move slowly. She ached to touch him. Every part of him. She pressed herself toward his body, her breasts flattening against his harder chest. His cock sprung up, hard and promising between them.

"I do nae want to wait."

"Nor do I, lass. I swear it seems far too long since I held ye."

His hand cupped the two halves of her bottom and lifted her up. The head of his cock probed the folds of her sex, seeking out the opening to her passage. Torin let her down slowly, and her knees slid over his hips, spreading her thighs wider. His cock found its target, finding her flesh wet and willing. Shannon wrapped her hands around his shoulders, but she was impatient, her body yearning for complete intimacy.

"More, Torin."

"Exactly what I have planned, lass." His hard length began filling her. Desperation began to pound through her, making her shake with anticipation. Everything moved too slowly, and she whimpered once again.

A low growl was Torin's reply. He thrust upward, giving her the last of his length. She didn't have time to demand that he begin moving. Torin lifted up off his knees and pressed her back against the bed. The bed wasn't as sturdy as the one in his room. It shook, the curtains dancing.

But Shannon had no attention to give to such things. Her focus was directly on the man pressing her down. He gave her enough of his weight to make sure she remained beneath him. His hands pulled at her hair to lock her head in place, and buried deep inside her, his cock was rigid and throbbing with need.

"I swear ye will wed me, Shannon McBoyd, or I will not let ye off your back until ye bend to my will. I cannae exist without ye."

His hips moved, drawing his cock up and out of her before plunging down with a hard thrust that shook the bed once again. It forced the breath from her lungs, too much sensation rushing through her to contain. Torin covered her mouth with one hand, smothering the sounds she made.

"Hush, sweet Shannon, we would nae want to be interrupted just now."

There was a wicked edge to his tone, one that sparked more excitement in her belly. She bit him once again, causing him to jerk his hand away out of surprise.

"Then kiss me."

"With pleasure, lass."

There was more than enough pleasure for both of them. Torin fused his mouth on top of hers while his body began to pump against hers. She lifted her hips to take each thrust, his hard flesh sliding against her clitoris each time. The pleasure was intense, and it refused to be controlled. She became frantic, lifting faster and pressing harder against her partner. Her hands dug into his upper arms, her fingernails cutting into his skin, but all Torin did was snarl against her lips. Their kiss ended because they were both focused on the actions of their lower bodies. Torin buried his mouth against her hair, and she pressed her face to the warm skin of his neck.

Rapture tore them away, each fighting to contain their cries. The bed shook as Torin rode her hard through the burst of pleasure, his own breaking a few strokes later. His seed drew a second unleashing of delight from her, making her gasp in surprise. Her body straining up to catch every last drop of his offering, she felt it burning into the walls of her passage and shook with enjoyment. They both collapsed onto the bed, their breathing rough, satisfaction spreading a warm glow over them.

❧

"Lundy will nae be pleased that you plan to wed."

Shannon kept her voice low, still fearing that their sanctuary might be shattered. She felt Torin stiffen, the hand gently smoothing her arm stopping.

"Ye're right about that, lass. It almost makes me want to have the man in church when we take our vows." There was no missing the frustration in his tone, although he tried to hide it by grinding his teeth together.

Shannon pushed her hand against the bedding to rise enough to see his face. The moon granted her only a sprinkling of silver to make out his expression.

"My McBoyd blood will give him more reason to raise his voice against ye. We should nae wed."

He growled, a soft sound that betrayed how deeply he felt about the matter. A second later he flipped her onto her back, capturing her wrists and pressing them onto the surface of the bed. Her breath froze in her chest because he had never treated her so while they were intimate. She felt like his prisoner, and she strained against his hold, but he kept her pinned, allowing helplessness to sink into her.

"Stop it, Torin. Ye are being a brute."

The grip around her wrists increased, threatening her with pain. He lowered his body until his weight felt crushing.

"I may have brought ye to Donan Tower tied around me, Shannon, but I never forced ye into my bed."

He blew out a harsh sound before rolling back onto his back. The bed shook when he landed. Shannon was suddenly alone. The night air carried his warmth away from her quickly.

"I am correct, and ye know it, Torin."

He sighed, sounding tired. He turned and lay over her again, only this time it was a secure hold, light and full of tenderness. His fingers stroked along her jaw.

"I do long for a family, but if I wanted a wife who would bear my children out of duty, I could have contracted a bride years ago."

She reached up to place her hand against his cheek. "Ye want more."

He sighed. "I want love. My parents loved one another, and it tormented them to think that I lost position because of their choice, but I swear to ye, Shannon, they were richer than the king for the love they shared. They gave me more than a position; they raised me in a loving home. My father refused the bride his brother found for him, so the girl was given to my father's half brother. Lundy is their eldest son. When my uncle died without an heir, Lundy argued that his mother's blue blood made him more rightfully laird of the McLeren. There were many McLerens who agreed."

"I saw them. It was the first time I felt McLeren colors were being worn by savages."

"His men are lawless. Keep that in mind when I set Brockton to watching ye." Torin smoothed his hands through the tiny hairs curling along the edge of her face. "I love ye."

"And I love—" She clamped her lips closed before the last word crossed them. Torin's fist hit the bedding next to her.

"Why do ye deny me the words?" His voice was stiff.

"Because if ye stay with me, Lundy will have that much more reason to argue for yer place. I cannot change that I am McBoyd. Ye need a bride who brings ye position to match yer own."

He smothered a harsh bark of laughter. He buried his head against her throat and kissed the tender skin there. He tipped his head up so that he might whisper in her ear.

"Ye do love me, Shannon, else ye would never fight to protect me. But it is I who will stand as yer protector. Isn't the fact that I am here proof of that?"

"Did ye truly sneak in here?"

He lifted his face, and the moonlight illuminated an arrogant smirk sitting on his lips. He rolled over, taking her along with him. He pulled up the covers and tucked them over her bare shoulder.

"Ye should sleep while ye can, lass."

"The earl might still decide to hang me with my father. He said he wanted to think on the matter."

A low growl shook the chest that pillowed her head. "He no doubt fears the strength of our clans if we wed. That is something I will need to discuss with him."

"My stepmother is with child. The McBoyd might still have an heir."

"Best ye hope she births a daughter."

A shiver rippled over her skin. "I know. The earl told me to go see my father. I went down to the dungeon to see what Archibald Douglas saw fit to give my father and his sons."

Torin heard the fear clinging to her voice. He ground his teeth together, fighting the urge to dress and challenge Archibald Douglas right then. It was a torment to listen to fear in her voice and to know that she did not fall into slumber because she wondered if the remaining hours of the night were her last. He wanted to protect her from that, and storming into the lieutenant general's chambers was not the way to begin a successful campaign.

But he would prevail. Torin watched the horizon turn pink and then golden, all the while holding his beloved close.

He would see victory, or he'd give Lundy what the man craved... his own death.

❧

"Enough, Lundy McLeren."

The Earl of Bothwell, lieutenant general of Scotland, glared at Lundy McLeren.

"I've heard all I need to from ye. She's a female, and it would nae be the first time the daughter was spared as long as she was wed to a man who would keep her under control."

"But—"

"The lieutenant general told you that he has heard enough." Joan Beaufort emerged from her seat behind the large tapestry. Lundy McLeren's face turned red when she glided up and refused to leave him in privacy with Douglas. She narrowed her eyes.

"I am also regent of this country, sir, and I tell you that alone means you shall be finished. I agree that they would be a good match and that their union would bring peace."

"But she is the daughter of a traitor!" Lundy shouted.

"Leave, Lundy." It was the earl who spoke, and his guards stepped forward to enforce his will.

There was nothing else the man might do. He sent a fuming glare at the earl, but when he gained no decree to remain, the guards stepped farther toward him. He stomped from the room, and the door shut calmly behind him because the men stationed at the doors had been raised in the palace. High emotions were not unusual. They performed their duties with patience and diligence, whether the matter was grave or not.

"Ye will remember yer place, Joan, or I'll have ye sent to tour the northern country. With a full contingent of my men to see to yer protection along the way, of course."

The queen lowered herself, gaining a brief grunt of approval from Douglas.

"His repetition was becoming difficult to stomach. I meant to help."

"It is the lairds of this country who need uniting. Lundy stands to become one of them. Offending him is nae in our interests."

Joan moved slowly away from Bothwell. She was walking over dangerous ground, but the arrogance in the man encouraged her. Men always thought themselves so intelligent; sometimes a woman needed to best them. Even if she must do so by being clear and crafty, so as not to allow them to notice that she was gaining what she desired.

"If you give him what he wants, when he becomes laird, he will think he can bend you to his will anytime he argues with you."

Bothwell stood up, his face reflecting his rage.

"Ye have a point there, one I do nae care for."

Joan lifted her eyelashes to stare straight at him. "But if ye allow Torin McLeren to keep Shannon McBoyd, the McBoyd will most likely settle down to planting instead of feuding."

Douglas narrowed his eyes and turned pensive.

"Ye hide behind yer demure behavior very well, madam."

"I am a woman. That is my place. But I listen a great deal, and Torin McLeren has powerful friends in Quinton Cameron and Connor Lindsey. Lundy McLeren annoys more men than he impresses."

"Maybe, but then again, Lundy will do anything I ask of him, so long as I give him what he wants."

"If you keep Torin McLeren happy, you will have a good force to call upon when you need it, because he will have a happy home that you allowed him to build with your mercy."

The earl sneered at her. "What I should do is send ye on that tour. Ye are regent in name only, madam. Do nae advise me on matters of state."

Lowering herself, she forced her revulsion down to a place where Archibald wouldn't be able to see it. She detested the man so very much, but the lairds of Scotland would not follow her.

"I'll leave you to thinking the matter through."

"Aye, ye do that."

Joan walked from the receiving room, her heart aching for her husband even more, because of who sat in his chair now. But she would not let her son be displaced; that was her duty now. She would pray for Shannon McBoyd; it was all she might do. Bothwell would hang her or not, depending on his mood.

Curse and rot the man. Someday soon he'd face the justice he so richly deserved.

But that would come far too late for Shannon McBoyd.

She was at his mercy.

❧

Shannon looked up when someone rapped on the door. Torin crossed his arms over his chest and watched the door.

Quinton Cameron came through the door with Connor Lindsey pushing him. Cameron froze when he got a glimpse of Torin. The retainers guarding the door both looked stunned. Shannon turned to look at Torin.

"Ye really did sneak in here?"

"Well, not alone, he didna." Connor sent her a wink before he turned and tossed a coin toward the retainers. One of them caught it and held it up for inspection. The two men shrugged and shut the doors without a sound.

Connor smirked. "Their orders are to keep ye in here."

Cameron grinned. "Aye, well now we're all in here together. I fear the lass's reputation will nae survive."

Shannon frowned but didn't let the man's teasing bother her. That little flame of hope that had begun to flicker when Torin appeared gained strength when she looked at the three lairds. They represented some of the most powerful clans in Scotland.

Connor suddenly turned deadly serious.

"We've business, lads."

❧

Archibald Douglas was the fifth Earl of Bothwell. There were relations in the man's family who disputed his claim to the title. He enjoyed power, and becoming lieutenant general appeared to suit him. Torin studied the man as the wide doors were opened by his servants. The Earl of Bothwell knew how to intimidate well; he sat with his back leaning against the chair while Torin was announced.

He sat on a raised dais that was covered with a lavish Persian rug. The chair he made himself so comfortable in was a throne. It was carved lavishly and inlaid with mother-of-pearl. Behind him, tapestries were hung from the ceiling to complete the regal setting. The only thing missing was a crown.

But the man didn't truly need that when the royal guards stood on either side of the dais. The dowager queen sat behind him on her own dais, and young King James II was nowhere in sight.

"This is a foul bit of business with the McBoyd, Laird McLeren."

Archibald Douglas didn't sound sorry. Torin inclined his head before staring the man straight back in the eye.

"I never thought it anything but that, my lord. It was my clan that brought ye the proof in this plot."

The Earl of Douglas fingered the large ruby ring that sat on his fourth finger. The thing was worth a fortune, but it was also a symbol of his position in Scotland now. James II was seven years old. He was king in name only; it was Douglas who would rule, so long as he was able to watch his back.

"Laird McBoyd will hang at sunset, along with his sons. Every last one of them shook hands with Atholl and raided yer holding of White Hill."

It was a kinder death than Torin expected for the traitors. Archibald drew a stiff breath.

"It's time to finish it. I'll leave the torture to the English. I'll send the priest to them and march them off to the gallows the moment they're finished confessing."

"They'd best make a good job of that."

Douglas spit on the floor. The two large hounds sitting at his feet didn't even flinch; obviously they were accustomed to their master's habits.

"Ye have my thanks and that of the dowager queen, Laird McLeren. Yer loyalty is truly proven."

"I want it rewarded."

Archibald Douglas gripped the ends of his armrests, his fingers closing around the carved wood until they turned white.

"I'll reward whom I choose, Laird McLeren. As laird of yer clan, ye owe loyalty to the true king. Such does no' require rewards."

"What I want shouldn't be here at all. I took Shannon McBoyd, and she is mine."

The earl chuckled, an unfriendly sound that made his dogs perk up their ears.

"And it was my authority that took her away from ye."

Torin felt his teeth grinding against each other. "My men know whom to respect, and I'll remind ye that I came to ye instead of settling my score with the McBoyds as most of my men wanted."

"Or what? Ye will side with yer men and nae respect my authority?" The earl leaned forward, his face darkening. "Mind yer words, McLeren. There's plenty of room at the gallows for another rope."

Torin smiled at the earl, which sent the man back in his chair.

"That will leave ye Lundy as Laird McLeren. If ye would rather have that sniveling whelp helping to watch yer back, send me yer priest."

Douglas suddenly chuckled. He slapped the arm of his chair while his dogs stood up and began pacing around his feet.

"I would have sworn that Lundy lied to me, but

ye do·love her." The earl laughed some more before drawing in a deep breath. "Ye poor fool."

Torin only shrugged. "It is something I'll nae argue against, but I find it a pleasant affliction to have. If ye plan to hang Shannon McBoyd, expect to see me standing beside her."

Douglas sobered.

"I should send the priest to ye for those words alone, but ye are right about me no' wanting that cousin of yers leading the McLeren. Lundy will make a pissy laird, who will whine endlessly when he isn't acting like a king in his own right."

Torin glared back at the man, refusing to cower. "I want Shannon McBoyd. I stole her and had her first. She belongs to me."

"Ye've got courage, man; maybe foolish courage, but it is there."

"Stop toying with me, Douglas." Men had died for less-forceful tones in this same room. Torin didn't care. "A Highlander keeps what he steals. The Douglas know that tradition well. I'm going to wed her and watch her belly grow round with my child."

"Her father will enjoy knowing that, but ye are right that a Highlander is entitled to the woman he stole." The earl snapped his fingers, and there was a rustle of fabric. Shannon appeared in the next moment, her face bright with temper. But she held her tongue, biting into her lower lip to remain silent.

"Go on with ye, girl."

She looked at the floor to avoid telling him what she thought of his making a gift out of her, but she walked across the distance between them, sending relief through Torin. He clasped his fingers around her wrist and felt her tremble. The earl studied her for a moment.

"Go on, McLeren. Never forget that I have paid the debt I owe ye. Insult me again, and I'll give ye that hanging ye just asked for."

"I'll remember both things, my lord."

Torin offered the earl a quick nod of his head and a slightly longer one for the queen before he turned and pulled Shannon from the room with him. She tried to jerk her wrist from his hold the moment the throne-room doors closed behind them. He tugged her behind a tapestry instead, setting her back against the wall. He lifted her up and pushed her mouth open with his.

Shannon pushed at Torin's shoulders. The man didn't move, did not make any motion that indicated that he felt her squirming in his hold. Instead he kissed her, hard and without mercy.

It was perfection.

She wanted to melt against him. Her hands gripped his shoulders, trying to absorb the fact that he was real. Her lips clung to his, moving in unison and kissing him back with every bit of anxiety that had tormented her.

"Torin… I need to catch my breath…" Her heart was hammering so hard, it threatened to burst through her chest.

"No, ye just want to argue with me for saying that ye belong to me." He pressed another kiss against her mouth, following her when she tried to pull her head away. She finally pushed herself up, above his reach, by flattening her palms on top of his shoulders.

Torin snarled softly at her, using his hands to pull her back down.

"I swear I'll spank yer arse if ye say one word in argument."

He meant it too. Shannon placed her fingers over his lips, delicately tracing them while she drew in the breath her racing heart needed.

"Ye scared the life out of me by asking to be hung." To maintain her composure, she smothered a sob that broke through her resolve. "I swear I cannae bear such a thought. I'll be yer mistress. Ye need to please yer clan and marry an heiress with blue blood."

"Ye'll be my wife."

She shook her head, biting back the shout of joy that she wanted to give. He suddenly let out a curse that shocked her with how dark it was.

"Ye will wed me, Shannon." He spit out another curse before framing her face with his hands.

"But I'm nae with child, Torin. I'm sorry, but I know I am not."

"I do nae care. I love ye, woman, and ye will marry me. It will bring peace to all but Lundy and his followers. I refuse to spend my life trying to please him."

He tried to press another kiss against her mouth, but Shannon flattened her hand against his mouth once more. Her heart was full of happiness and devastated too.

"Ye will lose too much by wedding me. I won't allow you to do that. Yer love is enough. I swear I will never grow discontented, even when ye bring home a bride."

He wrapped his fingers around her wrist and pulled it gently away from his mouth.

"What I must have is ye, sweet Shannon. God has blessed me with a woman I love; we'll nae be greedy by debating the matter further. Swear that ye will wed me."

"I cannae. Ye must think of ensuring that Lundy does nae gain more favor among the McLeren."

He growled and pulled her away from the wall. With a hand wrapped around her wrist, Torin took her down the hallway and into the receiving room. Conversation flowed softly from the nobility waiting there. Music filtered down from the musicians playing in the alcoves, and then Laird Torin McLeren knelt on one knee in front of her.

"Will ye become my wife, Shannon McBoyd?"

Her heart froze, and the conversation died. Silence surrounded them; even the music stopped. Torin had spoken loudly enough to have his voice bounce off the walls, and everyone waited to hear her reply.

It was gallant beyond compare. Her protests died in the face of his public declaration. How great a love must it be to see him embracing it when she brought him nothing but her own love in return. Nothing but herself. It was the stuff that legends were written about, and her heart swelled with it.

"Yes."

Soft applause filled the room. The musicians played a fanfare, but most importantly of all, Torin pushed back up to tower over her with a smug look of satisfaction on his face.

"Ye are arrogant, Laird McLeren."

He shrugged and renewed his grasp around her wrist. Connor Lindsey appeared next to his friend, looking every bit as smug.

"Aye, lass, and a barbarian, I hear."

Torin aimed a look at his friend. "I learned everything I know from ye."

"Glad to hear ye admit it. Now are ye getting married or no'?"

The grip on her wrist tightened. "I'm getting married."

"Good. I want to kiss the bride first." Connor Lindsey stepped right between them and clasped her face between his hands. A second later the man kissed her. It was no sweet salute of her mouth, but a full kiss between a man and woman. Connor Lindsey stole her breath, for the man knew more than his fair share about how to kiss. She finally shoved him away and felt her cheeks burn when he chuckled at her. He winked before turning to smirk at Torin.

"Better get to it, before I steal her."

"Not before I get my turn to kiss the bride."

Quinton Cameron looped a hard arm around her waist and pulled her against his body. His kiss was unique, just like the man, and he gave her no mercy, demanding a deep kiss just as Connor had. He spun her back toward Torin, and she heard Torin's chest rumble with a growl. His friends smirked, but Torin held her tightly, and that was what mattered most. Quinton raised an eyebrow.

"Of course, lad, if ye move too slowly, I might be tempted to get the lass to the church before ye."

Torin renewed his grip on her wrist and shot her a look full of excitement.

"Shall we, lass?"

"We shall." Torin took off at a run through the hallways. His boots echoed between the stone walls along with her laughter. They ran like children... They ran like lovers.

∞

The gloom of early spring gave way to bright weather. It warmed her face while they traveled back toward McLeren land. Her husband looked ready to burst with pride, but Shannon was too happy to take issue with him. She caught him watching her and felt her cheeks heat. If the man never told her he loved her again, she would not question his feelings, because they were there in every glance he sent her way.

They climbed higher into the hills, and the heather was blooming now. Shannon grinned when they sighted the towers of Donan Tower.

"Why are ye still calling it Donan Tower? It is a castle."

Torin tilted his head to one side. "Well now, lass, I suppose I should have expected that ye would begin changing things now that we are wed."

She scoffed at him. "Well, husband, far be it for me to mention to ye that there are three towers, and that clearly makes a castle."

He shrugged. "We're working as fast as the weather permits on the fourth one, lass. Ye'll just have to wait for it."

He smirked at her, clearly in the mood to tease her.

"But ye still want to call it Donan Tower?"

"I want ye to call it home."

He leaned across the space between them and hooked an arm around her body. With a smothered cry, she found herself pulled over to his horse in a tangle of her gowns. Shannon clung to him as the ground felt like it was spinning beneath them, but Torin never faltered; he held her firmly in front of him while they entered the village. People were outside, working the newly plowed fields. The blacksmith was busy, the clang from his hammer filling the air. Women looked up from the bank of the river where they were washing laundry, lifting their hands to shade their eyes so that they might see who was on the road.

They rode onto the bridge and heard the bell in the church begin tolling. This time it was a welcome sound, ringing in happiness that the laird was returning. Once they passed the raised gate, they heard a cheer from the men gathered along the curtain walls to view them.

"My wife!"

They sent up a louder cheer; this one startled several birds off the rooftops. Baeth squalled like a girl from where she stood at the top of the stairs. Shannon turned to look at her husband's face.

"'Tis only home so long as ye are here." She watched his eyes glimmer with satisfaction and tenderness, and, more importantly, love.

"But 'tis still a castle, as any right-minded soul could tell ye."

❧

Shannon knelt next to her trunk with only a single candle to illuminate the dark chamber that she'd first been given. The room was quiet now, as though it were waiting for something or someone to come and breathe life into it once more.

That would not happen tonight.

Shannon lifted the lid, the leather hinges creaking in the silence. Very little was inside. She reached for her folded arisaid, which had been sitting on the table in Torin's chamber just as she'd left it. Running her fingers over the scarlet and blue threads, she stared at them before sighing.

Her father was dead, and his sons too. She couldn't even lament their passing from this life, because she honestly felt that they might be more content now that their positions of earthly life were removed. Her stepmother would be. Fate was being kind to the child bride her father had taken to gain a rich dowry. Word had arrived that her stepmother had birthed a daughter. That little girl was the most welcome girl baby in all of Scotland, for she would be allowed to live and maybe someday restore honor to the McBoyd name.

Shannon placed the McBoyd colors in the trunk. She closed the lid, sealing them in darkness. For now, the future belonged to her life with the McLerens. This was her home.

And it was the most wonderful place she might ever have imagined.

A soft step in the doorway drew her attention. Torin stood there, concern etched into his expression. His eyes were dark and unreadable, but she felt his love. His attention moved to the hand she still had lingering on the top of her trunk. He stretched out a hand in invitation.

"Are ye ready, lass? My chamber is too cold without ye."

She stood up, pinching out the candle before reaching for that hand. His fingers closed around hers, gently, firmly sealing them in a grasp that sent two tears down her face.

"Then I shall warm it for ye, my love."

～

"Push now, mistress."

Shannon would have liked to tell Baeth that she hated her, but there was too much pain for her to do anything more than snarl. Her entire body was dripping sweat, and her fingernails dug into the arms of the birthing chair. Looking down, she stared at her swollen belly, still slightly amazed to see herself so round so soon after marrying.

"Push harder."

"I am pushing hard!" And it felt like her body was ripping open. She felt her baby being forced from her, fighting to be born. The birthing chair made it easy for the child to use gravity to assist in its birth, the wide legs supporting her spread thighs, leaving room for the midwife to crouch between her legs and catch the infant.

"I've got it, mistress. Just one more push."

Shannon bore down and groaned through the final, agonizing contraction. Her child began to wail, sending tears down her cheeks.

"A son, mistress, a strong son for the McLerens."

Shannon cursed. The midwife and the maids looked shocked to see their mistress using such profanity. But in the next moment they giggled, because birthing rooms were always full of surprises and it didn't matter if the mother-to-be was high or low.

"But he's strong and healthy, mistress."

"I wanted a girl because everyone has been telling me how much Torin needs a son. Well, I'll decide what I have, nae anyone else. Everyone needs to stop telling me what to do…" She stopped because another contraction went through her; thankfully this one was much milder. "That hurt too much. I hate giving birth."

But her voice grew softer as she heard the soft cry of her baby. The midwife finished cleaning him and held him up for her to see. Tears flooded her eyes and fell down her cheeks unchecked. She suddenly didn't understand why she was angry at all. The tension and pain diminished, leaving behind nothing but happiness. Shannon reached for her son with a pleased sob on her lips and fresh tears sliding down her face.

"Oh… look how perfect he is…"

"Does that mean ye are pleased with a son, madam?"

The midwife snorted with disapproval, but Torin didn't heed her. He walked into the room, in defiance of tradition that dictated he remain behind the door. But his eyes glowed with love, and Shannon didn't care what anyone else said about the way things were supposed to be done.

"I suppose a son will do, at least until ye give me a daughter." She fixed him with a hard look. "I want a daughter, so ye'd best just know that now, Torin McLeren. Do nae be surprised when I birth one."

Her husband chuckled at her. "I shall do my best."

Maybe it was love that he'd needed, Torin thought as he looked at his son and the woman who had given his son to him. Lundy and his ambition suddenly seemed so funny that he wanted to laugh, but his cousin was not important. Kneeling, he touched his son for the first time.

Love was perfection.

About the Author

Mary Wine is a multipublished author in romantic suspense, fantasy, and Western romance; now her interest in historical reenactment and costuming has inspired her to turn her pen to historical romance. She lives with her husband and sons in Southern California, where the whole family enjoys participating in historical reenactment.